A NOVEL

SILAS DILLON
OF CARY COUNTY

CLIFFORD SCHRAGE

NEW YORK

NASHVILLE • MELBOURNE • VANCOUVER

SILAS DILLON OF CARY COUNTY

Published in New York, New York, by Morgan James Publishing. Morgan James is a trademark of Morgan James, LLC.
www.MorganJamesPublishing.com

The Morgan James Speakers Group can bring authors to your live event. For more information or to book an event visit The Morgan James Speakers Group at www.TheMorganJamesSpeakersGroup.com.

ISBN 978-1-68350-283-8 paperback
ISBN 978-1-68350-284-5 eBook
Library of Congress Control Number: 2016916584

Cover & Interior Design by:
Megan Whitney
Creative Ninja Designs
megan@creativeninjadesigns.com

In an effort to support local communities, raise awareness and funds, Morgan James Publishing donates a percentage of all book sales for the life of each book to Habitat for Humanity Peninsula and Greater Williamsburg.

Get involved today! Visit
www.MorganJamesBuilds.com

CONTENT

THE VIEW FROM HERE

Now that I'm forty, up higher on life's hill, in the ministry, and a dad, I'm able to recall the account of my childhood without plummeting into a hole of bitterness. As I sit in my den at my desk I realize that recalling hasn't been as painful as it once was.

I carry the weighty luggage of my childhood, understanding that what may have crushed me has strengthened me. My childhood is now a limpid film in the panorama of my memory, and I simply accept it. Those early storms somehow worked like purposeful winds wafting me into the ministry, holding me here for fifteen years.

Hearing the racket my four children and six foster children make at play in the other room as they're stranded indoors this rainy July day, with an open book before me I discover something so visibly close that I've missed it. It's this: people who aren't loved die—no matter—whether love never reaches them or they refuse it, they die without it. People need love.

I was taught that human beings have the mental space to recall all, even details into earliest childhood, and I believe it. There are morsels from even my early infancy that I can recall with precise illumination, but there are, of course, dark lapses as well. A blend of varied ingredients—older informers, clear memory, God, and a lot of my own imaginings—have all furnished me with details, imploring me to tell my story.

I am Silas Dillon. I'm an orphan, or like an orphan. Unlike David Copperfield, I know I won't turn out to be the hero of my life. Like Huck Finn, I'd drifted further downstream into misfortune: my pap's lost and drunk too. Like Uncle Tom, I'd been placed into many places.

I'm a child of humanity. I was a pitiful orphan type while my mom lived, or at least had a heartbeat. I spent time with her—from time to time—while her life scarcely smoldered. She slowly rotted before she reduced to ashes, could never quite ignite herself, could surely never kindle me. You could call me an orphan of the living. So because of her wretched incompetence, I was placed "into" other homes, other arms.

As I recall, I did spend some time with mom. The court's paradoxical catering to her condition, while I was supposed to be the patient, allowed her to attempt to care for me.

You want to know my mother. Her looks? She was really very beautiful. She was of Jewish and Irish extraction, born and "raised" on Cary Island. Her parents were not as unbalanced as she. You need to know that she was chemically dependent, and so emotionally unstable that some of the professionals called her schizophrenic, but they weren't given time enough with her to make sure diagnosis.

Early on, she adamantly remained unwilling to release me for adoption, leaving me on Cary Island, in Cary County's laggard, yet rigid foster care system. There on that island she breathed the briny air too, wearing a valid label mentally ill especially when it gave her some special rights. There I, Silas Dillon, tried to grow fruitfully, while planted in the soil of alienation, anger, and ruin, attempting to grow on Cary Island and the promontory of a binding foster care system.

Outwardly denoting the best interests of children, the system impeded me. I was frail, bi-racial, repeatedly transplanted like one of those ornamental trees in one of those landscaped yards, from plot to plot, seemingly unfitting and unbecoming anywhere, moved interval after interval, interrupted from one dwelling to another, with roots stuck in the same ball of earth, attempting to thrive, scarcely watered, dying. From birth to late adolescence, the painful episodes of my life are chronicled in these pages.

Now at age forty I am really not bitter, but I do want prosecution, want sentence passed on the bureaucratic delay and poor judgment done to the well-being of kids lost in a system. I don't want pity. I want the county court—the whole system itself—indicted!

Cary County is an island. It is cramped in New York Bay, across New York Harbor, with a population of three hundred thousand, with the imperial skyline of fortunate New York and its vain lady of liberty in sight on one side; Brooklyn, Queens, and affluent Long Island on another; industrial New Jersey on another; and the blue Atlantic on the other. Here on this island the disruption and neglect of what Jesus Christ called "the least of these" carries on. Cary County is like other real places. And Silas is like other real people who happen to be orphaned.

This story intends to blow a trumpet by bowing a violin. Listen closely. There are things here on Cary Island, like all those real places, that prevent souls like Silas Dillon from connecting cords, from spreading roots, from receiving love. There are bad things and the neglect of needful things that induce humans to be turned into maladjusted adults, stunted trees. There are all these wobbly parts within this confused child welfare system which make too many castaways like Silas, and fewer stable homes with doors open for him. There are things that could prevent these like me from being turned into stunted ones.

More about Cary Island: Like the rest of suburban America, innumerable houses of worship stand with steeples and spires, crosses and committees, pews and altars, ministers and ministries, boards and bake sales, deacons and elders, bulletins and announcements, crusades and choirs, tithes and tongues, sacraments and rites, and a lot of other religious commotion. They stand in mortar, rise with stained glass, in red brick or pretty white, on the bedrock of Cary Island, supposedly on the foundation of the book that declares "Religion that God our Father accepts as pure and faultless is this: to look after orphans and widows in their distress and to keep oneself from being polluted by the world." This verse, fitly set as the hub of the pragmatic wheel of real Christianity, is what all the other spokes of canon, order, ordinances, and churchianity are meant to be connected to. But the spokes are broken; the axle's slipping; the rim's deforming, and the mechanism needs to yield to the mechanic.

This indictment is not against that formidable, invisible army-roster, that fire-resistant file in the book of life, that assemblage which Christ builds and knows, which all of hell falters before. This trumpet is blown to awaken those sleeping ones. This match is struck to light a fire.

I, Silas Dillon, sit with my fist to my chin, elbow to desk, gazing onto the wet streets, through a wet pane of glass, postponing pastoral phone calls, recalling without pain some of that former pain, some of that former joy.

ONE

CUTTING THE CORD

Cary County Hospital was warm on my birth night, while Cary Island, lashed by a below-zero wind chill down from Canada, froze outside. Its grassy bedrock was wrapped with a hard coat of snow. My birth mother Maureen heard the wind's shrill moan while she herself moaned in pain. My arrival came on a moonless starry night, late, January 31, minutes shy of February.

Her cervix was open, her back aching. My father wasn't there to help her, to rub her back and comfort her, to talk with her, or pray with her. She didn't know which of the twenty or so men she'd embraced that month nine months earlier was my father.

passed and Mommy was wheeled into the delivery room where all those vital provisions were.

"Not much longer," Dr. Cohen said.

Jill the kind nurse on duty helped prop her up in that big chair so her muscles could push me out easier.

"Your first baby, Ms. Dillon?" she said. Her youthful energy moved about the room, working as she spoke.

"Second."

"So you're a veteran. That's great!"

"I guess." Maureen winced.

5

"How old is your other child?"

"Two.

"How nice."

Maureen didn't reply.

"So he'll have a brother to play with."

"He's gone," she said.

"Gone?" Jill briefly made eye contact while she kept stepping about the room, tucking, sliding, pulling, working.

Maureen groaned in agony, shouting with a contraction. Sweat beads erupted on her forehead, descending, collapsing down her cheeks. "Had to give him up." Tears erupted from her eyes, descending, sinking with suddenness, dripping, mixing with her sweat. "For adoption." She looked across the room avoiding both of their eyes.

Dr. Cohen listened, scrubbing his hands.

"Must have been very hard to do, Ms. Dillon." This young nurse didn't pause from working. "Sometimes it's the most loving though." She wiped Maureen's face with a damp cloth, tenderly, now avoiding talking, not wanting to bring other pain.

"I try not to think about it. I hope he's good. I try not to think about him much." She breathed heavily. "It bothers me." She breathed with concentration, rhythm.

Silence—only the sterile *clinks* and thin echoes of the delivery room, a cough from Dr. Cohen. Maureen braced against another contraction, breathing, straining, hollering. Water broke, gushing like tide. Her loud hollering embraced the room, seizing everything. It would be soon.

"He's in Connecticut I think. In the country—a quiet town somewhere." Maureen stared at the blackness of the window as though looking toward Connecticut, out at the black color of glass, at the darkened reflection of the room on glass.

She felt that compelling pressure, suddenly an urge to push, and she hated this arduous work. She screamed; she cursed. My head moved down in the typical, little by little way with each contraction, down the narrow passage, from the warm world of the safe womb, to the astonishing opening where this shocking, offensive world is.

"Push, Maureen! Breathe! Okay. Easy now," Jill held Maureen's hand, because she'd no husband there to hold it.

"What kind of night is it?" Maureen squeezed this out amid her pushing.

Jill looked baffled.

Maureen breathed. "The weather?"

Jill didn't want Mommy's thoughts to digress too much now. She wanted her to focus. "Well, it's cold. Temperature dropped. It's windy. Hear it?" Maureen nodded. She could hear the wind.

Outside, on the other side of the large, dark, reflecting window, the cold gripping wind swirled across the starry, winter-sweetened coast. The falling tide roared, squeezing and thrashing and white-capped, bloated between Cary Island and the mainland, surging swollen, rushing reluctantly and pushed under the two-mile bridge, through the deep, ice-banked, narrow strait out from New York Harbor into the cold, hostile Atlantic. This strong watery gush, governed by the clockwork of the veiled moon, shouldered its way with the force that once pushed aside the land, reshaping even its firm bedrock foundation.

"Here's the head," Dr. Cohen said, clasping my head and frame with firm and gentle palms, with sensitive, reactive fingers.

A minute later I slid out, big and blue and shining. I began to cry, screaming out loud in the normal way. I was held and shown to my mother. "A boy," Jill said.

Mommy did not smile. The doctor cut the umbilical cord—that huge detaching stride away from my mother. There was no pain.

I altered into the lovely, soft pink, and I was wrapped in a warm, white towel. Maureen didn't reach her arms for me. She was tired. There was no dad to walk me around in his arms, to kiss me and talk to me. But this tender nurse Jill held me and talked to me for a few minutes, and she kissed my small head. Then I calmed and rested.

I slept for a long time in one of those little glass beds where all the other newborns slept the same way, and I was fed from one of those little bottles like the others. There in that county hospital I was treated like any other brand-new human being. I was special because I was a human being, different from other creatures.

No one lied to me yet.

The next day Maureen held me for an hour, and she fed me. I loved that. I loved her. Her voice sounded similar, yet dissimilar from the way it sounded when I lived inside of her. It was clearer, closer. "Silas. Silas," she kept saying. She named me *Silas*, which means "to borrow." She tried hard to make contact with my eyes. She named me after her grandfather, Silas Rosenberg—a tough, hardy, hardened Jew who'd come to New York from Europe, whom she could only faintly recall from her own hard, untidy childhood.

"Silas. Silas," she kept saying. I wanted to linger here, to remain close to her, but something troubled her. She was restless.

She kept shaking, rising, pacing, standing by and staring out the window. She was sweating , clutching her fingers, folding her arms. Sometimes she held her hair in her fists. She cursed. She cried, biting her nails, her knuckles. That gnawing, narcotic craving in her mortality had plainly become a colossal, gripping incubus which refused to release her.

On the second day, she got herself dressed, signed papers with the foster care agency, and left me. She hastily paced out of the warm hospital into the sunny, long-shadowed winter suburbia of Cary County, deserting me, cutting the cord of our bond more deeply, scarcely glancing back. She thought to herself that it would be temporary. I lay, without knowing what I waited for.

T W O
SYCAMORES

Like most of the houses on this island, this one was tall and slender, packed tightly like canned sardines, separated from the neighbors by narrow driveways—confined, crowded—the same way Cary Island itself was hemmed in in New York Bay. Like the others it was a hundred years old. It was owned by a vinyl siding installer, ironically cedar shingled, painted forsythia-yellow, with forest-green trim and front door, and with a steep, eight-stepped stoop. Mature, motley barked sycamore trunks lined the street, their elbowed limbs shading even the roofs; their firm roots lifting the concrete walks. This was where I was placed for an undefined march of time. It was in this house, under these trees.

Of course at that time I didn't understand all the things that were happening to me. I never wondered what the people in charge with my life were doing to me. I never wondered where the good people were, why the people who were supposed to help me along weren't. I just sort of congenitally went for the ride, sucked my bottle, wet my diaper, ate, cried, slept, and trusted. I had no questions. I didn't wonder what was to be done with me. I had no understanding of my situation, had no others' to compare with, to provoke me to coveting, wanting, or gloating over what I had or didn't have. But I needed love, and I innately felt that need. I didn't cognize that I needed it; but there was a yearning, a deep aching, a concrete feeling need; and I was at the mercy of my temporary caretaker for it.

This lower middle class vinyl siding installer, Earl Madden, was my first foster father, a fifty-year-old father of two grown married daughters who were then living out of state. Earl was small in stature, with red, wrinkled, weathered complexion; he'd a wiry build, balding, graying, with thick black eyebrows, with hard hands and thick fingers—hands that had held a hundred hammers, always with a cigar in his mouth. Chronically angry, especially pent-up when business was slow, "Go to sleep!" he'd shout from the first floor up the stairs, into the corridor, through a closed door, into my crib, into my tiny ears, penetrating beyond my blaring baby-wailing. He had a furious scraping voice. "Shut up!" he'd roar, as though I understood. He'd curse, click open cans of beer, and raise the television's volume—a ballgame, the news, an old movie, smothering my cries.

My placement into Earl's custody, into one of his bedrooms, was a slight—yet secure—expansion to Earl's irregular income. Earl unenlightenedly felt he was retrieving his tax money from the county. When work was steady for him, baby life was nicer for me.

I spent a lot of hours alone in the crib. My diaper was changed often enough to avoid detrimental cases of diaper rash. I did get a sense of being cherished often enough to survive, though. I felt a bit treasured when I was held by Mommy Sophia (Mrs. Madden) as she fed me with the formula bottle. She'd hold me, rock me a little as she hunkered her large, loose, turnip shaped body on the couch to watch the succession of sitcoms, drifting lost in other worlds of episodes, smoking menthol cigarettes, coughing, hacking, chewing sandwiches, often scolding Joseph, another ward of Cary County, their four-year-old foster child. "Joseph, stop that! Joseph, get down here! Joseph, don't touch that! Joseph, eat your lunch! Joseph, be quiet!

Joseph, get off that! Joseph, watch out for the baby! Joseph, not now! Joseph, what's wrong with you!" It was almost poetic, almost comic.

I was placed on the floor in a little reclining seat. I'd sleep long naps or gaze around, making sounds with my mouth and involuntary jerks with my limbs. Sometimes I was left in a room this way, alone with Joseph, at Joseph's mercy, for minutes at a time. Joseph would pull at my arms, sit on me, twist my nose, press toys against, drop them and slam them on me, play with me like I were a toy or like a pet, make me laugh, cause me pain, frighten me, and make me scream. I still have a dent-like scar on my skull from Joseph. Joseph didn't know better. There was something raging within him too, a hunger for warmth that he couldn't control.

At this juncture in Mommy Sophia's life of employment, her options were either these doldrums of around the clock childcare, or back to the horror of working around the corner at the drycleaners or the supermarket as a cashier or some other place like these on the boulevard. But she couldn't punch out at the time clock and call it a day with me and Joseph. We brought in less money than a job, but "caring" for us was easier.

Once on a weekday afternoon of one of Earl's jobless weeks, while Earl sat in his recliner drinking beer from a can, as I sat placidly in my reclining seat on the couch, as Joseph played with blocks on the floor, and Sophia sat beside me watching one of those vulgar weekday talk shows, the two of them conversed, which didn't happen too often.

"Soon's the ballgame starts I'm turnin' this bull off!"

She ignored him, her attention charmed by the television.

"Hear me?"

"What?" She didn't look at him.

"The ballgame's comin' on. I'm turnin' this bull off!" His voice raised. Joseph glanced at the screen, but immediately returned his attention to his tower of blocks.

She made no reply.

"I can't believe people get on television like this with all their horse hockey!" He sipped his beer, slid a fresh cigar out of his top pocket, peeled off the cellophane, inserted it into his mouth, tucked it deeply into his jaw, struck a match, and puffed.

"Look Mommy. Look Mommy!" Joseph wanted Mommy Sophia to see his proud tower. She wouldn't look as the television screen seemed to absorb her.

"Look Mommy. Look at my tower! Look at what I made!"

"Okay. Okay. Good Joseph. Good!"

The female talk show host engaged a studio audience with their comments and questions—bracketed by her directives—to a married couple on stage who were on the threshold of divorce, who had two small children, who vehemently argued with each other over each of their attachments to their parents and each of their parents' involvement in their personal and family affairs. The combative, sarcastic, bitter tones—somewhat fake for effect—continued in time slices between commercial breaks, regressing, deteriorating, producing nothing salubrious whatsoever except to mesmerize, entertain, and enslave idle people like Sophia in their living rooms. At one climactic heated moment, the enraged wife vaulted to her feet shouting and pointing at her husband, shoving him once as he snickered, exacerbating her. Part of the audience laughed, part cheered. If this was real, then their marriage was ruined.

"This is droppings!" Earl commented again, but he kept watching, keeping the channel, holding the remote, puffing. "You always watch this horse hockey?"

She ignored him.

After a little while I began to fuss, hungry and crying.

"What the heck's he want now?"

"I don't know. I just fed him." Sophia remained fixed on television. I hadn't drunk from my bottle for three hours.

"Give him his pacifier!"

"You give it to him," she replied. "I don't know where it is. Why don't you get up for once! I just sat down!"

The pacifier was hidden underneath me.

Sophia had been seated on that misshapen couch for twenty minutes. "I'm not gettin' up. You get up for a change!" Her halting voice and jolting body threatened, as though she'd physically conquer her small framed husband.

He rose, scowled down at her with a wolfish glance, grimacing as though he smelled something rotten. She visually seemed to melt, flattening slightly from this higher perspective, making her width apparently wider, making her appear—in his semi-intoxication—in her immense brown house dress, immersed in the couch's motley brownness, becoming part of the couch as her slouching, fluid wideness sank it.

Earl entered the kitchen but couldn't find a pacifier; so he took a half-filled bottle from the counter, marched back, and handed it to Mommy Sophia. My eyes brightened, happy to see this milk. Earl swallowed another long sip of beer and then let out a tremendous belch. She stuck the bottle in my mouth and situated a small blanket so that the bottle would prop up and she wouldn't have to hold it for me.

Once I finished, my stomach hurt, so I started to fuss again, and more so. I cried, and I cried loud. After about five minutes of this, the Yankee game came on. Earl raised the volume so he could hear the commentator over this howling of mine. More minutes advanced, and now I was screaming in panic. I needed to be burped, I needed to release the gas in my belly, but no one would pick me up and do it. My face grew red.

"Shut up kid!" Earl growled.

I kept screaming. A prolonged minute passed.

Earl now stood, leaned, putting his glassy-eyed, weathered, unshaven face almost against mine, shouting, "I said shut up, kid!"

This only made me cry louder, harder, more afraid.

Joseph stopped his block piling to look. He looked scared, afraid he'd be yelled at next; but then he yelled at me, mimicking Earl virtually comically.

Earl turned to Sophia, who finally moved to pick me up. "Can't you do anything with this kid? His voice is goin' right through me!"

"He's just a baby! What the devil's the matter with you?"

"Put him in his crib or something."

She patted my back a few times, but not enough to help. She walked to the stairway and heaved her enormity upward, ascending slowly. Each stair creaked. The banister tottered, rocked.

Upstairs she plunked me into my crib, wound up my whirling mobile of airplanes, and closed the door, muting my screams which continued another ten minutes, until relief finally came to my stomach, without assistance, naturally bursting in burps like Earl's. Awhile later I fell to sleep as tears dried on my face.

I was at the mercy of my caretakers. They never played with me, never smiled at me. They plainly neglected my life. I wasn't a full person. Within me remained an uneasy, insecure, unsafe feeling. Sometimes it felt thicker than at others. It sat in an instinctual way, like a squatting frog, as in a swamp, deep in the recesses of my senses. It hurt like pain. I cried and hated waking from sleep. My stomach and the muscles around my ribs sometimes ached from so much crying. Sometimes I felt like I'd completely shut down. Fear, grasping me from the deep cryptic structure of my existence, became a gnawing, cranky ache--a spasm of agony and a weighty vacancy of serenity that seemed to have an ever-present personality. It was an emptiness with substance. I wish I'd known words then.

The acrid, slouching Maddens simply didn't sense that I had feeling or significance, and their callous ignorance and negligence damaged me. They didn't know. I couldn't communicate, so they couldn't infer. I wanted them to love me. I couldn't hate them for not loving me. I didn't know how to hate. I longed to respond to tenderness. To the Maddens, eating, sleeping, keeping warm, dry, and under a fever was all a baby needed. But I craved more. I lived so fiercely alone, but I couldn't tell them.

They didn't tickle, cuddle, or adore me. I was like a pet they didn't like very much. They never talked to me, unless Sandra Jackson my case worker was there for a visit. Then they pretended. Each month she'd come to check on me and the Maddens. She had thirty other cases to keep up with. The time and effort that the social workers from the county agency New Blossom put into their cases were essentially left up to them. They could accomplish the meager minimum with the lives of each of their cases—paperwork, showing up in court, making their minimal number of visitations. They could pretend for their superiors; or they could invest an extra mile of exertion, time, interest, and work to make changes. Fewer social workers could find room to do this.

The Maddens didn't directly hit me or hurt me, except for two times.

When I was fed, sometimes I spat out, spraying, making noises with my tongue fluttering and lips vibrating, like babies do. Joseph would laugh. I would laugh. Mommy Sophia prevented that in different ways. But once when I was eleven months old, being fed mashed carrots from a jar at the high chair, Joseph came over, wanting to play and laugh, and stuck his tongue out, making that sound, prompting me to imitate.

It was winter, December, and the weather had been nasty and icy a few days. I had a cold and didn't sleep well that night, waking, crying repeatedly, waking everyone else as well. We were all cooped up. Mommy Sophia was in a bad mood that afternoon.

"Joseph, stop it!" she shouted. With a mouthful, I let loose, mimicking Joseph. A thick shower of mashed carrots ejected with force, speckling Mommy Sophia. She thrust her huge torso quickly backward, dropping the jar, then spoon, quickly sliding her chair a foot backward. I spontaneously burst with ecstatic laughter at her sudden recoil, thinking maybe she were playing. I wasn't sure though. Orange dappled her face, hair, glasses, blouse, and she simply stared in a momentary pause. Joseph laughed, and for some reason she seemed to descend into a chagrin, a shock, then an infuriation. Her expression collapsed, sinking into a fiend's. She cursed—a shout—with her face an inch from Joseph's. Terror swarmed the kitchen. He ran, and then I could hear his crying from the other room. She wouldn't strike him because New Blossom didn't permit hitting, or any spanking, and he was old enough to tattle. She stomped to the sink, turned the water on, saturating a dish towel, ringing it, wiping her face, shoulders, hair, removing glasses, cursing, washing away orange carrot.

I watched her, startled. I'd been happily opening my mouth spoonful after spoonful, distracted in playing with a toy, banging it on the plastic tray; but now I was afraid, motionless. My face froze, and I began to scream. My loud bellows, red face, tears, and carrots in and over my mouth incensed her further. She saturated the towel again, and with all of its watery weight she threw it at me with enraged force. It slapped me in the face with a soggy thud, smothering me, wrapping me. My neck and tiny head dashed back, banging the back of the chair. She washed my face violently. I suffocated, drowned, choked, was silenced, screaming inside, hearing her gnashing curses and words. Soaked, I finally caught my breath and mustered up a scream. She wrung the towel out over my head, her corpulent face wiggling, contorted with a furious grimace. Again I choked, drenched, silenced in a half-pint of water. She slapped me once more with this weapon, jolting my head to the side.

Once at fourteen months old, having one of my bad nights, my stomach ached with piercing cramps. I couldn't stop crying and screaming, pleading for mercy as I stood in my crib in darkness behind the closed door where I could hear the television muttering and Earl Madden murmuring far downstairs. Then I heard Earl's stomps ascending, my door opening, Earl's shouting through drunkenness and darkness, "Lay down and go to sleep! Hear me? Hear me? Lay down!"

I gaped at him with tear glazed face, squinting from the hallway's sudden lighted brightness, in terror. Earl slammed the door, sealing me back into the darkness where he remained silent for a minute. Two minutes. Again I began my screams, terrorized. The stomach pain ruled me. Darkness enclosed me in fear, confusion, and dread.

After another fifteen minutes Earl Madden's stomping murmurs ascended toward me a second time. The door whirled open. I could see his frothing face in the glaring hundred-watt hall light. I caught my breath from bellowing, feeling the hopeful pause of life and relief, thinking maybe I'd be rescued by someone. I saw that it was Earl. I felt fear. He moved toward me, reaching, abruptly buckling my head with his palms pressed against my temples, lifting me in this way—by my head—yanking my face rashly up to his so that my timorous eyes were fixed into his burning sockets, so that my delicate running nose grazed against his beer laden breath. Earl banged my slight knees and feet against the crib bars. "Lay down and go to sleep! Are you gonna lay down and go to sleep! Ha? Ha? Ha kid?" Partially dangling, partially leaning against the rail, My frail weight suspended, hung from Earl's callous hands, from my own head, by my flimsy neck. Earl tossed me back into the crib, flinging my frame against the bars on the opposite side, bouncing my slight weight onto my twisted foot and ankle on the stiff mattress, whacking my head on the rails.

Again Earl slammed my essence back into the darkness with the loud door, and he descended, stomping. Clearly, he wanted me to be quiet and go to sleep, but it certainly wasn't clear to me then. I whimpered, sobbed myself to sleep, still locked in an intense stomach pain. Yes, I was at the mercy of these, my foster parents.

In the warm months, I spent a lot of time outside, playing in a playpen in the shade of a wild cherry tree in the tiny yard that spread only twelve times broader than the playpen. I managed to remain content unaccompanied, sometimes for hours, until I became hungry, agitated by a mosquito, or frightened by the neighbor's barking Rottweiler. Sometimes Joseph played out there with me when Mommy Sophia was in the kitchen keeping us in her sight. There were times, in those balmy blue afternoons, Joseph would wander off. He would make me laugh and sometimes keep me interested in toys, his antics, little things in the yard. These times were my best at the Maddens', amusing diversions which quietly brought ease to my distress.

Like other babies, I loved the routines in life, like the morning cartoons. I felt a faint security in routine. The familiarity of my setting made me feel immune, ironically safe. The unfamiliar made me feel anxiety. With all my other struggles, a predictable course of simple daily affairs brought me reassurance, shielding me from fears. I needed the conditioning, the expectation, the regularity, the repetitions, no matter how oblivious I was to my misery. Ruptures in the routine, rearrangements, unexpected, clangorous surprises brought me dread and quiet panic.

Fridays were mountainous days. Disruption came on Fridays. That's when Sophia took me for my weekly noon visit with my birth mother Mommy Maureen at the agency.

We crossed the bridge into Brooklyn, withstood traffic, arrived downtown where Mommy Sophia left me and Joseph for two hours in the eight story New Blossom Children's Services office with our birth mothers. (Why the main offices were in the heart of Brooklyn rather than on Cary Island was because the city courts were there, and family court is an active place for the agency's lawyers and social workers involved in foster cases like mine.) Anyhow, Mommy Sophia loved this two-hour hiatus. She got a break for two hours. Whenever Mommy Maureen didn't show up though—which happened now and then—Mommy Sophia grew furious. She had to spend an hour one way in traffic, another hour to get home, and didn't get her break.

She was stuck with me in Brooklyn for two hours until Joseph's visit was finished. She was rough with me then, impatient, jamming me into the stroller, yanking me out, changing me violently—everything was done brutally. She took out her anger for Maureen on me.

Maureen Dillon was a stranger to me. As soon as I became nine months old I had that common sense of abandonment each week when I was handed to her for two hours. As there was no attachment, she was just an intruder, causing an attachment disorder, and she couldn't understand this. I was placed into her shaky hands. She endured my crying and those visits, but she was also angered by my snubbing her.

She loved the idea of getting healthy and keeping me. She hardly spoke, barely smiled, strove to force herself to get out of her enslavement to despair, out of her physical prison of addictions, out of herself, for me, or really for herself to keep me. I was her link to normality and sanity. Custody was an emblem, a symbolic badge to the world and herself of wellness and competence. Custody of my life was a manifest victory to her self-respect. Mommy Maureen's custody of her baby was for herself; it was not so much for me. She craved that applause.

She didn't know how to love her son, but she wanted to know and pretended to know. She knew how to give birth, but couldn't nurture. Her awkwardness at even holding me was evident even to me. I cried for half an hour sometimes. The consoling pacifier in my mouth as all that could tranquilize me.

Maureen was in a drug and alcohol program appointed by the agency. She had to attend, cooperate, extricate herself from her addictions, and maintain residence before a judge would consider granting her custody. She had to stay in the care of a psychiatrist. She had to show up for weekly visits, and she needed favorable weekly reports from Sandra Jackson.

Once when I was fifteen months old, after a visit with Mommy Maureen, in my exhaustion I fell asleep on the way home in my car seat. This I always did, but I usually woke up either before they returned home or once the car stopped in the driveway and the engine was turned off. But I kept sleeping this one time because I was extremely tired. So Mommy Sophia let me sleep in the car. It was about three o'clock, sunny, early April. The forsythias were beginning to bloom, the grass beginning greening. The sycamores extended their great bare arms as though sheltering, safeguarding. Wind gusts and breezes swirled. After about twenty minutes I awoke looked around, yawned, stared in a reverie, rubbed my eyes. This went on for about five minutes, until I started to become aware of my aloneness in that car, until my isolation among the faint sounds of the suburban streets and the murky noiselessness within the interior of the car seeped into my understanding, and until the hunger in my stomach made me hunger more, intensifying. I started to whine, appealing, wondering where exactly I was and where Mommy Sophia was. I wanted relief. I spotted my pacifier which had fallen to the car seat , but I couldn't reach it.

I recalled interactions with Mommy Maureen that Friday afternoon. Motionless recollections, memory glimpses and utterances flashed back. After minutes of whining, I whimpered and sniveled until fear gradually grabbed me, and I began to cry.

No one heard me, and no one came to rescue me. This continued until five o'clock, two hours alone there in the small world of the car. Terror, panic, and dread seemed to envelop me, smother me. I wrestled, grappled, tried to untangle my way out of the snug confinement of the car seat. Frustration. Rage. Fright—All these tormented me, giving me a puzzling desire to hurt myself.

Mommy Sophia assumed I still slept. A fusion of the television, the telephone, assumption that I kept sleeping, thoughtlessness, and carelessness forestalled her from checking on me. My hands and feet grew cold, diaper sodden, saturated, burning my skin. For two separated stretches of fifteen minutes I stopped crying, caught my breath. But then the terror returned.

Finally Mommy Sophia came for me, and when she opened the door she heard a howling scream, red-faced, with tears and mucus and saliva glazed over my face. This annoyed her. "All right, all right, it's okay, it's okay, you're all right, be quiet, be quiet, sssshhhh, ssshhh!" She said these things quickly, brusquely, in a scolding tone. Her fleshy, whiskered, squinting face was close to mine as she carried me in. I looked at her, hunting for a trace of love, comfort, pity, anything in her expression as she merely looked about the neighbors to see if anyone noticed as I cried. She was only angry.

It took me another two hours to get myself together after that, sitting, losing my breath, catching my breath, sniveling in distress. I felt a deep puncture of depression in my small heart. Mr. Madden and Sophia felt nothing that night. I slept in my crib exhaustedly until late the next morning, under their roof which I could never call mine, under bright and windy stars, under the long limbs of the deep rooted, growing sycamores.

THREE

SNOW CLOUDS

Mommy Maureen's efforts to reform herself satisfied a lenient judge—Judge Clement—who chaired a bench at the county's family court. Family court cases were many and daily in urban Cary County. Silas Dillon's was the seventh of twenty-three that crossed this judge's bench that particular February Thursday. Like another part in the assembly line, it was just another case, just another decision in the run of decisions. His mood that day was a little detached. Part of these judgments yielded to the conventions of New York's law, while the other depended on the umpire—his mood, his insight, his angle. Mommy Maureen was to be felt sorry for. Most people pitied my mother. She remained wretched, pathetic, and I was all she had to be proud of in life. People pitied her for that. She'd made mistakes she was sorry about. She cried, and did it publicly—before boards, at hearings, in court. "I just want my baby," she'd said often, sobbing. Rooms full of people got quiet and patient. Like I said, she was pathetic. This judge's heart rightfully thawed for her, but deludedly overlooked me, Silas Dillon of Cary County, in the shadows.

I had just turned two when this change began. The agency was to serve in watching closely by having a social worker recurrently drop in on the children unannounced to see how mother and son managed. She knew this.

Molly Fresh, a new social worker recently out of college arrived that next Monday morning to the Maddens' to bring me to my mother. That morning uncovered itself with a cold, still, colorless chill and an expectancy of forecasted snow. Mr. Madden had left for work. He didn't say "goodbye" to me. Mommy Sophia woke up early, dressed herself and me, and packed my things into a trunk and two boxes. Molly arrived, bundled, scarved, buttoned, knocking on the front door. Lifting me, Sophia opened the door. Thin cold air intruded like a spirit.

Small, slender, simply pretty and childlike with shoulder length, wavy brown hair—"I smell snow in the air," Molly said, stepping in, shivering, opening her coat collar button.

"It's going to snow," Sophia said, closing the door.

Molly looked down at my stuff on the floor by the door. She then looked at me, smiling. "How are you today Silas? You look so handsome. You're going to your mommy, ha? Aren't you?" She seemed to speak loudly. Her thick Brooklyn accent uttered quickly.

I just stared, holding one hand with the other, pulling my fingers. I did this when I was nervous. Sophia tried to put me down on my feet, but I clung to her, whining; so she held me, not wanting any contest. I'd never met this person Molly before this meeting, but I did feel easeful with her, never feeling that way around Sandra.

"I heard a lot about you," Molly said to me, looking into my eyes, speaking with a child's voice. "I've been reading his reports," she said to Sophia now with her adult's tone. "He seems to be pretty well adjusted here. I really hope this transition is a smooth one. His mom still seems sort of shaky to me." Molly talked with her hands clasped together, looking at me, then at Sophia, then at me. She seemed lively, and like she wanted to hold me; I liked her. I leaned for her and she reached for me, happy, lifting, holding me. She was much lower to the ground than Sophia—with probably a five-inch difference.

Sophia wrapped me in my coat, hat, hood, mittens, handed me back to Molly, and carried my things to the van. It seemed like my leaving was something I was eager for, but then outside in the stinging cold, before I was put in to be taken to Mommy Maureen, Sophia kissed me, holding my hand. There were tears in her eyes. One leaked down her cheek in the cold air. She smiled sadly, perhaps with regret. I watched as she walked up the steep porch into her house with her thick arms folded. She looked back once before closing the door, before the van shifted.

This car seat was large, high, different—one that enclosed, felt safe, yet unfamiliar. I was harnessed in, seated by the window in the first seat behind the young driver from the agency, beside Molly. The radio played. The heat whispered warmly, and the view from this van was so much higher than the view from Sophia's car. I sort of liked this.

This neighborhood I'd grown familiar with looked somewhat altered from this height. I stared out at the utter yellowness of the house in the gray backdrop of sky. Sophia opened a curtain to look. The driver looked into his mirrors, swiveling his torso, cautious, shifting into reverse. I could hear the beeping warning as the big vehicle moved into the street. The driver kept looking into his mirrors, his long pony tail remaining around his neck on the front of his shoulder. Out in the street, he shifted into forward, turned his wheel, driving, moving down the long street toward the boulevard, passing the bulky, thick sycamores which, like the blinking of my eyes, browned out my vision with quick successions as I looked out at the colors, looked away from this nice stranger Molly, passing—continually passing—shapes and colors and movements and bare life of the humanity of this cramped island. I wondered where we were going. I was moving. I didn't know it, but I'd never come this way again. I had no choice but to just go for this ride, to be taken, controlled, under authority, to be moved within the stiff movement of this rectangular, metallic-blue steel, through the gray air that would soon bring a storm of cold snow.

We crossed the island, near its fringe by the ocean. It was not a nice area, but the beach at New York Bay was three blocks away, and I could smell the seaway salt even in the still cold air. Mommy Maureen lived in a fourth story tenement dwelling. This was Bay Street, and it was jammed tight with parked cars, coercing the driver to double park. Molly released me from my seat and carried me as the driver grabbed my trunk and followed.

She opened an old, narrow door inviting us into this brown brick edifice. Once inside, this driver lit a cigarette. The smell reminded me of Mr. Madden's cigars. The blue suddenness of its aroma sweetened the moldy, rank smell of the foyer and hallway. I had to tilt my head back to see because the hood of my coat had pushed my woolen hat down, shielding my vision.

Inside was dirty, scrawled and scribbled with marks and graffiti—fouled white, with warped colorless tiles. The worn stairway creaked and the dilapidated banister wobbled loosely as though it would fall.

Molly and this man climbed. We heard murmuring. Sounds of voices and cries of children from behind doors resonated, pealing through metal doors with a thin, clear scraping.

This was an unearthly place—spooky, cubicle, thin echoing, dark. We elevated, trudging, with happy steps. Molly kept talking to me with a nice tone. "We're gonna go see Mommy. This is where ya gonna live, Silas. Hear the kids?" She breathed heavily. On the second landing, she stopped to rest, placing me down a minute. "I need a rest, Paul."

"No hurry. No hurry." He smiled, placed the trunk down, dragging on his cigarette.

I watched him with his head tilted and with complaisant lips sealed. He didn't look at me. I held my left hand with my right, continuing to nervously pull my fingers through his gloves. Molly pulled my hat up off my eyes so I could see better, and I looked at her. She looked momentarily intensely into my eyes, and she smiled. I didn't smile back, but looked away, quiet.

"Do you want to walk Silas?"

I nodded.

She took my hand, stepped up, and I followed—moving, rising, so slowly, one step at a time, with concentration.

"That's it. That's it. Big boy. Good."

I felt good about this. I felt proud. We ascended the rest of the way like this—slowly, ascending, around, around, spiraling. And as we moved, I looked down—carefully—at the steps and my small white sneakers. Right foot first, left following... the remainder of the way up—twenty-eight steps toward the unexplored, toward something new that I knew nothing about.

Molly looked at the top of my head, and at these steps, wondering about my future—the near future—and my life on these steps, in this hallway, with this woman, my birth mother Maureen, whom we verged upon.

They found the door on the fourth floor—number forty-four. Molly had been here before, doing her job by getting things in order in the process of reuniting a troubled mother with her two-year-old son—inspecting, writing reports, being nice, counseling, scrutinizing, admonishing, advising, urging, caring, talking, warning.

Molly waited until Paul caught up with the trunk. He was out of breath, with his half-consumed cigarette burning, protruding from the corner of his lips. He set the trunk down. "Here we are," Molly said. Her tone was a blend of a childish voice an adult voice, a preoccupied thoughtfulness toward this approaching encounter, this approaching trial of days with my unsupervised stay here.

She knocked on the wooden door. Footsteps. The door knob turned. The door opened. I glanced up. Mommy Maureen was smiling. Her red-brown hair was wet, dampening the front of her blue denim blouse as she'd just showered. She looked lovely as she bowed down to look at me, noticing fear in my eyes. "Silas," she said, reaching. I allowed her to lift me.

Mommy Maureen removed my coat and Molly stayed half an hour as I clung to her for asylum, as the persistent distress I felt around Mommy Maureen wouldn't leave me. I wanted my pacifier for solace and I kept asking for it, "Pafis! Pafis!" with tears, but neither of them knew what it meant as Sophia had. Neither knew how much it meant to me, and Sophia never told them. This frustration with the repellent, fetid smell of that apartment made me scared as I remained standing between Molly's knees—as though behind a shield—while she sat, talking to Mommy Maureen. She tried to encourage me to approach Maureen who held a stuffed bunny, dancing it on her knee like an inferior ventriloquist—pretending that the bunny sang to me. A crazy, tiresome song she created ad lib:

> *Silas is a little man. Silas is my friend.*
> *Silas, won't you be my friend.*
> *Silas, come and see me.*

She repeated this over and over, pausing between, staring and smiling at me somewhat insanely as I simply probed the inside of my mouth with my index finger, watching her scrupulously, then the bunny, her, and the bunny again, confused, disconcerted. The song seemed so obtuse to me even then, and she seemed to go in and out of her mind. She overdid this bid for my affection as the bunny's dull, crooked face actually made me feel like it really didn't want me, as much as it didn't want Mommy Maureen to bounce it around that way.

Molly remained patient. After the fourth dreadful chorus, reaching her arm up, Maureen made the bunny jump up high and slow, mimed its scream with a high-pitched *wheeeee*, flipped it over in the air, suspending it as though there were no gravity, and then made it fall quickly, landing on its mushy head with a loud, abrupt, *plplplplup* sound hastening from her lips and tongue.

Now I laughed, smiling, moving closer. This absurd little violence made it all seem so ridiculously funny as Mommy kept emitting that *plplplplush* sound from her extruding tongue, making the asinine stuffed bunny smash its head onto her thigh repeatedly—flattening its face—to keep me laughing, smiling, near her.

It wasn't obvious to me then, but she wanted me near her not because of fondness, but more so that Molly would be persuaded there was some bond between us. Maureen was always on stage, performing, proving, auditioning—even before outsiders, strangers in public. It had something to do with her mental form. So she performed with this bunny repeatedly, as I laughed afresh each time.

Paul had been waiting in the van all this time, probably smoking. When it came time for Molly to leave, she gave Mommy Maureen some more instructions, and then dropped down to her knees, saying to me with an obliging inflection, "Goodbye now Silas. Molly has to go now to see some other boys and girls. Molly will come and see you soon Silas. I love you. You are going to live with Mommy now. Okay? Molly will come see you, okay?"

I just gawked at her. She looked at me patiently, with her mind a little bit ahead, thinking about other responsibilities. She stroked my crimped, light brown hair and smiled, gazing into my trusting eyes. She tenderly squeezed my bronze colored cheeks. "He has the most beautiful blue eyes you know Maureen," she said earnestly.

"I know he does," Mommy responded proudly.

Amid her many job concerns and cases, I really believed Molly cared about me. She stepped out and closed the old door, and I was now left alone there with my birth mother for the first time since I was left with her in that hospital room after my birth.

Mommy Maureen carried my trunk into the adjoining little room, which would be mine. Besides a white dresser subdued by dark blue Yankees' baseball logo and a used crib, there was nothing about this room that would be engaging for a two-year-old. The walls and floor badly needed painting and refinishing, and the old, high wooden window needed cleaning. Looking up through its glass

I could see only smudges and the sheer, stark whiteness of the sky behind. I could hear the wind pressing lightly against the rattling window. Snow began to fall as I could view from my angle an intermittent large flake finding its resting place against the pane and sash.

My first day was exhausting. Mommy talked and talked, often with her face right up to mine. She required complete attention. I watched television and played a little with the few toys Mommy Maureen had there. I cried twice in my fear, crying "Pafis, pafis," but my cries did not bring me my comforting pacifier.

I fell asleep for an hour on the couch. All day I could hear noises, noises above the ceiling, footsteps, voices, some hollering, banging from the apartment next door, and loud music on the other side from the apartment there. It was such a loud, low old place. I could hear horns on the street, and of course all day Mommy talked, rambling to herself, to me. She talked to me about things as though I were an adult, rambling as I listened bewildered, quickly learning to just ignore.

"Dipa. Dipa," I said at about noon, pulling at my pants so she'd know to change my diaper. She never thought to check. While she kneeled and changed my diaper, and as I lay on the dirty floor beneath her leaning torso, she talked: "You're two now. If you think you're gonna go in your diaper much longer you got another thing comin! Sit still! Lay still I said! I got enough goin' on here. There's a movie comin' on at four I'm not gonna miss so I don't want you whinin' about nothin'. Jasmine and Carl are comin' by tonight so I want you to be sleepin'." She rambled with her speech like this often. In her eyes were waves of buried anger alternating with looks of far lostness and crazed glares.

Snow fell for hours that day, but I couldn't see it falling as the flakes blended with the white sky. The only visible accumulation was what huddled against the pane. I climbed onto a chair which stood against the wall under the window in the living room and stood to see out. This brought me to a complete other world. It was dusk, and the snow stopped falling, and it began to clear. Like a seagull from an unmanned crow's nest of an old mast, I looked from this height, out, down Bay Street toward the east where, over some roofs, I could see the gray-green of the bay and the soft splatters of white caps surfacing, sinking, surfacing, sinking... The sky seemed lavender, almost touchable. Across the quarter mile distance and beside the ocean the visible lights of Brooklyn flickered, with a sparkling commotion from Coney Island and the Shore Parkway's snake of headlights moving toward Manhattan, around Bay Ridge. I just stood there looking out, looking for life, spellbound by the color, the white, the humanity, the shattered overcast, the sights of the urban streets of Cary Island.

By nightfall the heavy clouds had moved east and the stars polished the blackness with a cold, shiny brilliance. I had to press my face against the pane to see, to avoid the reflection of myself and of the ugliness which opened behind me.

Mommy's two friends Jasmine and Carl arrived, but they didn't pay any attention to me. Jasmine was a very dark-skinned lady, about thirty. She spoke with a Haitian accent, and she didn't smile—not once—and she seemed angry, and seemed to stay that way most of the time they were there. Carl was thin, not as dark as Jasmine, with a shaved head, silver jewelry bulging from pierced flesh on his face—ears, brows, nose, lip, tongue—a dark goatee, a quiet, ominous stare from black irises and pupils that seemed to peer through thin, crevice-like fissures.

Another older man named Jack entered with them. He seemed about fifty, only he was white, slovenly fat, partially intoxicated, and even though he dressed in a dark blue business suit and tie, he appeared bedraggled as his tie hung from his neck, and his white shirt draped untucked.

They then opened little plastic packages of heroin, syringes, spoons, straws, and matches. They lit flames, strapped their arms, squeezed their fists, craving, famished. Mommy and Jasmine injected this into their veins as I watched, and Carl inhaled it through a thin straw, vacuuming it directly into his wide nostrils.

Jack wanted nothing to do with this heroin. He was here for something else. He waited patiently and just sipped brown alcohol from a small flask he kept in his pocket. I could feel something diabolic in the atmosphere of the apartment, and it made me nervous, even frightened. All three of these heroin users felt their rushes of euphoria, the transient soaring painlessness, and they groaned with sighs of pleasure and sick laughs, followed by lapses into apathy. There was energy—a fallacious energy. Numbing painlessness, a rest which wearied and a beguiling painlessness which dug its ulcerous wound paradoxically deeper, held them. This was my birth mother's perpetual appetite, to find freedom from her pain—pain from whatever it was that weighed heavily in her from her past, pain from her broken relationships, from all the self-inflicted wounds and those from other inflicted humans, pain from regret of mistakes made in her own selfishness.

After a while Mommy Maureen went into her bedroom with this enormous man and his bottle of booze. She remained in there for an hour while Jasmine and Carl watched the television, and while I sat, observing, pulling my fingers, gouging my slight finger nails into my own skin, distressed, wanting to sleep, wanting someone to hold me, rock me, observing their cadaverous deadness, excitableness, and feverishness, walking to the chair to look out at the night, seeing lights outside in the darkness, seeing my own frightened reflection. I cried for about one minute—very hard—with violent screams, and then I simply stopped. Jasmine kept looking at me with dead, mean eyes: "Shush! Shush boy! Now shush!" She shouted with her Haitian, demanding manner.

That big man finally came out, without his tie on, carrying his jacket, with his giant shirt tucked in now, and his pants pulled and belted a little higher. His thick flesh shook and jiggled as he walked.

He didn't even look at me. It was as though I didn't exist, as though I were nothing, like a cat. There was this indulgent aura, this permissive indulgence with carelessness that amounts to hatred that came out of this man. None of those present knew of what people were involved in this big man's life, but whoever they were, they were not better because of him.

Mommy came out after him wearing nothing but a very long tee-shirt over her underwear. She came right to me, with a nervous energy, with talking, with confusion, with hurry. She lifted me as I reached for her. "You're going to bed!" she said, and that was all.

She dropped me into my crib without changing me. I didn't go to bed that night with my pajamas on. She didn't even take off my sneakers. I cried for a minute, but was so tired I just drifted off into sleep. I woke up twenty minutes later in the darkness, and cried again, but this time I kept crying, screaming until my mother returned for me. She brought me back out into the living room.

It was finally time for giant Jack to leave, and as Jack and Carl walked toward the door, there was no conversation. Carl said, "Good, good," as he quickly counted a fist full of bills Jack passed onto him. Jack tipped his heavy head back, swilled a long gulp from his flask, scuffed his lumpy mass out the door and closed it behind him. I could hear his stout steps in the hallway as his rhinoceros-like massiveness moved toward the stairway. Then, suddenly they could hear a shout, a descending clamor, a crash, more pained collapsing shouts that seemed to jerk vociferously out of his wide mouth, with more clamorous crashes, shouts and uproars of Jack's plenteous flesh as he fell for maybe fifteen steps down the rickety stairway. I imagined the whole building shook. Inside, Carl stopped his motion, listening. Silence. A giggle burst out of Maureen's mouth, while Jasmine palmed her mouth as she watched Carl and Mommy.

Carl stepped out to see what had happened. "Ya all right? Ya all right?" I could hear Carl saying in the hallway.

Big Jack's moans returned: "Yeah. I think so," he said with a dilatory, growling,

Time lapsed, and Carl came in with his goatee and gold adorned face, laughing.

"What happened?" said Jasmine.

Carl could barely get it out, trying to speak through his overwhelming laughter. "He fell–" laughter. "He fell. He fell down the stairs!" Crass, stoned laughter followed.

"He fell?" Mommy said. Then she burst out in laughter, and kept laughing.

They all laughed for a long time. Huge Jack limped and staggered to his car.

This little deviant group laughed like demons. They scarcely spoke to one another, yet they adhered together like ill parasites bleeding energy from each other. This sick laughter was the only semblance of joy they expressed, and that quickly withered.

After everyone left, Mommy fell asleep on the couch. So when I became tired, I curled up on the other end and slept as well. I was so tired, and I needed a bath too. I felt a little bit safer with these strangers gone. Mommy was familiar. Sleep was my favorite place. It was the taken for granted, soothing dressing of an exhaustively lonely day. I had no thought of tomorrow. God, or tomorrow itself, or both would care about all those things there; but of course I didn't know or believe that then. I just slept, breathed, and dreamed of sights I'd seen from that high window, and dreamed of Carl, Jasmine, Jack, Mommy, and other monsters.

FOUR

APPLE BOUGHS

Molly's third surprise visit from the agency was the one that caught me alone in the apartment. It was an April day, like the day Mommy Sophia left me in the car a year earlier—a sunny, breezy, kite flying late afternoon—more than a month after the day I was placed here.

Molly climbed the long stairway, knocked, and spoke at the other side of the door: "Maureen! Maureen!"

When I recognized Molly's safe, amiable voice, I ran to the door.

"Silas honey, how are you? Are you okay honey? Is Mommy there Silas?"

I replied with one-word answers: "Mommy. Door," and with some two-year-old, unintelligible words too.

She knocked on the door harder, calling, "Maureen! Maureen!" thinking maybe she was asleep, or in the bathroom. She waited patiently. Finally, "I'm going to get the man to open the door Silas, okay?"

I was silent, turning the door knob, playing, jiggling it, curious.

"I'll be right back, honey."

Molly went for the building superintendent to open the door. I played contentedly with the knob. Other times when there were knocks on the door I stood silently, in stationary fear, until the unknown visitor left.

Maureen was somewhere on the street for two hours, a risk she'd taken—maybe ten or twelve times. There were times she'd take me with her, but usually I was too much of a bother, especially when she'd get high. She really was proud of me, but none of her friends in the street or in their flats found me adorable. Once she left me alone all night, but fortunately I'd slept through most of that one. Many of those hours were lonely, tear-filled, terror-filled hours; some were quiet, imagination filled, play filled hours. I manufactured imaginary friends to play with.

On at least a dozen nights that month Mommy Maureen had different men visit her. She'd take them into her dark bedroom for about an hour, and then they'd just leave. One man visited three times like this. None of them ever talked much. Most of them were apparently ordinary men, well-thought-of in their business spheres, men with families and jobs and responsibilities, but also obviously with sordid secrets.

Maureen frequently got high that month. I sometimes watched her inject her vein with the syringe, and usually curiously inquired, "Dat?" asking what it was she was doing.

"Medicine. Mommy's medicine," she'd say.

"What dat, Mommy?"

"I said medicine!" she said louder.

She never sat me down to read me a story or tell me a story or just talk to me. Her thoughts were always somewhere else, planning, worrying, racing, struggling.

Finally Molly came back with the superintendent and a policeman, just in case Mommy had returned and would cause some trouble. Molly had full authority from the court to move me. As she gathered my few things together, the men waited. I stood by the couch watching when the policeman looked at me and saw the fear and alarm in my inquisitive eyes. He smiled at me, but all I saw in his smile was his mouth. There were no words, no eyes. He was tightly packed with dark blue and squeaking leather, with sternness, writing things down in reports, with sunglasses on, ignoring the radio that kept speaking in static from his waist. The old superintendent of the building curiously walked around the messy apartment, murmuring low. These alarmed me, I started to cry.

Molly came from my room with my stuff jammed in my trunk. She knelt and hugged me saying, "It's okay. Ah, it's okay, Silas honey. Everything's going to be all right. It's okay, baby." She continued to hug me and pat my small back until I stopped. Then they left the apartment, making their slow descent down the feeble stairway. Molly kept talking to me, filling me with soothing words, occupying my thoughts with hopes, saying things I wanted to hear, promising me candy and juice, making me laugh, teasing me, making funny noises, tickling, distracting, aiming to make me feel secure. I laughed nervously with tears on my face all the way to her car.

We drove a few blocks down this street—Bay Street—which I'd observed so often from the high window standing on that chair, through this urban din; and we stopped at a convenience store for that juice and candy. It was one of those old general stores with those creaky wooden floors and a peculiar sense of crookedness. Four stories of apartments piled above it. Molly used her own money to buy me lollypops, chocolate covered raisins, juice, and a toy—a little monkey that danced in a circle when I pressed a hidden button.

When they stepped back outside into the sunlight, what was unusual was that in the lot beside the old building there lived the remnants of an old apple orchard—five tremendous trees with limbs intermeshed in their white blossoms—like lacework—grown closely locked together through the years like intimate human lives. They stood there in noticeable ambivalence, out of place, unobtrusive, surrounded by the municipal congestion, looking aged, mature, and graceful, full of fluffy whiteness, wisdom, and with stories to tell from Cary County's rural past. If these beautiful, full-blossomed trees could have seen and spoken, they'd reveal with lament the passage of change that had taken place. They stood poised among all the other commotion of structure and alteration like the resilient, buoyant, nineteenth century "tall" ships by the piers at South Street—seemingly lost beside, but at the same time shining bright sites beneath the newer colossal structures in the financial district on Manhattan Island. They stood poised like white haired aged patriarchs and matriarchs, aside and unassuming as ones might at a family reunions, quietly observant, brimming with secret sagacity and sage secrets, heavy with a sorrow over the change, brokenness, pace, and departure from the old ways, quietly moved by the plight of their grandchildren and great grandchildren who lived fragmented by divorce, separation, remarriage, in blended, jumbled, and mixed up homes.

Molly and I sat beneath these exquisite white apple boughs on a worn wooden picnic table. On one side breathed the busy street; on the three other sides stood graffiti-ridden walls. In the sheltering white shade it seemed our skin was made bluer.

"Molly loves you."

I fixed my little eyes on Molly's.

"Molly loves Silas," she said, looking at me, handing me chocolate covered raisins. Her eyes kept watering up as she gazed at me, broken over my being neglected and left alone in that apartment. I devoured the candy, enjoying eating in hunger.

"Mommy loves Silas," I repeated. I couldn't say *Molly*. I couldn't pronounce my *l's* yet. This was an antilogy. She poured more of a mother's love on to me than anyone had, and I clumsily called her *Mommy*.

"Molly. Mollllly," she said, teaching me the l sound, stretching the l's.

I watched her, chomping on my chocolate covered raisins, drooling.

"Mollllly!"

"Molmy," I replied, partially attentive to the little monkey's dance as I repetitively pressed the button.

"Molly."

"Molmys."

She laughed. Her youthful, blonde radiance and simple manner found me adorable. I found her so pleasant to be with, a magnetic adult I'd not experienced except for when I first entered, born in the hospital with that nurse.

I laughed, copying her, still chewing and drooling chocolate. I kept saying "Molmy" because of the reaction from Molly, because it brought me an unconsciously sought for approval.

She rubbed my golden frizzy hair and touched my brown smiling face. "You're so bronze," she said. "Oh you're so beautiful. Do you know that?" She leaned her pretty face close to mine, adoring.

This made me feel so good inside. "Bonze," I said, nodding. I simply agreed to anything her tone led me to agree with. I didn't know what bronze meant. I knew she thought I was handsome, maybe unique looking. I knew she loved me. I felt and welcomed such an authentic acceptance from her, and I wanted more. I loved her, or at least I loved her love.

"Oh Silas, if I were married and didn't have to work, I'd take you home with me and make you my boy."

I nodded again, eating my candy, happy in ignorance.

I could have remained there under those apple tree canopies forever, eating chocolate, securing attention from Molly; but that wouldn't be. She sipped soda from a straw and we sat quietly awhile listening to the sounds of the street—cars, voices, clatter, clangs, bells, and clacks; we sat quietly absorbing what would one day become just a memory, a dream that faded or blurred, and then it was time to get back into the car and go.

Once again I was fastened into a car seat willing to go wherever I was taken, only this time I was handed a big lollypop to hold with my free hand, while my other hand clutched my toy possessively. Molly gave me a big kiss on my cheek, and playfully said—"Will you marry me, Silas? Will you be my husband? I need a husband," she said to me.

I nodded again. My puerile, uninstructed, faultless expression in agreement was what she was after.

"You're so funny!" she said laughing. She moved into the front seat, started the engine, and drove into the sunny glistening traffic. While she drove, she began to sing, and this arrested my fascination and focus. She sang half to me and half to teach me, that comfortable old song:

> *Jesus loves me, this I know*
> *For the Bible tells me so.*
> *Little ones to Him belong*
> *They are weak, but He is strong.*
> *Yes Jesus loves me. Yes Jesus loves me.*
> *Yes Jesus loves me, the Bible tells me so.*

"Sing with me, Silas!" She looked at me through her mirror, and she sang again. She sang with a strong, sweet, purposeful voice—admiring God, teaching me. She kept singing through it—three times, four times. Soon I joined in in my baby way. It stayed in my head for the rest of that day and night, and would emerge again from time to time, and I would just sing it in my clumsy way. At that hour I felt happy to have this person who loved me in my nearness, this person who made me feel well.

FIVE

FLIES

For two weeks I stayed in the Cary County Children's Center, which was formerly an orphanage administratively adjoined to the agency in Brooklyn, but which was physically in the center of this island. It was a tremendous house that really wasn't a permanent orphanage anymore: it was just called that because once, years ago and for a century, it had been an orphanage. Now it was just a holding coop, sort of a place where kids like me were kept when we were initially removed from abusive, dangerous situations, during transitions—changeovers between homes—until "fitting" foster homes could be found for placement. Ideally, guardians who treated foster kids as their own—with love and rightful intention—were the sort the agency appealed to.

Molly worked very hard for me—as she did for all of her assignments—to place me in good foster care, with preferably both a foster mother and father. Of course I didn't know this, but for the time being I just thought that this was where I lived—in the Cary County Children's Center, and the way every kid lived—in this big, seascape mural papered room amid rows of cribs and beds; and the other big, cityscape mural papered room amid three long tables and a dozen highchairs where all the kids ate and were fed beside the big, sizzling, clanging kitchen; and the other big, farm mural papered room, the playroom filled with toys and noise and kids and sofas and chairs and a big-screened television, with cows and pigs and chickens plastered on the plaster walls.

I didn't get to see Molly a lot here. She was busy working—visiting foster homes, on the telephone, in the Brooklyn office where she was making good impressions on her superiors and talking with lawyers and judges about kids' cases. But when she came here, she visited me and other kids she knew. She always made contact, physical contact, with touches, with hugging and kissing. God she made me feel good.

I was never alone or bored here. There was too much stimulus: battles, crying, activity, shouts, laughter, people coming and going. It was a busy, noisy place even though it was only half-filled with kids. I lived here for two weeks, but those weeks passed swiftly. The young people who worked here weren't the most loving to me, but I always ate and had my physical needs met. It was here that I finally became toilet trained. I wanted to be like Billy, one of the bigger kids (a three-year-old) here who knew how to use the toilet. The young workers who cared for us worked effectively hard to get the two-year-olds trained.

During this particular year—like many others—there lingered a scarcity of foster homes, a need that led the agency to advertise the need to people of the island and the surrounding boroughs. Advertisements emphasized the need, the benevolence factor, the reward of personal satisfaction, and the frequent opportunity for permanent influence through permanent adoption. Monthly, monetary county assistance was rarely a motivation factor because it amounted to only less than a dollar an hour on a twenty-four hour a day basis.

Many of the foster homes had even more than three foster children lodging at a time. The ideal foster homes were hard for the agency to crack open. People—even church people—just didn't see the need, or even care to get involved, or see it as a "calling," or want to see. That's just the way it was, and always had been. Oh, there was sympathy. People perfectly capable would enter, observe, think hypocritically "Someone should do something. Isn't it sad? People need to get involved. Oh, isn't this heartbreaking, these poor kids," or things like this; and then they'd feel perfectly justified because they felt pity. But their affect would end there, making no difference. There was this clear, tragic avoidance—among many—this clear fear of any encroachment into their ease. This pitiful self-preservation was itself pitiable. Molly and workers like her were always angered by this, and often outspoken.

On one afternoon in particular, it was sunny, humid, still. For some reason during that May the orphanage was full of flies, flies that I had to keep brushing from my face, perpetually buzzing about my face, always stealing, stealing moments of time in swats, brushes, and head shakes; stealing peace, order and rest, seemingly hungry for something on my and others' skin, or just plain eager to annoy. They were useless things, parasites, noise makers, annoyance makers, time wasters.

Molly was there that afternoon, and she was bothered by the flies and the heat. She was introducing the children to a certain couple—Mr. and Mrs. Comforti, thirty-five-year-olds, parents of two of their own—potential foster or adoptive parents. They came to possibly choose. They weren't forced there, but neither were they there entirely voluntarily. He was a lawyer: Anthony Comforti, Counselor at Law; she stayed at home. They had a textbook house and situation. Standing in the huge playroom Molly said, "They all come from different situations, some worse than others."

Mrs. Comforti, with a strained expression from a tanned, golden-earringed, shiny-lipped face, said, "What's the matter with so many parents? Why can't they get their acts together? Why won't they take care of their own kids?" These weren't questions she wanted answered. They were statements. She recognized lack of responsibility.

"I know what you mean," Molly responded.

"I mean all these kids—and more—just dumped on society and tax payers!" Now Mrs. Comforti was recognizing—maybe—her responsibility.

"It's the way it's always been."

"Tst tst. So sad. And they're so cute!"

Many of us kids weren't very cute.

Attorney Comforti looked at his Rolex. He had an appointment or something. He was a law guardian for some of the kids here, and some in the foster homes. It was his job. He worked a lot at family court where Molly spent a lot of time. That's how Molly got connected with this couple. Molly's guess was that he was more willing to be open to taking in a child than his wife was. But beyond his occupation, this was the closest he got to these orphans, us homeless kids.

"Oh, we're going to talk about this, certainly," Mrs. Comforti said, eager to leave, avoiding any pressure from Molly. She fidgeted with her fingers on her pearl necklace.

Noticeable silence. They walked, looked into the sleeping quarters, into the big kitchen, into the dining hall.

"We were thinking of moving out to Long Island. Might that throw a wrench into the works if we take a child?"

"No," said Attorney Comforti.

"Not at all. Not at all," said Molly. "We have a lot of homes—even Suffolk County."

"I told you that, honey," the attorney said to his wife, somewhat chafed.

She looked at him especially strained now, embarrassed.

"Well I don't remember Tony. This is all so much at one time. How can I remember everything about all this?"

Molly felt awkward. She didn't know how to back off at this point. After some hesitation, she said "Mrs. Comforti, we have a two-week program—two nights a week you can come for two hours each night. It's an eight-hour orientation—gets potential foster parents acquainted with everything they might have to face. We create typical scenarios. We screen. You might find this is not for you. But our hope is that you might find yourself challenged and eager to help a child with your means. Some of these kids have a lot of baggage; that's for sure—a lot of hurt and history. We aim to fit each family with the most fitting child. We put your foot into the water first. We don't just thrust a bunch of kids on anyone at once. It could really be a rewarding challenge—for your two children as well."

Mrs. Comforti avoided eye contact with Molly. Molly had a way of burning through with her deep gaze. It was obvious that this lady was hedging. Molly could pick that up now having a few months of experience with people.

The Comfortis looked at each other. Couples have a way of reading and communicating volumes to one another through subtle glances.

"We're going to talk about this Molly," the attorney said.

Mrs. Comforti said, "You have an appointment don't you, honey?" She was eager to get out, away from Molly, us troubled kids, the persuading and dissuading air there, and all the flies. To her there was something very unrefined, even un-American about all of this talk of taking in children. She had the perfect family. A special, distressed child as an addition—even temporary—might rob them of all they'd worked toward. What if members of their extended family found this upsetting? What if friends found this repulsive? What if vacations, visits to salons and malls were hindered? This was all too sudden, threatening the apple cart.

Mrs. Comforti had an expression of pain on her face, like someone had just poured dirty water on her.

"Somebody's got to help, Mrs. Comforti. These kids need homes. None of them deserve or asked for this," Molly said.

"Yes, I think we know this."

"If you know of anyone willing, please direct them to us." I could hear the spleen in Molly's tone. She wanted them out, away. "Well, we'll say goodbye now. Goodbye." There was a sarcasm, a "shame on you" in her intonation. Molly was shooing these people away, like they were the flies she'd been waving her hands against, as though they were parasites. She wanted to get back to productive work. She was committed, and it showed. She'd thought the Comfortis were beautiful trout, a fine catch, parents for one or some of us, but they turned out to be unavailing, fruitless.

As they exited, Molly griped to one of the child care workers, "I got better things to do than sweeten stuck up snobs! What's the matter with people?"

"Well at least they came. Farther than most people get. I guess they can't be bothered."

"Who knows, maybe they'll be back. Out of our hands. Another possible is coming at four. We'll see if they show, then I have to make some visits."

A few sets of possible parents visited that day, wasting time, not committing. They buzzed around the orphanage like flies.

The flies buzzed the rest of that day. The warm sun shined over Cary Island until the evening made its descent into darkness. Soft zephyrs of air blew, carrying gentle scents of lilac and rose, cut grass and salty brine through our screens as we were put to bed. Two-year-old life at the orphanage for two weeks wasn't really bad, at least for us two-year-olds who didn't know what we didn't have, or what we needed.

SIX

GULLS

Daddy placed his gigantic right hand over my head. It felt like his fingers enfolded me, enveloping more than half of my head. His fingers were like protective wings of some big mother bird. His other hand held my shoulder and arm. His thumb across my chest was like a ping-pong paddle. Mommy Lucinda placed her soft gentle hand on my back, seated on the couch behind me with her eyes closed tightly—I imagined—as they always were when she prayed. Daddy knelt on one knee beside me on the carpet. Even kneeling he towered above me. I simply watched his inch-close, large red lips and his black, whiskered skin and his tightly shut eyes as he prayed for me. His voice was deep, buried, rich, mighty: "Lord Jesus, You have placed this child Silas into our home, giving us charge over his life."

He hesitated. I listened for a moment to the purring vibration of the nearby air conditioner.

"Yes Lord. Yes Jesus," Mommy Lucinda agreed.

As Daddy continued I could feel his breath, even his heart, it seemed: "Lord your word welcomes us to come to you. Lord your word promises us many things Jesus. Lord we lift this child to you now."

47

At this point I expected them to lift me up. They didn't.

"Jesus," Daddy continued, his voice raising, deepening: "Heal this child we ask. Place Your mighty hand upon this child! Let him breathe, Lord! Open his lungs! Jesus, we present this child to You. You've created this child! You've breathed the breath of life into him, now help him respire, Jesus!"

I could hear my own belated wheezing between his sentences.

Mommy prayed aloud now: "Dear Jesus, we again dedicate this child to You. Cause him to grow up in You, Lord!"

Daddy would add, "Yes, Lord! Amen, Jesus," repeatedly while Mommy led the praying.

"Make him a man of God, Jesus. Protect him. Keep him we pray. Keep him from the evil one. Surround him with Your angels! Swing open gates for this child, Lord"

At this point I had an itch on my back, and I tried to reach it from over my shoulder. I squirmed, twisting. "Itchy," I said.

Mommy Lucinda felt my wriggling, and while she closed the praying, saying, "Thank You for hearing us, Jesus! Thank You for the cross where You died for us, Jesus," she thoroughly scratched my back with her long, lovely nails, orbiting her smooth brown hands. She scratched and scratched, and it was satisfying ecstasy for me. Then she turned me around and hugged me, pressing my head close against her neck, kissing my head.

Daddy rose to his height—way up by the ceiling—five inches more than six feet. He'd played basketball in college, and was quite good at it. He pulled my nebulizer from the hall closet, plugged it in, poured a measure of medicine into the nebulizer reservoir from a dropper, and delicately placed the mouthpiece over my nose and mouth, strapping the elastic band around the back of my head, and then he turned the machine on. Vapors discharged, slowly emanating. Vapors formulated to alleviate asthma such as mine puffed up, floating. Remedying mist to assuage grim asthma—caused from my mother's heavy smoking while she'd carried me in her womb—evaporated into my lungs and into the air. I breathed, rested, cooperated. I don't know how or why this cropped up, but I was diagnosed with this one night last year as I couldn't breathe, when I was four.

Mommy inserted a video tape so I could watch a cartoon as I sat, allowing the medicine to work. The air conditioner's purring and the nebulizer's lulled murmur were muted by the voluble varied sounds from the television.

"Comfortable Silas?" Daddy said with his hearty voice.

I nodded, eyes fixed on the television. For half an hour I sat—watching—immersed in the simple plotline of the show, breathing, widening my airways, immersed in the regenerating vapors and as happy as a five-year-old could be.

Molly had found me this place, these people—one of these rare, marvelous foster homes—after I'd waited at the orphanage. For three years my foster family had treated me like one of their own. They only had one other—a ten-year-old, Justin. Their name was Sparks: Max and Lucinda Sparks, Pastor and Mrs. Sparks. Yes, Daddy was a minister, a Pentecostal minister.

They wanted to adopt me, especially now since I'd been with them for more than three years, right into this hot July. What held up any adoption proceedings was the law—the law that provided rights—extended rights—to my Mommy (Maureen) who was holding on, who—because she seemingly made efforts to improve, because she was in a special unhealthy category—had rights, who because she had been making some faintly potent efforts toward rehabilitation, had acquired some forbearance from the courts, even after the mistakes she'd made. What averted any adoption was the dawdling of the courts combined with the loitering of the New Blossom agency and the hesitation of Judge Clement.

The Sparks lived here on Cary Island right beside the little church he pastored in. I had a real daddy whom I idolized and a real mommy whom I loved to be near. These three years were so agreeably pleasant, like Joseph of old in his naming his firstborn Manasseh, I seemed to have forgotten all my former anguish. Or maybe it was because I was only five.

Justin was the best big brother any five-year-old could have. He always took me places with him, even when he was amused with another ten-year-old friend of his. He took me fishing and swimming at the nearby docks and beach by the bay in the summer. He pulled me around on his sled on snowy winter mornings. He taught me how to swing a stickball bat and play handball. He read books to me—like the children's Bible. He made me laugh. Sometimes I got on his nerves of course, and he'd get very angry and frustrated, wanting to be away from me; but generally he was patient, untiring, unruffled. He sort of liked being a big brother, having a brother, I guess.

Justin was very protective of me. If I'd do something wrong in the house, he'd cover for me, prevaricate for me, protect me. If there was something on my plate that I hated to eat, he'd eat it for me; or if he didn't like it either, he'd furtively dump it into the garbage so that I wouldn't be denied dessert later before bedtime.

One time we were in the bathroom and he was showing me how to do pull-ups on the towel rack, which was made of porcelain—adhered amid porcelain tiles. He'd been taking fitness tests in gym class that week, so there was this enchantment and immersion in this at home as well, manifested in standing broad jumps in the hallway, sprints with his watch as a pretend stop-watch on the sidewalk, and sit-ups by the television. Anyway, I had to participate too. I was hanging from the towel rack in the bathroom: "Stretch your arms down all the way! All the way!" he said, teaching. "Now pull! Pull up! Pull your chin over the bar, all the way! That a boy! That a boy! You can do it! I knew you could!" He was imitating his gym teacher—Mr. Thew—a young gym teacher whom he'd idolized. As I was doing this, luxuriating in Justin's Let's play school, suddenly everything came tumbling down, crashing down, shattering down in a loud breaking and clattering. It was an avalanche in tiles—half the wall! The adherent grout provoked the domino effect. There was this cloud of grout dust; this still pile of tiles, mostly broken; this sorrowful, dull incredulity in the air between us; this panicked, frenzied stare—my eyes to his, his to mine; this disturbing scramble in Justin's thinking for a fiction for Mommy. Our ears rang. It was actually very resounding. From downstairs, it must've sounded like the whole upstairs of the house caved in, imploding.

Mommy Lucinda came running up the stairs. Pausing at the top of the landing, listening, curious. "Justin?" she said inquisitively, investigatively, a little frightened about what she might find.

With hesitation: "Yeah, Mom," Justin responded with a forced casualness in his tone, with this strained "everything's normal here" craftiness in his whole manner. I stood silently awaiting.

"Where are you?"

Halting. "In the bathroom."

"What was that noise?"

I could hear her walking this way.

"What noise?" Nobody laughed at his question. Justin hurriedly snatched up the towel from under the rubble on the floor, and he quickly took the towel bar from my fists; I yielded.

"That loud crash," she said demandingly loud, walking, verging upon us.

"Oh that."

Mommy Lucinda entered. "Oh my," she said, covering her mouth, eyes wide.

There was silence for what seemed a long time. We both stared at Mommy, fearful, thinking of Daddy. Her eyes gaped at the mess;

they rose up at me, then higher at Justin. Her hand remained over her mouth, as though this helped her think.

I looked at Justin. His black skin seemed to look more effulgent, as though he blushed. He looked at me, and I imagine my burnished complexion changed—maybe paler—as well.

"Justin, what happened? Are you hurt? Are you hurt Silas?"

"No Mommy."

"Justin what are you two doing up here."

I never would have gotten in trouble for this, because Justin brought this all about, spurring me, pretending I was his gym student. But at ten, he actually thought I'd be scolded since I was the towel bar gymnast, since my body was the one that physically hung from the fixture. Perhaps he believed he would have received some of the blame since he was older and knew better and didn't steer me away from this; but still he didn't want me to catch any castigation from this. I know this. He loved me. He really had this protective, sheltering nature about him. She waited for a response. He balked.

Finally he declared, "I just dried my hands, Mom."

Her look was one he couldn't read.

"I swear, Mom. I just dried my hands and this happened."

Silence. A blend of disbelief, and what looked to me like delight, arrested Mommy's face.

"I had to wash my hands, and then I just dried my hands," he said again, sounding somewhat more convincing.

But this was even funny to me, because Justin never voluntarily washed his hands.

Mommy Lucinda's expression of astonishment, bewilderment, and rage thawed remarkably into a trifling smile, which erupted into a tremendous grin, which then softened into giggling, and then just sweepingly liquefied into bursting laughter that kept running, and running. She slapped her thighs, bowing her torso up and down, covering her mouth, roaring with laughter, dripping with tears of laughter. Then I began laughing my usual, nervous, confused, fake laughing. Justin allowed himself to smile—at Mommy. Mommy really tried to control this because she didn't want Justin to make light of any "embellishment" which basically amounted to lying—on his part; but she couldn't. The absurdity, the preposterousness of the wall of tiles collapsing because of a simple customary act of drying hands was just too much for her on this day. This was medicine. This produced part of the medicinal joy of life for my Mommy Lucinda on this day. How we must've looked—our juvenile expressions—Justin's bright black face and my blue-eyed, bronze, innocent look beside a pile of mischief's evidence and destruction! By the sound of the sudden crash she'd feared meant blood, she must've found this relieving! "I just dried my hands! I swear!" These words will be forever clear in my memory's ear. Justin really was a good big brother to me.

A couple months ago in June, we were at the docks fishing for flounder (Justin showed me how to cast and use a reel too), and two older boys who were about eleven or twelve—one black, thin, and wiry and the other white, chunky, and sloppy—came over on their bikes looking at our four flounders in our bucket. "Hey Sparks, what's up?" Lamar the black one said.

"Nothin," Justin said. Justin gazed at Lamar once quickly, then stared back at the water where his taut line sank with hook, sinker, and bait.

"Caught a few ha?"

"Yep."

"What are ya usin'?"

"Sandworms."

This Lamar had his intruding hands in our bucket, handling our fish, pulling them out, helping himself audaciously. Two seagulls cried directly above us. His friend Lee, who also went to the public school with Justin, remained on his bike without a shirt on, in shorts, and with his bare feet flat on the loose blue stone. They were both in sixth grade, while Justin was in fifth.

"Look here Lee. Look at the little flounders these guys are keepin'!"

Lee got off his bike, letting it fall, clattering on the stones. Without cringing in pain, he walked on the stones like he had shoes, and he squatted beside me, bumping me boorishly, obtruding. I stepped aside with my line in the water, looking at him, at how dirty he was, at both of them hovering over our bucket like the gulls overhead, looking at Justin, at them, then back at Justin again. The afternoon sun suddenly slid behind a high spread of cloud, became shadowed, removing the squinting from our eyes. The smell of salt in the air, seaweed and mud from the low tide, and putrid fish from the nearby fishing boats continued floating into our nostrils.

Justin looked at me. I could tell he sort of evaded Lamar particularly. He was not pleased they'd arrived, and wished they'd leave. He remained quiet. Everything had been so nice and calm five minutes earlier. Now there was a bad, thick, pernicious feeling in the atmosphere.

This kid Lee got up with his hardened, dirty feet, insolently approaching Justin. "Hey, let me try your pole, Sparks," he said, placing his hand above the reel, grabbing.

Reluctant, irritated, yet not wanting a confrontation, Justin released, but with a bit of hesitant authority in his voice, he said, "Okay sure, but just for a couple a minutes."

"How long ya been fishin'?"

"Hour," Justin said.

"And ya only got four?"

"Caught two crabs and an eel too."

"Threw 'em back?"

"Yeah."

"What ya throw 'em back for?"

"Don't want 'em."

This other kid Lamar looked at me. "Who's this little kid?" he said to Justin, rather than straightly talking to me.

The sun slid back out from behind the cloud. Brightness immediately gleamed. My brows lowered. I didn't like this attention drawn toward me from this kid.

"My brother. Silas."

"I didn't know ya had a brother."

"So."

"Don't look like ya."

"Well he is."

Lee centered his attention on his line in the water. We could hear gentle slaps and splashes as the small choppy waves hit the tarred bulkhead beneath us. I could see a gray striped tabby cat on one of the fishing boats seated on the gunwale looking at the gulls overhead.

Lamar reached his long, black, wiry arm toward my fishing pole, and with an uncertain, testy daring said, "Let me see your pole kid."

My brows lowered further. I was quite a bit shorter than he. "No!" I said firmly, briskly stepping a few feet away. I stared out, stiffly boring my eyes and head straight out at my line, at the fishing boats, at this cat.

"What do ya mean no?" Lamar remarked with a bit of a startled giggle, with a manner that inquired from me who that I thought I was. It seemed the gulls laughed too. One landed on top of a wharf post nearby, as though to see.

"No!" I said simply. This grasping, self-willed bully made me mad.

Lamar's hand clutched my pole, pulling a little. I tried to jerk away from him.

"What's your brother's name, Sparks?" He pulled my pole.

"Silas. His name's Silas. What are ya keep askin me for? He can talk."

"Silas!" I shouted.

"Sparks. Hey Sparks, your brother Silas won't let me use his pole."

He wanted Justin to take care of this. He felt he had some power over Justin—a kid a year younger than himself whom he knew, whom he felt would probably comply. There was this understanding of reputation, position, and hierarchy from school, and perhaps in my foster family as well.

"So, it's his pole. Maybe he don't want ya usin' it."

Though there was a detected uncertainty in his voice, I could hear a recognizable exasperation from Justin. I felt I had his support at this moment. "It's my pole!" I said, without looking at Lamar, pulling. Lamar would not let go. He had a sick kind of grin on his face. "It's mine!" I screeched. This kid was obviously stronger than I, at this point having only one hand on the pole. I tried prying his fingers from it, but they were rigid, unmovable.

He then placed his horrible skinny fingers and palm across my face and pushed. I resisted. We both became angrier. "Let go, kid!" he grunted, demanding; and then he smacked me.

While Lee kept fishing, looking over at us, Justin stepped over and he too grabbed my fishing pole. "Just leave him alone Lamar. He doesn't want you to use his pole, so leave him. You think you're a tough guy hittin' a five-year-old. Big tough guy! Hittin' a kindergarten kid!"

"What are you goin' to do about it, Sparks, ya twerp!"

"Nothin'. Just leave him, come on." Justin was not that much smaller than Lamar. He was trying to make peace here, pleading, but he was angry too. No one would let go of this pole. Six hands now—four black and my two brown—clasped tightly. At once, there was a flounder on the line. Justin could tell first. "He's got one. He's got one! Come on, let go Lamar. Let him reel it in. He's got one!" I still wonder why this timing worked this way, what the reason in the heavens was that this fish now took the bait. There was something humorous about this, even though I was just slapped by a big kid.

This only made Lamar more persistent. He looked at the two of us, angered that seizing this pole didn't come as easily as it had with

Lee, angered that he wasn't having his way and that a mere fifth-grader and his little brother hindered that, and all that before the eyes of his partner Lee. He would not surrender. There was silence and stillness a moment. It seemed all three waited for someone to yield. The flounder pulled and tugged. It was a big one. Lamar kept staring down at me, at my face, at my hair. "Hey Lee," he called. "Look at this little imp. What is he anyway? Is he a nigga or a white boy?" He laughed. His anger over this struggle brought him to flinging these insults. "Hey, it's a white nigger. Look at him. He's got light hair!"

Lee giggled.

Who's ya daddy, kid? You wanna be black or white? Your momma's a whore!" I didn't know what this meant, but Justin did, and this made him even madder.

"Shut your mouth, Lamar! Let go! Why you have to do this?"

Lamar began to thrash, walloping his elbows violently. Finally he had pole to himself. I let go first, as I began to cry—and then Justin, not because Justin surrendered, but rather because he was ready to fight, unafraid. He launched a hard punch at Lamar's face, hitting him squarely in the nose. This angry courage from Justin so surprised Lamar that at first he just stared at Justin, aghast. Then, to save face before Lee, he had no choice but to drop my pole to retaliate. I quickly retrieved and began reeling in my tears. By now Lamar's nose was bleeding, dripping over his white shirt, splashing on Justin as they wrestled, upright. Suddenly Lamar, trying to free from the grapple so he could punch Justin, swung Justin around, tossing him wildly against a huge, iron trash can. The can toppled, spilling trash, and Justin fell into it—ants, fish guts, and all. This was quite a stage.

Justin stopped a moment. Lamar wiped his face. "Give?" he said.

Irate, breathing heavily. "Leave us alone!"

They were both breathing hard.

Lamar stood there thinking what to say. He kept wiping his nose, looking at his finger, wiping across his sleeve, bloody, nervous, feeling defeated.

By now I excitedly pulled up my flounder. "I got 'im! I got 'im, Justin! Look, I got 'im! It's a big one!" I'd completely disregarded the tension of the fighting now. It wasn't until later that day that I thought about how proud and secure I felt with Justin as a big brother. It was a nice fish—twenty-two inches—still the biggest flounder I can recall ever seeing. I let it hang from my line, feeling its weighty sensation as it flopped and curled itself with strained life, shining white and glistening brown and flat, bending my rod.

In his defeat, Lamar advanced. He wanted my pole again. I scurried, with my back to him, with the pole pointing toward the gulls, with this fish dangling, swinging like a tetherball. Catching me, he reached around, trying to grab the handle. I could tell he wanted to mangle my fish, pole, or both. We circled around together some, beneath the circling gulls—around and around—grappling. I burst into a raging scream, but somehow freed myself. As I turned, before Justin could seize him again, the huge flounder swung circuitously— from my jostling and jolting—with momentum, with speed and springy heaviness, around, colliding with a perfect smashing slap onto the side of Lamar's head. For seconds there was silence. Then Lee began to laugh, loudly. Then Justin started laughing, and I laughed too. We couldn't stop laughing. Wiping his face of his own blood and all this fish slime, unable at this instant to wipe away this humiliation, frustrated and disgusted he lifted our bucket and tossed our other four fish into the bay.

As I was ecstatic about this big fish, the sudden loss of those small ones really wasn't too despoiling.

By now Lee was waiting on his bike. Justin caught Lamar by the tail of his bloody shirt and furiously wrestled him down again. Lamar was at an emotional disadvantage now, as he was shocked by

Justin's bravery, as he bled, and as Justin, replenished with fuming adrenaline, held him down, climbed onto him, sat on his midsection, and pinned his wrists to the stony floor, shouting: "Why'd ya have to come here? Why can't ya just leave us alone? Why can't ya leave my brother alone, ha?"

Lamar was clearly beaten. Lee watched, but that was all. Kids at school surely heard about this one. These things didn't matter to Justin; he never wanted to fight, but he fought for me, to protect me. He loved me and I'll never forget him for it.

One block from the church down the shadowy street in the theater parking lot a group of boys—eight-, nine-, ten-, eleven-year-olds—often assembled to play stickball. Justin's leadership flair was evident there. Being ten, vocal, and the best player—he was esteemed. Judging fair or foul balls, close plays, balls and strikes were, as a rule, yielded to Justin: he played fair. Justin was always a team captain, and Eddy or Tyrone—eleven-year-olds—were captains too. The game began with flipping a coin, and the winner chose a player first, and they'd alternate until scrubs—Clyde or Joey—eight-year-olds—were left standing quarantined alone. I certainly should have been one of those; but even though I was six, the worst and a hindrance, Justin always mandate that I was permitted to play. He picked good players first to win, then me third so I wouldn't feel left out, so he could—with his shepherd's heart like Daddy's—watch out for me and coach me.

One sunny spring Saturday morning before the matinee cars entered, we had a game going in the cool shadow from the high west side of the theater building. We'd played six innings—a close score, tight, tense. One inning we were winning, the next losing. It was like that. As the morning crested into noon, and that great shadow shrank, and the sun strengthened, Justin said, "Last inning!" as we took our positions in the lot between innings. Now the other team scored two runs, putting them ahead by one. I was out in the out-field—the fourth outfielder—behind the centerfielder against the fence. My job was to chase the ones that really got away. Justin was the pitcher—almost always. A white chalked square on the red brick wall was the strike zone, even for little guys like me.

Now we had last licks. Needing two runs to win, bottom of the order, Justin offered us deficient hitters a pep talk: "Now just concentrate! Keep your eye on the ball! Don't look away when you swing! Hear me, Silas? Don't look away! Okay?"

I nodded, wide-eyed.

Jamal got a double. Then Pauly and Clyde struck out. The last batter—I was up. At age six I understood the game. I didn't want this pressure. I usually struck out. Sure, I'd have loved to be the hero, but everyone knew that would be unlikely. I clutched the sawed end of the broom handle without choking up.

"Don't be throwin' him no curve balls, Eddy! Just fast balls! He's only six. It's not fair."

"If he wants to play, he's gotta take it! What do you want—me to let him hit it?" Eddy kept turning his hat, fixing it, keeping it backward, wiping sweat, nervous, aggressive, dog-eat-dog, mimicking some favorite Yankee or Met pitcher of his, as though on the mound. His bright blonde hair and brows appeared blonder in the sun beside his navy-blue Yankee cap.

"Yeah," agreed Tony from deep at short stop. With his hat down over his brows and head tilted back I couldn't see his shadowed eyes. His tone was clear though: he was agitated. He wanted to win.

"He's just a little kid, Eddy," Sammy shouted. Sammy was seated with his back against the brick wall, knees up beside his cheek bones, brown hands clasped over brown shins.

"Aright, aright, aright!" Eddy consented. "Just fastballs, but I'm makin' sure they're fast!"

I stepped up to hit. The bottom of the strike zone was up—a little below my waist; the top of the box was over my head. My participation really was a bit ludicrous. Eddy went through his professional wind-up. The pink Spalding came darting unimpeded. I let it go, looking at the box. Sure enough—outside the box by two inches. Ball one.

"Come on, put it in there, Eddy," one of the guys out by the fence said.

Eddy pitched again. The pink sphere ripped forward. I swung, missing. I looked at Justin with my eyes wide. "Was that a strike, Justin?" I wondered if I should have swung.

"Right down the pike! Come on, you can hit it, Silas! Watch it close!"

Eddy pitched again, and the pink blur came zinging by—right at me—and I stepped back, looking. It was two inches in the box. Either I was too close, or he did curve it. I looked again to Justin for support, saying nothing. He just stared, arms folded, kicking the wall gently—frustrated—letting his rubber sneaker bounce back delicately. Strike two.

For the fourth time, I moved into the box and prepared myself. I felt myself beginning to wheeze a little. Eddy's wind-up began, finished. He released. The pink globe came speeding, inside. I focused, stepped, swung, connected, pulling—pulling so much that the stinging pinkness of the rubber ball surged with as much speed at Marty—a tall, skinny Italian kid on our team standing a few feet from third base. I initially felt so good about the way I met that fast ball, but soon the instant ego breathed its last when that hard rubber orb smacked the side of Martin's face with a ping, boomeranging back into the lot, making most of the kids laugh. Half of these laughers tried to conceal it, snickering; but a few—including Justin—ran to his aid when he grabbed his face and fell to his knees. He was okay. It was just a stinging spank as the ball was soft enough to be innocuous.

When Martin recovered, I stepped up again. I noticed Jamal on second base, his black skin shining in the bright sunlight. He squatted with his hands on his knees, eager to dash to third. Eddy wound up, impressed with himself. Again, a fifth time, the pink ball came shooting forward. It seemed this little sphere was the entire earth—the whole world, a world of importance—and hitting it, in my mind, meant pleasing Justin, which was my whole world. Unsure, then decisive—I felt I should swing, and as I did, I turned slightly, watching as the ball—a soundless pink line—passed me. Strike three.

A few fielders cheered. "Yeah! We win!" Justin and our guys just sat, stood, picked up their gloves and sticks, looking with expressions that seemed to have braced for this. I felt lost, under, and I wondered what Justin would say. I'd seen him mad before, and I didn't like it. I hated letting him down. I didn't approach him.

"Why'd ya turn your head? Why'd ya take your eye off the ball?" I heard his sudden voice. I could tell he restrained himself, as though there were this infinitesimal, controlling governor inside of him, cautious, restraining. Irritated, disappointed, he continued to force his baseball coach voice: "Why in the world ya turn your head when ya swung, Silas?" He tried his best to keep this—all this, this game—in the right perspective.

"Sorry, Justin."

He said nothing.

I stood. I kicked the wall. I wanted to die.

Then, immediately, he came to me. He must have heard something in my voice. He put his hand on my shoulder, pulling me against him. "I'm sorry. I'm sorry," he said, reinforcing, wanting it to sink into me. Many of the guys were watching this now. He didn't care though. They knew I wasn't "really" his brother, but they did know that I was treated better than one-maybe—if I had been.

"You didn't do nothin'," I said.

"You did real good, Silas. That was hard. You can't hit those pitches. You're just six. He throws fast. That was hard. I'm sorry it came to you being up with two outs like that. That's not fair. You did good. It's just a stupid game. Come on. Let's go get a soda." We both just stood there a minute, and he kept patting my back. My head remained against his chest. The other guys were walking away, but they kept looking back.

"You're startin' to wheeze aint ya? You okay?"

"I'm okay."

We picked up our things and walked the familiar block back home. Mommy Lucinda was an artist. She had a studio, a whole room in the attic of the big parsonage where she painted, where she taught Justin and me—and sometimes a few of the other kids in the church—in water colors, acrylics, sometimes even oil paints. Wet winter days were best for this. I'd get my enormous smock on (an old shirt of Justin's), cover my shoes in plastic, stand before a vastness of a white-painted used canvas roosted on a bulky easel. Mommy pinched out little blobs—a multihued work of art itself— of color onto a pallet. I can still recall the tranquil thrill I'd felt back then, breathing in the smells of the paints, solvents, and musty roof rafters there, eager to create, following her careful instructions.

At five this was so pleasant—being near her, being trusted with her paints and brushes, hearing her praises, absorbing her approval and kind tone as she spoke. I toiled to be sure I held the brush and pallet the way she taught, and focused to mix the paints properly with the knife. Even after concentration I got myself slopped in paint—sometimes even in my hair. I wanted to do right and hear her say, "Very good Silas," the way she sometimes did.

I attempted to copy Mommy Lucinda's scrupulously refined land- scapes and seascapes up there. Those one hour excursions took me into another imaginary setting. From her fabricated world, I aimed to create mine; and it became a setting I delighted inventing as my imag- ination escorted me into that blended world of hers and mine: onto a high crag gazing out over a lake and a range of mountains, beside a sunlit shore of a green and white-capped sea, into a shadowy forest where a thin brook strolled its own way. I still go back up there— in my mind—into her attic from time to time. I recall the feel of her hugs and touches, her words which I'd so desperately needed then. I still smell her, returning there—in my mind—onto this island in

New York Bay, into that varnished church, that parsonage beside it, that warm accepting kitchen, that second story room Justin shared with me, where he shared his toys and baseball cards, where I'd stare out the worn window toward the docks at that old urban street where we'd play stickball, at the gulls which seemed always to soar overhead in wind, crying, hovering, seemingly protecting like encamping delivering angels. I was so happy there, and that was the happiness I'd ignorantly longed for when I'd stared out over the streets from Mommy Maureen's repellent apartment years earlier.

Once after one of those visits with Mommy Maureen I had a terrorizing dream, waking me into tears. I was back at that place—that horrible apartment Molly liberated me from—in that dismal, dingy hallway. I had this paralyzed feeling—like I couldn't move, couldn't even shout or speak as that Maureen clawed, snatching my colorful pallet and brush out of my hands, tugging off my smock, seizing one of Mommy Lucinda's paintings—green grass, blue sky—pulling at me, at my clothes until I was naked, furious, helpless. She was dirty in the dream, and in a nebulous way all of her dope paraphernalia were all about her, and needle scars were all over her skin as she raged, trying to plunder my joy. In my terror, frustration, and powerlessness I scratched and gouged at my own face—self afflicting—in my dream, in my sleep.

Mommy Lucinda came to me that night, turned on my light, hugged me, swabbed the lacerations on my face, held my head against her shoulder and rocked. "It's okay Silas. It's just a bad dream. Everything's okay, see, see—here's your room. Mommy's here. Justin's here. It's just a bad dream." Then she prayed like she did often: "Sweet Jesus, give this child of yours peace. Hold him in Your arms Jesus. Let him rest in your sweet presence. Calm this child. Touch this child. Let him know You love him. Let him know You're true." She hummed softly, high-pitched—some hymn we sang at church. She hummed angelically, rocking until I descended back to sleep.

SEVEN

CICADAS

It was when I was eight that I first had this incipient awareness of my distinction from other kids. At eight I acquired that budding consciousness of shame about my situation, the mystery of my biological father, and my birth mother Maureen's incompetence. I was a foster child. People all about me—at school, at the agency—often referred to me that way. Sometimes I was called *the foster kid* in the neighborhood. In plain English I was a bastard—begotten and born out of wedlock, illegitimate, and worse. I guess eight is too early for a kid like me to think heavily about such things, but I did. I thought too much; and I knew a lot too. Older kids in that neighborhood taught me things, and I understood, very well.

It was then, at eight, that I began to battle embarrassment. I wished I could say with truthfulness, "My mother's dead," or even, "My mother doesn't want me," or "My mother's sick and dying," rather than that she was a drug addict and incompetent. I always wished I could say with truthfulness that my dad was buried, or that he was sick and dying, or even that he was half nuts, a drug addict, incompetent, or a drunk, rather than say, "I don't want to talk about my dad," or say truthfully, "I have no idea who my father is." There is an undeniably shameful stigma in having this kind of a messed-up background in this part of the world. I understood rationally that it wasn't my fault, but it still attached itself to me. I was the one in it. I was ashamed of it. I felt oddly at fault, almost culpable. It was a passive inexplicable sort of guilt.

It was then, when I was eight—just before school (third grade) began in September—about a year after I'd had that appalling dream of my messed-up mother yanking my art stuff out of my hands, that Molly was assigned to come one Saturday morning to take me reluctantly back to Mommy Maureen. Daddy and Mommy Sparks had been contesting this for a year—in court, at the agency, in prayer. They invested their own money on a lawyer to represent them with their insufficient rights -and to a legal degree—to represent my best interest. I can remember Daddy even used this ongoing, painful ordeal as subjects and metaphors in some of his sermons. They loved me a great deal.

My court-appointed law guardian, Leonard Levy, was scarcely involved. I think he was slack and lazy, certainly inconsiderate. He had tens of other cases. Maybe if he'd become acquainted with the actual pulse of my being—stepping beyond the clerically sterile biography of my life documented on the agency's reports and recommendations around my case, leaping over the thick paper of Silas Aaron Dillon: 056-53-0263, beholding more than glances of words on formal forms of my history, caring and moving aggressively closer to me—touching, seeing, meeting me and all those in my life—maybe he would have made a convincing case before a busy judge's bench, despite all of the support Mommy Maureen got. Maybe I could have settled adopted at the Sparks' home. Maybe this disruption could have been avoided. An ugly prowling monster of red tape in the system bound so many people's lives. If anyone in the system had weight before a judge's bench to make a case for an orphan of the living, the law guardian certainly had the muscle. He could turn the judge. He could make the case. Too many of these "overseers" chose to be willfully atrophied.

On the other hand, an awful lot of vim, impetus, and focus seemed always to guard and insulate Mommy Maureen. She was pregnant now—again—carrying her third fatherless child. Again, her prostitution made my unborn half-brother's father a mystery also. She was infected with HIV now too, which meant this third offspring might be infected as well. The latest social momentum to keep siblings inseparable in the system now made it possible—even encouraged—for her to have another chance at caring for me. That new social concern for the continued union of sibling groups was really for those poor kids whose cords with their brothers and sisters needed to remain bound for their stability and comfort, while their temporary disunion from their parents was more than enough of an emotional upheaval on them. Nevertheless, I and my not yet born brother fell into this judicial classification, even though no bond existed. Mommy's court-appointed attorney shoved, jammed, and squeezed this whole situation through this family court loophole.

Added to this, Mommy had a couple of special interest groups behind her. Her contracting HIV put her in a special phylum too, providing her with some distinct rights and attention from these groups. So the focus somehow got circuitously directed onto her pitiful quandary. That social concern for the messed-up single parent who'd never had apt assistance in ordering her life often had a tendency to put the vulnerable offspring into the shadowed backround. Because I was still very young and "resilient," it was presupposed I'd rebound once Mommy Maureen's life became composed.

The absurdity in the attention toward my yet unborn half-brother was that had someone with influence in the system known about Mommy's pregnancy early enough, a quick abortion would have been encouraged. But now that my half-brother would have his rightful right to life, an awful lot of upheaval and change was wrongfully quaking for his and our "benefit."

Justin, Mommy and Daddy Sparks, and I had been preparing for this for two weeks now. The judicial ruling had been adjudicated on August 20, setting this date—September 4—allowing us this span for embracing farewells and bracing ourselves. I was experiencing the roughest disruption. This was the saddest hour of my brief life. From my eight-year perspective, I survived horizontally, propelled by forces I could barely understand much less control. I was a casualty. As far as I could see things vertically, there was just sky.

No one heard Molly's car pull in the driveway as we all sat silently in the purring of air-conditioning in the living room that Saturday morning. We all wore shorts—sitting, waiting, anticipative. It was hot and humid. No one spoke at length—just words, phrases. My old trunk was jammed, heavy, and boxes were packed. All my stuff—the tangible contents of my life—was a neat assemblage in the middle of the spacious floor, resembling a small Midwestern city in the plains—huddled, vulnerable, braced against the forecasted touchdown of a tornado.

Three knocks on the door thumped like fatal blows, bringing sudden fear. Mommy Lucinda's eyes pooled with teardrops again. Everyone but me arose. Daddy went for the door, looking back before opening.

Light and Molly entered. Daddy closed the door behind her.

"Hello Silas. How are you? How are you Mr. Sparks, Mrs. Sparks, Justin?" Molly said. Her sweet, familiar voice always brought me respite.

"Not so good. Not so good, Molly. We're trying," said Daddy. He looked at Molly, and at me. He forced himself to sound positive about all of this, for my sake. "We're going to miss Silas being here every day, for sure." He paused. "Well, you know all this."

"I know. Oh, of course." Molly was bothered this change thrust upon me and on the Sparks', but she too aimed to be optimistic.

"But everything's going to be well for Silas. He's going to be just fine. The good Lord's going to be with him, and he'll be fine.

He's a brave boy, and he'll be just fine. And we'll get to have visits—lots of visits, right Silas?" Daddy's deep, healthy voice was replete with paternal promise.

I just stared at the floor. I wouldn't look at Molly, Daddy, anybody. Daddy reached his big hand around my shoulder and pulled me against his large frame, hugging me. With my face buried in the hidden security of his shirt I felt the ingenuous freedom to just let go and cry. I let it explode, but with silence. My little heart was broken. Angry grief simply ruptured. I felt forlorn, with a grave sensation of defeat, the kind I'd felt at bat that day playing stickball. I felt that desperation, that hopelessness I couldn't do anything about. I felt that weird sense of responsibility, like it was all partially because of something I did or didn't do. I didn't want to go with my crazy mother. I was happy here, and I felt secure here. "I don't want to go!" I moaned, muffled by his side. It was a plea, a "Somebody do something!" entreaty. I began to wheeze. Crying hard never helped my asthma.

"I know. I know son. We don't want that either." Daddy almost cried too. I'd never seen that big strong man cry before as he'd always had some knack at restraining it. Even in the pulpit he had a proficient way at holding back his tears. I vividly recall a Good Friday sermon—during communion—when with resplendent words Daddy Sparks took his congregation back to the crucifixion. The manner in which his uncomplicated English disclosed human beings' sin recounted Jesus' innocence—His surging bleeding, and the violence He'd endured—made even children cry that night. Somehow he'd been able to hold back his own tears. He'd wanted to cry, but he'd wanted more so to communicate. But now he cried, and he wasn't ashamed.

Mommy Lucinda cried, and then Justin, but he ran into the other room to hide his cries. He felt desperate too. He loved me. Molly moved over to Mommy Lucinda and hugged her. "Everything's for some purpose, Mrs. Sparks."

"I know. I know."

"I don't know what it is, but there's a plan. We've nothing else to hold on to."

"I know. We gotta trust. I know, Molly."

"This is so wrong. This is so wrong," Daddy added.

Molly put all her sympathies into thinking hard. She didn't know what to say.

"This whole system's messed up," Daddy said.

"I know it is, Mr. Sparks. I agree. That's why folks like you and me are in this, trying to make a difference, trying to join our little bits of force to turn this thing upside-down, trying to chip in, doing our best to bring sense into situations, like Silas's." Molly hesitated. I think she could have cried, but she'd been working in the system long enough now—certainly not insensitive—but tough, accustomed to cases like mine, ventilating her anger and disagreement by working hard rather than burning out and growing too emotional.

She took a deep breath and spoke again: "We were all prepared for this—really. We were all warned about things like this happening. I was warned when I was getting oriented to my job five years ago. You were told about this sort of thing very possibly happening. We'd all been briefed about the system and the courts. It's not all 'happy ever after.' We try, but too often—it's not 'happy ever after.' It's unfortunate, but little ones like Silas never get that preparation. He's the real sufferer. Yeah, we hurt!" Molly was nodding. "But Silas, and many like him, are in the middle. Laws are messed up. The whole system is."

This motionless air of sad agreement amid this little group stood there. Daddy stood so tall, brawny, solid. "Well, we can keep praying," he said, wiping his eyes.

"And we will," Molly said.

"Max, maybe we can pray now," Mommy Lucinda said.

Daddy reached out his big hands. We all joined hands. Justin returned. Daddy began with his deep tone: "God you know the end from the beginning. We've asked you for this child. We ask Lord that you shelter this boy. Continue to work in his life. Keep him, Lord. Give him a heart for You, God. Lord, our hearts are broken—" Daddy choked up with tears. I felt his hand placed on my head the way he had placed it there often. "Lord, heal our hearts. Work this out for good, Jesus. Have your way. Amen."

We embraced, crying, and we all lifted items of my belongings from the floor, stepping outside. I didn't know then that this would be the last moment I'd spend in this house. A thick intensity of heat collided with me as I stepped out of the air-conditioning. The sauna-like burst of heat that early September afternoon accosted us; and the suburban honks, hums, mowers, brakes, kids, machinery, and common disorder met me like the world did when I was first born here on this island, into this county system, over seven years ago. Leaving this home—its safeness and sanctuary—was like leaving the womb.

Above these discordant sounds of suburban mankind, from the trees in the humid heat a steady buzzing, screaming, sibilant and consonant sound permeated. The cicadas relentlessly made their diabolically monotonous droning in the canopies of trees in the hot humidity. They seemed to—as a matter of their course—keep still in the trees, refraining from leaf hopping. Their locust-like stout heads, whisker-like antennae, colossal eyes, sucking mouths, and two pairs of large, branch-veined, pellucid wings were all hidden, invisible to us. We could hear them though. Their presence was real, though invisible. Their hellish sound penetrated, even forcing us to raise our voices so we could be understood in speaking as we made our way to Molly's car, carrying my cargo. They seemed to cheer in a fiery triumph, in some sort of fixed, apathetic conquest. Their drum-like tissues beside their abdomens shrilled fiendishly louder than I'd ever heard—soaring, falling, holding, piercing. Those cicadas were ugly, demonic looking creatures; and they were veiled in the trees, except for one, for sometimes in their infrequent flight one might smash against a wall and fall.

That's what probably happened to this one. It sat on the hot cement stoop in a corner striving for sound, life, flight, rest, or something—against the siding in solitary and colorful blackness—remote and separated from the triumphant, fiery heights of the many others. It sat apparently struggling, defeated. Before I descended the stoop, I reached my foot over (I felt anxiously compelled in my sad anger) and stomped—crushing, crunching its intricate insect form into mush. I felt power. I wiped my foot, and then proceeded downward toward Molly's car, into the course that was appointed for me, toward my uncertain destiny which people were plotting for me.

EIGHT

WILD CHERRIES AND YELLOW-JACKETS

Molly drove me twenty miles across Cary Island from the ocean side where the honest horizon remained uninterrupted, where if we just turned our heads and looked to the east, bright Brooklyn seemed like a subdued pleasant place in the distance. She took me to the New Jersey side where there were fewer trees, industry, a narrow channel separating the states, ships, tugs, barges and a smell of chemicals in the air. The air-conditioning in her car was cool, and the music cheery. I felt a little numb from my grief, yet with the windows closed, sealing me from the world that I watched, the bleeding in my heart caused by the ripping from my place at the Sparks' family seemed to stop. Of course, I didn't consider it then, but how long healing would take depended on whether infections could be deflected.

Mommy Maureen's place was in a halfway house called Crossings House—a New York State funded program and facility—a tremendous three-story stone building on Channel Turnpike, a busy roadway paralleling the deep bulk headed channel. We turned in the driveway and drove under a car port into the back where several cars parked on a new asphalt lot. It was like going to the doctor's or the dentist's or a restaurant or someplace like these. It wasn't like going home, for sure.

Nine other women who were also trying to beat drugs lived with their children here too. This was a new and special program—for cases like Mommy's, an alternative to dispersing kids into foster homes and letting the drug addicted parents continue to ruin themselves, where hopefully moms would cooperate, mend, and learn to be responsible. There were a lot of mixed views among the social professionals about this sort of latest, costly approach. Around the clock counselors and child care workers lived here, while therapists worked there during the day. Taxpayers doled out an awful lot for this.

We parked the car and opened our doors. The thick heat collided against us again. I heard only a few cicadas in a nearby tree as I looked around. Next door I noticed a very enticing swimming pool in the ground with no one in it, and a basketball backboard and hoop on a garage at the head of a driveway. Behind was a large vacant lot. The sound of the turnpike was blustering, noisy. As in a park, a row of picnic tables lay on the lawn beside the parking lot. Adults and kids seemed to be coming and going out the back door. Some sat on the spacious wrap around porch. This place was busy, definitely different, clean and neat. So far, the only negative was that pregnant Mommy Maureen was inside waiting for me.

I stood behind the car by the trunk while Molly got some of her papers and things and locked her door. High-rise, outmoded apartment buildings beyond the lot emerged in the gray haze with visual offensiveness. I hated that urban county on that irritable day.

"We'll bring your things in in a little while, Silas honey. Let's go see Mommy and meet some of the people first okay?" She put her arm around my shoulder.

I was sure she had already met "some of the people" already, and that it was just my turn now. I somehow couldn't bring myself to being phony, putting on a sham, simulated smile right now. I really was very angry, furiously frustrated inside. I couldn't act that way to Molly, however. She'd always been too genuinely good to me these years.

I felt like I wanted to die. I intended to be cold and aloof to Mommy Maureen. This was all her fault. Why did I have to be her little band-aid while she tried to get herself fixed?

As we walked toward that porch I looked down at the hot asphalt, at my high sneakers, at my brown legs, my blue shorts. I pulled my Yankee cap down over my brows so my petulant, anguish-stricken eyes wouldn't have to look at anyone else's.

"You okay, Silas?"

"Yeah."

"Sure?"

"Yeah."

"You want to talk awhile before we go in, honey?" She tried to get me to look at her. I wouldn't.

"No."

"Sure?"

"No. I mean yeah. I don't care."

We were quiet as we slowly strolled, and I imagined she prayed. I'm certain that whatever she thought about, surrounded me. Her thoughts were never wrapped up with other business whenever we spent time together. Whenever Molly was with me, she remained unconditionally wholly with me.

She steered me to a picnic table in the shade of a wild cherry tree, and she sat opposite me, speechless a moment. A trifling breeze blew, stirring some leaves, cooling, lifting the scent of newly cut sparse grass. Fallen wild cherries and black stains of rotted ones blotched smattered on the table and benches, and yellow-jackets maneuvered, hovering above the smatters. A little sparrow landed on the other end of our table very nearby, pecking at crumbs, ignoring the tiny cherries. I wondered if it were fearlessness, carelessness, trust, or just desperate hunger that brought it so close. Its little head jerks made me thing it glanced at me. We could faintly hear its little talons scratching the warping wood until it freely flew away, out of our sight. A long minute passed.

"Silas."

I didn't look up.

"Silas, look at me, look at Molly."

Somebody entered into a car. Doors slammed. An engine started. Tires rolled.

"Silas, honey."

I still didn't look up. I kept fearing Mommy Maureen would notice we'd arrived and would come charging down the steps off the big porch with a whole lot of garrulous, confused words out of her grating, cigarette smoked voice box. I looked across the deep, debris-filled lot in the back. I wanted to run into it. It hung hot and dusty, but I wanted to run into it anyway, and keep on running until I dropped, died, or found my way back to Mommy Sparks. I felt like pulling my hair. I felt like killing myself. Suddenly I felt Molly's index finger on my chin, gently lifting my head. I grabbed my hair through my hat and squeezed hard. I pressed, mashing my two elbows against the table—hard. I took my top teeth and bit down on my bottom lip—hard. I screamed within myself, within my being, tightening all my sinews. I burst with keen bitter cries and tears once again. It was like the salted, seaweed besieged locks on the nearby channel opening, and a current of tide rushing through. My tears dripped, puddling on the wooden table-top which quickly absorbed, sopping them up into its seasoned dryness as though—like a brief deluge of rain on a wide parched desert—they were insignificant, paltry, nothing. I took my knuckles and struck the wooden seat, letting my head fall flat onto the table, feeling my tooth puncture my lip as I'd still been biting, watching my navy-blue Yankee cap tumble to the ground.

Molly quickly came to my side, rubbing my back. "I know. I know. It's okay. Cry it out. It's good to cry Silas. It's okay."

She did comfort me. Even though she didn't cry with me, she really made me feel that what she said was so. She had such a motherly strength. I felt safe crying with her. As I reflect now, I can see that she was perfect for that social work. It was her calling. She fostered me.

I raised my head when I noticed the blood from my lip dripping on my shorts and mingling with my tears as I lingered there. At once I looked into Molly's kind eyes which immediately noticed my bleeding, swelling lip.

"Oh Silas, you're bleeding. You bit your lip, honey."

I said nothing, wiping with my fingers.

"Here," she said, rummaging through her handbag. She pulled out tissues and wiped my chin and mouth. She took fresh ones and gently placed it on my tooth-wide wound and pressed, holding her hand there. She looked at me—into my eyes—and shook her head with a small smile. "You're a silly boy, you know it," and she laughed a bit, hoping I'd follow. I didn't. She hugged me and kissed my head while she held my lip. We sat there like that for a long time. Mommy Maureen didn't come out. After a while Molly said, "Here hold this against your lip."

"Okay," I mumbled.

She took out another tissue and wiped my eyes, and then she leaned and lifted my hat from the grass, wiping off clippings. She stuffed it on my head sideways and pinched my cheek, saying, "You're a silly boy Silas" again, smiling. "Listen to me little fella. Everything's going to be okay. Everything's going to be fine. You hear me? You'll be able to visit Mommy and Daddy Sparks and Justin from time to time. You never know, if this doesn't work out, you'll go back there. But we hope this does work out. We all want your Mommy Maureen well. We all want what's best for you. This is the way your Mommy wants things. She wants you with her, and people in the court—the judge wants you here. They say it is best. So there are just some things in life we can't control sometimes. We can't always have things impeccable."

"What's peckable?"

"Impeccable. It means perfect, faultless. We can't always have things impeccable. We try our best, and we pray. You hear me? You can call me up whenever you want. I'll be around. I'll be stopping in on you and Maureen a lot." She paused. "You hear me buddy?"

I nodded.

We walked to the house, up the steps and into the small foyer. She told the receptionist that I was Maureen's boy, and she asked two of the workers there to take my stuff from the car up to my room, handing them her keys.

The receptionist dialed an extension upstairs and Mommy was on her way down. She scurried down sunny and grinning, wearing shorts, happy to see me. I don't think I'd ever seen her move so fast before. She'd gained weight, and her face revealed it. I could only recall her being depressed, strung-out, high, perturbed, or deranged. She lowered to her knees, placing her white hands on her thighs, and she looked at me. Years had been passing. I was growing. I was too tall for her to kneel like she did.

After the last litigation in court, when the very real possibility that my adoption by the Sparks' had been pending, and Mommy had been granted some more time to get rehabilitated, some parents' rights advocate somehow got through to her the truth that she ought to take very seriously the courts' very patient yet persistent stipulations that she cooperate. She needed to regularly take her long ago prescribed medication, which sedated her as far as her melancholy went, so that when the court ordered mental health study progressed, she'd be deemed rational and fit. She needed to regularly take her newly prescribed HIV medicine—AZT—to forestall the onset of AIDS. She needed to choose to get into a program to free herself from the heroin grip. She needed to make evident some conscientious efforts of planning, of getting employed, of focusing on parenting skills—for me and my unborn brother. Meanwhile, eight years—my life—had slipped by. I was a toy, a pink stickball to be bounced around, a plaything—to her, something to be fancied for her own gratification and selfish serenity. This whole concept, this theory, this thought came to me in a more elementary, puerile way— then, at eight years of age, while she kneeled before me saying, "Silas, my love, I missed you so much. Give me a big hug and kiss."

My expression remained constant, with my hat low over my eyes, with my eyes diverted. I noticed the bulging beneath the white cotton maternity blouse from her abdomen, the sign that a new human would be crossing the threshold of this world. It was five months away— around my ninth birthday. I wished I were dexterous enough to appeal to her and communicate to her in a sophisticated, adult manner that she ought to let the Sparks adopt me. I was impetuous; it just came out: "I don't wanna live here. I wanna go back home."

"Silas!"

"No. I hate you." I turned away, around, facing Molly, looking down.

Mommy looked up at Molly. Molly said nothing. I imagine now that Molly had surely appealed to Mommy to do just that even before all the courtroom business. Molly had probably aimed to convince her that that would be best for me, and that that would be the most loving and selfless thing to do for me, for my emotional health, for my future. There was this open adoption possibility as well, where the birth mother could legally keep contact and have visitation privileges after the finalized adoption, so that cord—however strong or weak—could remain connected. Mommy had always refused. She clung, unyielding. She wanted me to herself, for herself.

Molly's expression—her peacemaking knack—somehow told Mommy that I'd come around. She lifted my head again with her finger under my chin. "Silas, Mommy's going to take you to your new school today if she can. If not, on Monday. You're going to like it. It has a whole new wing, and a brand-new gym, and a baseball field. And Mr. McMaster the principal is a very nice man; and Miss Karessi your teacher, and Mr. Kemp your gym teacher is looking forward to having you in his gym class because he's heard you're a good athlete. He loves the Yankees like you too!"

"How's he know? Who said I'm good?"

"Well, me, and Daddy Sparks."

"Oh." I said. Molly's words somehow magically lifted me. I thought about my baseball glove. I straightened my hat. The expression on my face—my countenance, my eye contact, my look of wonderment—announced to Molly that there was a flicker of hope here, for now.

"And now that you're eight, you can join the soccer league in the community!"

"Wow, that's great!" Mommy responded from her knees, moving a little as two little ones passed with their mother out the door onto the porch.

I don't think Mommy knew she was going to bring me on a school tour at all, and I found it typical that Molly had taken time to make these important contacts for me, that she was interested enough to know all this; and that Mommy didn't know this. Looking back now, I know that it was more than part of Molly's accountable duty for her salary, it was concern. I also know that my disgust for Mommy's inadequacy was merciless, rooted from bitterness, lacked any understanding, yet was normal for an eight-year-old.

"What happened to your lip, Silas?"

"He bit it."

"I bit it."

"You got blood on your shorts. You okay?"

"Yes."

"Come on," she said, rising, reaching her hand for mine. "Let's go wash up."

I began to follow. One of the workers handed Molly her keys. "Silas, I'm going to leave now. I'll stop by Monday morning, and maybe I'll go with you and Mommy to the school, okay? School starts Wednesday, so we want you to know your way around."

I walked toward her and hugged her goodbye.

She rubbed her fingers through my crimped, twisty hair. "You have my number. Remember. I'm here."

I nodded. She left, and I went into the big bathroom downstairs to wash up with Mommy Maureen. One of the young childcare workers—a heavy black girl who was very talkative—pulled out some peroxide from a cabinet and poured it on a washcloth and pressed it on my lip. It burned, stung, fizzled; but I submitted, knowing it was good medicine.

NINE

THE CHANNEL

Hundreds of years ago, Welsh settlers founded this island, naming it Cary, which means "rocky island." Underneath a blanket of stony soil, thick bedrock kept this plot firm through eons of storms. The surface soil's pebbly temper had always made this place agriculturally impotent, yet the island had always been more of a trade center, and at one time—during the great Atlantic slave trade—it had been a northeast center for trading, buying, selling, trafficking, investing in, and auctioning human beings—Africans, slaves.

My life was like this island—a hard, craggy place. And I often felt like one of those who had been auctioned off, put on the block, sold to any bidder, torn from my ties.

Now I was trying to bond—sort of—with Mommy Maureen, and it wasn't easy or working. She was volatile, unpredictable. She was flighty, moody. One hour she'd be happy, talkative, energetic; the next hour she'd be biting her nails, pacing, staring, weeping. One day she'd be friendly and loving to everyone in this domicile—to the other moms, the workers, all the kids. The next day she'd be unsociable, solitary, locking herself away in her room, even from me. One week she'd spend petulantly cross, breaking into fits of rage over nothing—cursing, frustrated, throwing things at walls. Another week she'd be considerate, warm and tender, doting, asking if I was tired or hungry or felt okay, holding doors for people, smiling, greeting. One night she'd sleep soundly, the next she'd be up, scratching her head, sitting, getting up, straightening her room, secretly smoking cigarettes by the window.

My asthma was as unpredictable as my mom's moods. I always had my safeguard inhaler with me, since I'd outgrown the nebulizer. Besides that I'd developed eczema which seemed to blossom redder, itchier, and rawer as months passed. I was often applying prescription creams for that too.

I liked to be in school. I felt safe there. I didn't like learning and books though; so I didn't work too hard, unless I liked the subject. Sometimes I liked social studies—not history, but the global studies—geography and the differences between the world's races. English was tolerable—some of the storybooks we read, a few of the poems. I never put effort in math or science. It was during math and science I'd stare pensively out the window, or get fidgety and distract other kids and get Miss Karessi mad at me. Math demanded concentration and paying attention. Science was uninteresting. I invariably failed math and science.

Two-thirty meant the last bell would ring and I'd get on a big bus with those elementary school kids who had normal homes, except for Kyle and Tyrone who lived at the halfway house with me too. Not knowing what was up with Mommy made me hate the anticipation on the ride home. Sitting on the bus for a long time was not a bother to me. I liked red lights and parents at stops who'd detain the driver for asinine reasons. A lot of rain meant a slower ride home too.

One day in December when we got on the bus to go home, Tyrone got an idea: "Hey, let's get off the bus at Joey's stop today." His white teeth and white eyes beamed.

I was confused. I looked at him.

"Ya mean at the bridge?" Kyle said. Kyle's white skin, thin lips, red freckles and hair were so counter to Tyrone's jet blackness and ample lips. My complexion remained somewhere in between.

"Yeah, let's go across the bridge to Jersey!"

I pondered: it wasn't very cold; afternoons at the residence were especially ho-hum since the sun set so early this time of the year. This was a great idea! We were learning about the states and where they were on the map, and this seemed like a bright and shiny idea for us to brag about to other kids. "Yeah, then we can just run home along the channel!"

Kyle seemed reluctant, but the pressure of our outnumbering thrill made him fold. "Aright, just a minute though."

We got off the bus at Joey's stop, about a mile—four or five stops before ours, with the several other kids that got off there. Usually Mommy, Tyrone's mom, or Kyle's mom met us at our stop in front of the residence. I wondered, as we furtively deboarded, who'd be there today, and what the backlash would be. The bus driver was inattentive. When the door unfolded, closing, and the bus thundered away, adrenaline filled me like amphetamine. This thrill had all of us beaming.

"What a you guys doin'?" Joey said.

"Goin' across," said Tyrone, pointing at the bridge. Eighty yards across drooped that other state, New Jersey, with all its motley, industrious clamor summoning us. In my memory, that fragment of New Jersey seemed dark, squalid, even evil from my eight-year-old perspective. This side, Cary Island, was secure, familiar, safe, sunny. In retrospect, there was this curious light and dark separation.

"Ya crossin' the Rock Channel Bridge?" Joey was awed. It was named this because of all the bedrock that had to be blasted out to build the bridge and all the bulkheading along the channel.

"Wanna come?" I said.

He wanted to. I could tell. His eyes were filled with amazement, watching, lured, hesitant.

Kyle was quiet, scared. At eight, our insane daring even made us skeptical that this was actually happening. It was all so accelerated, swift as the channel's current when the locks were opened.

"I can't." Joey said. "I'm not allowed to. I'll get in trouble." He squinted, looking westward where the bright sun had begun to set.

We climbed up the steep embankment to the highway. At the top we looked down at Joey, who still stood at the stop, watching us. He seemed so far, so safe, so removed from us, I thought. Joey had a mom and a dad, and he lived in a nice house, and he did his homework, and his hair was combed and clothes nice every morning.

Trucks passed, cars sped, exhaust emanated. We walked. Tyrone led the way, I followed, then Kyle. We didn't speak. There was so much noise from the whirring of passing vehicles, honking horns, and clamor from the factories across the channel that we wouldn't have been able to hear one another anyway. We just kept pacing, careful on the narrow curb that separated us from the four-foot railing and the channel on one side, and the hazardous highway on the other.

One man shouted out from his car as he passed in the deafening traffic: "What are you kids doing?"

Another shouted, "You kids wanna get killed?"

What a question! I didn't know if I was supposed to answer.

Another in the hurried velocity: "Get home!"

And yet another, a woman's screech: "No pedestrians on the bridge!" Her voice was awful. It could have made one's ears bleed. I didn't know what a pedestrian was then. I now imagine she read a sign to us!"

Each of these passing cries frightened us, not in fear of punishment, but because in our caution we were startled, jumpy. We didn't look back. We moved faster.

Finally we got to the other side, climbed over the four-foot railing—assisting one another, and running down the embankment.

The homes, marts, stores, and buildings on Cary Island looked so different from this side. Adrenaline drove through us. We kept walking, not looking back. We came to the sidewalk of the street that paralleled the channel like the route we lived on on the other side. We walked fleetly—a half mile—because we wanted to see the residence from this side. We could see it in the distance.

"Let's go back now," Kyle said with an urge.

We squinted, focusing, looking west. It was hard to notice if the bus was there at the residence still, or if there was any activity surrounding our absence. Twenty minutes must have lapsed since we got off.

"Let's go this way awhile." Tyrone's proposal was a calm demand.

I followed, and then Kyle—down a narrow lane for about a block. And then there was another lane we took, until we came to a lot, and some greenhouses.

"Look!" Tyrone pointed. We paced to where a shed and dumpster could conceal us. We sat there in the dirt, excited, feeling incongruously free in our little insurgency, catching our breath. The sun kept lowering, the air beginning to stab with cold. We zipped our coats. Then Tyrone picked up a rock; and with a delirious, wild grin he just threw it at the greenhouse. A pane broke. Then we could hear the glass break on the floor on the other side.

We giggled, listened. No retort from anywhere. We could faintly hear Christmas music playing somewhere in the distance. "God Rest Ye Merry Gentlemen."

"Watch this!" Tyrone picked up another larger rock. He threw it higher. It dropped onto the angling roof of glass, crashing again.

The lowest part of the opaque, filmy structure was green; the higher part was a lighter reflector of the orange of December sunlight and shapes of small buildings opposite the lot.

I looked at the rocks on the lot, noticing they were no different from those on rocky Cary Island on the other side. I watched Tyrone in his sinister ecstasy lift another, and throw. I listened as it crashed, and as the falling glass inside crashed again.

"Come on, it's fun!" he whispered loudly.

I reached for a rock, and threw, thoughtlessly. I reached for another. The mystery of this destructive pleasure, this aimless, effortless indulgence in the forbidden electrified me, actually mystified me as I kept searching, lifting, throwing, listening. Kyle followed, and the three of us continued in this aimless and randomly wasteful vandalism for a minute or so, until a light from within that end of that long greenhouse lit.

Suddenly panic struck, and the late afternoon seemed suddenly colder, so closer to dusk. We froze. Then suddenly—a voice—a loud, irate, old man's voice: "Hey you____ kids! What the ____ do you think ya ____ doin'!" His amplification slapped us with a terror of judgment. His cursing struck us like three blows. None of us could see him, but we knew that wherever he was, he was wild with anger. My heart pounded.

We bolted, at first speechlessly running, riveting our direction toward the bridge, the same way we came. Then I could hear Kyle crying as he ran.

"Don't worry!" I shouted between breaths.

It wasn't until we reached and began to climb the embankment on the New Jersey side that I started to wheeze; so I walked. I was out in front. Tyrone and Kyle followed, and walked as well. Tyrone was giggling; Kyle still cried.

We walked along that narrow curb again; and amid the danger on both sides I thought of Mommy Sparks, Daddy Sparks, and Justin; and I felt a trace of shame. I felt lost. For some reason, I recalled a certain Summer Sunday at that Pentecostal church where Daddy was Pastor

Sparks. I'd been seated in the usual front pew with Mommy Lucinda and Justin. Sunday School just ended. Daddy's text that Sunday was Matthew 3:7-9: "But when John saw many of the Pharisees and Sadducees coming for baptism, he said to them, 'You brood of vipers, who warned you to flee from the wrath to come? Therefore bring forth fruit in keeping with repentance; and do not suppose that you can say to yourselves, "We have Abraham for our father"; for I say to you, that God is able from these stones to raise up children to Abraham.'"

Daddy preached on practical Christianity, denouncing the gospel of ease. I remember his elevating a certain family's expression of love for people as a model for evidence of loving God, connecting it with his point. "Brother and sister Lewis crossed paths with a young preg-nant lady over in Brooklyn, unmarried, and already a single parent. Well this woman made up her mind to abort this child, convinced she couldn't afford another. Well the Lewis's committed themselves, offering this young woman that if she'd choose to give this child life, they'd make sure that for the first year they'd provide enough for his care. We have needy, helpless people all about us saints, None of 'em are inclined to come inside our nice churches or hear our empty words if words is all we got! But they might hear us if we reach out instead of just preach out—if you know what I mean. To reach people for God we have to extend ourselves, to give up our comfort. The Lewis's are showing God's love to this woman and her children!"

I remember Daddy's long, staring, breathing pauses. His flock would wait in silence. "We can't just love in word or tongue, but in deed and truth! We can't like John's crowd who called themselves Abraham's children call ourselves Christians and then sit idly by! Nonsense! We're frauds! Faith without works is dead!" He shouted, continuing, "We can't pretend, wishing, 'If I had a lot of money I'd open a home for kids!' Phooey! We start with one! We open our hearts and doors. We lay down our golf clubs and pick up our crosses! We sacrifice the nail salon and invest on a human being."

That's a sermon I recall. It has stayed with me. Daddy and Mommy Lucinda devoted their lives into human beings, and for some reason I thought about it now deeply as I wheezed and walked and shivered as the deadly cars whizzed by us on that dreary bridge, as the miry channel waters swirled below.

Mommy and Daddy Sparks and Justin visited me every couple of weeks. The people in the program said it was okay, but they weren't allowed to take me out, or visit for long durations. That was supposed to be for my benefit. They thought it might interfere with the "bonding" that was reputed to be forming between me and Mommy Maureen. The big problem was that every time they'd leave from a short visit at the residence, I felt that old ache again. I wanted to be with them badly. I could tell it hurt them too, and that made me feel both bad and good.

After we crossed the bridge, we descended the embankment on the Cary Island side, and the area seemed dull and quieter now than when the bus stopped before. Joey was gone, probably at home doing his homework, aiming carefully at something constructive with his mom or dad helping him. By now the sun was set and the purple-gray filled the east, bleaching the trees, darkening buildings, making them square two-dimensional structures. We kept walking. My feet, ears, and fingers grew frigid; but as I walked my wheezing subsided. To the west the sky glowed with bright scarlet, and every shape that stood before it was black.

When we arrived at the residence we discovered a police car in the front. We entered the rear entrance of the house, still speechlessly novice as wrongdoers to fabricate a unified story, and we found a nervous hubbub, a tense panic mixed with relief. "Where have you been? Why weren't you on the bus? You boys had us scared." Our moms were there. A nurse was there, with two of the workers. The policeman was writing.

"We were at Joey's" Tyrone said.

I and Kyle kept quiet, looking at each other.

"Well how?"

"We just got off at his stop."

Tyrone lied so masterfully naturally.

"Don't ever do that again! You hear me Tyrone Wilson?" His mother's thick black index finger was raised above his white eyes.

"Yes Ma."

We were fearful that the police were there because of all those windows we'd broken. We were relieved, but we were also unsettled. I had this inexplicable feeling that I had crossed something other than a bridge, traversed into something metaphysically secret, into something darker and dirtier than that part of New Jersey. I'd crossed over a line into the forbidden, a prohibited clime that was more ruinous than the West Channel Bridge we'd walked, one that would be ruefully easier to cross from that time forward.

Well I liked being in school mostly because I didn't like being stuck in Crossings House with Mommy. I looked for opportunities to get away from Mommy, like the one I just described. The psychology people at the residence wanted Mommy and me to be together often. That was program policy, because they were supposed to watch us interacting together to see if Mommy was capable. The funny thing was that they didn't "study" us much. They had a lot of meetings behind closed doors where they talked, drank coffee, wrote and read reports, making Mommy's and other people's files thicker. I now can't imagine how much money taxpayers paid for all this.

Back to school again, I'm not sure people like Miss Karessi embraced my being present. Miss Karessi was a petite, loquacious, ambitious young lady who wore little, round glasses. She loved kids; no doubt. She hugged them, touched them on their backs when she leaned over them looking at their work; and some hugged her. Once she hugged me, but usually she didn't, and that was probably because I was habitually dirty, tousled, sometimes reeking. Like many "serious" teachers, I recall her as one who wouldn't go out of her way, especially for one like me. I was a lost cause. She redirected attention to kids with hope, to kids with influential parents in the district.

A lot of the kids brought gifts in for her—little things like mugs with praises like "World's Best Teacher" printed on them, or packages of homemade things to eat, fruit baskets, or cards, nice pencils, and sometimes even gift certificates to restaurants. My guess, looking back, was that most of that was initiated by parents, or kids who'd probed their parents because other kids brought gifts in.

Once I slipped one of Mommy Maureen's nicer ashtrays—a heavy, glass, semitransparent blue one with a lighthouse, a bluff, a soaring gull, and Maine embossed in white, wiping away ash stains—into my backpack to offer as a gift for Miss Karessi. "Oh, how nice, Silas, but I don't smoke," she said so all would hear.

Some kids giggled, some laughed aloud. Picturing pretty little Miss Karessi puffing cigarettes at that moment did seem absurd.

"That's enough," Miss Karessi said to the laughers, forcing a change on her expression and tone.

I didn't know what to do in my angry awkwardness, so I walked quickly, carrying the burdensome thing, looking down into its deep florescent blueness back to my desk. When I looked back at her I could tell by the way she kept an eye on me that she probably regretted her reaction—her making that vociferous point so that the other kids wouldn't suppose she smoked. Finally, having thought hard enough, she said: "Silas I love Maine, and I could use that to put my paperclips in. Can I still have it and use it for that? Those trays don't have to be for ashes only! I really like it."

I quietly stepped forward as quickly as I'd retreated, and I thudded it onto her desk, returning again, staring at the floor tiles, less angry.

I did spend a lot of time—three or four visits that year—in Mr. McMaster the principal's office. After the second visit in December I could foretell his predictable, rehearsed speech which regressively lost its threatening intimidation. I guess he'd forgotten that kids have memories. It went something like this: "Mr. Dillon, your teacher works very hard, and your mother has great hopes for you. You are in this school to learn. Antics, fighting, fun and games..." His voice heaved with threat here: "It will not be tolerated!" He paused, looked at me through spectacles with grave, preoccupation and fake hostility. "Do you understand me?"

"Yes."

"Am I understood?"

I nodded.

"So you're telling me there will be no more problems with Miss Karessi!"

"Uh huh." I fidgeted, eager to get out.

"Now return to your classroom."

I'd bob my way out of his back office, through a little maze of women working at desks, around a high counter, and out into the hallway, mostly unaffected.

In classes I liked I didn't get into trouble. I was pretty good in art class back then, probably because of Mommy Sparks' influence. Mr. Tinge, an older, soft-spoken man with long gray hair tied in a ponytail and thick glasses magnifying blue eyes, often drew the class's attention to the things I drew, painted, or made, praising my work. He called me the Gauguin of West Channel Elementary School, probably because I made my human figures dark complexioned like Gauguin's primitive looking Tahitians. I don't know.

Music class usually included singing along with old, corpulent Mrs. Sonato and her piano. I never sang, and she never bothered me too much about it. She didn't stand up and walk around ever. Maybe she didn't notice. I'm still not too sure why—why I didn't sing or why she didn't press me. I'd always loved to sing in church with Justin and Mommy Sparks; but those church hymns and choruses somehow made singing feel good. But singing patriotic songs, or about ten little Indians and a dog named Bingo, even in third grade, seemed a lot less sensible. For a couple of weeks we played record-ers and learned about instruments we'd be able to explore in fourth grade. Otherwise, our voices—what we could do with our voices with inane songs—was the seat of passion with old Mrs. Sonato.

My best subject was gym. I liked it because I excelled. I'd always been coordinated, lithe, fast, aggressive, competitive, strong. A lot of that came from Justin's influence, and hanging around those older kids in the old neighborhood. Thick-chested, short-haired Mr. Kemp the gym teacher often employed me to demonstrate before the twenty other boys things like pull-ups or swinging a bat, and he usually called on me so he could demonstrate things like wres-tling moves or wheelbarrow racing or defending a basketball player. I always outwrestled my opponents, and I was often the last one out in the dodge ball contests. I won the *Best Athlete* award that year.

I wonder about teachers like Mr. Kemp and Mr. Tinge. Surely the fact that I came from a dysfunctional situation wasn't hard to discern. I believe they may have singled me out, applauding me partly because they sensed I needed it. For cast-offs like me, the little candles to go on required the fuel like those.

One day in November I had an exceptionally bad asthma attack at school. It actually began the night before, but gradually grew worse, and really peaked after running on the soccer field in gym class. I was suffocating. My inhaler at the nurse's office wasn't helping, so the nurse—not wanting to take any chances—called an ambulance. That was something. I got a lot of attention. The whole school knew, and many of the teachers in the front of the school let their kids look out the windows as the medical technicians wheeled me out and drove me away to Cary County Hospital where I was born.

One of the childcare workers drove Mommy, and she met me at the emergency room where I was propped up in a bed between high green curtains getting oxygen and some stronger medicine in a big nebulizer. She was so frantic—talking, blaming people, yelling, dramatizing, just generally in one of her backward moods. Security was called and took Mommy away into another room. I was especially happy to see Molly come. She didn't have to, but someone from the halfway house called her. She calmed Mommy down, and she calmed me down too. I somehow breathed better with her there.

Molly always had to explain things to people, professional people. That was part of her job I guess. She spoke low, almost to a whisper, not knowing I could hear, to a nurse and the emergency room supervisor: "Just understand, this boy's mom is sometimes unstable. She sees these situations as opportunities to gain some attention. She somehow feels she's the center of a great drama. That's part of her neurosis, Just try to respond to her genially and she'll be fine!"

"Yes, fine, thank you Ms.-"

"Molly Fresh. I'm the case worker."

"I see."

"Try to be gentle with little Silas. He's been through a lot—too much—especially lately. His asthma has been aggravated no doubt because of some of the stresses of displacement. He was taken last month from a long time placement—five years. He was growing quite secure, doing so well, but then the court decided to award his mother custody, in a special program—a trial basis."

The physician-supervisor listened patiently, nodding, saying "ummmm" and "I see, I see."

"Besides his asthma, he's recently acquired this horrible eczema. That's why his skin is the way you see it."

"Would you mind staying Ms. Fresh until the boy's airways stabilize?"

"No, I can stay."

I could recognize then, for the first time, how Mommy affected me, and could distinguish her affect from Molly's and others'. A light went on. Unlike some kids who love their negligent or abusive parents, I plainly didn't. Perhaps if I hadn't experienced a tender home like the Sparks' and didn't know any different, I'd feel different. But I was mad.

We stayed there another hour or so until I could breath better, and then Molly drove us back to the big residence by the channel in time for dinner.

After the holidays in early January the Sparks' came to visit me, and this time I could tell something was up. Mommy Maureen and other people at the house let us be together alone for once. It was like the old days. We sat in the big reading room on soft chairs.

"What's the matter?" I said.

"Well Silas, we're moving, away from here, to Ohio," Mommy Lucinda said.

"God has called us, Silas, to move on—a new pastorate, a church— for me to pastor in Cincinnati. It was very unusual how it all transpired, but He's made it very clear, son." Daddy's deep, confident voice reached my soul. It always felt like that when he talked. This news hurt me, but somehow I felt like there really was a great God that talked to him like that whenever he spoke to me so honestly.

"Oh."

Justin just looked at me, unless I looked at him; then he looked away. He kept swinging one foot up and down as he slouched in his chair. I could tell he didn't want to move away.

"Will I still see you?"

There was a long pause. "We're going to keep in touch as much as possible, son," Daddy said. Again there was a thoughtful hesitation. I could tell Daddy wanted to say things to me about how he felt about everything—about court, the battle, Mommy Maureen; but he restrained himself. There was this sort of controlling governor inside of him. He was frustrated, especially with her selfishness surrounding me; but he refused to disintegrate any honor I may have been developing in my attitude and opinion toward her. He spurned his temptation to embitter me by denigrating the courts or New Blossom Children's Services. He was so slow and deliberate to speak, so controlled and slow to anger, so careful with his words, so gentle with me.

Mommy Lucinda began to cry, and there was something about her crying that Saturday afternoon that revealed to me that she felt defeated, struggling with something in her faith, and it had something to do with me, and their lack of success at legally securing me for adoption.

Daddy did almost all the talking that afternoon. Recalling now, I can't imagine how much stress was on him at that time. It had to be overwhelming—pastoring, comforting his little family in all this business surrounding me, comforting me, moving, preparing for a new ministry, planning, making these decisions.... We were all going through an ordeal.

The wind blasted so cold outside that day. The sun shone and the shadows remained long—all through the day—as the sun hovered low, clinging close to the earth just a few weeks further than the solstice. I wondered, gazing at the coal-colored wild cherry limbs which kept bobbing up and down in the tossing wind. I merely wondered, gazing numbly through glass out the window. I felt freakishly alone, so monstrously alone.

"Honestly Silas, this is all so very confusing to each of us." Daddy said this, pointing to his own chest, toward Mommy Lucinda, and then at Justin. "We all love you so very much, and we all want you with us." He paused, searching for the right way to talk to me, careful for my heart, searching for the right tone, certainly praying—for God's hand to settle on my heart. He spoke with his own heart aching.

"Love you too," I said.

"I can't make you any promises. We'll be praying for you, son. For some reason God lets strange things—senseless things—happen in people's lives. We just gotta trust Him, son. There's nothing else."

"I don't want you to go."

"Look at me, son."

I was crying. He made me look into his eyes. He cried.

"You hear me, son?"

"I nodded." He made me brave. He wanted me to love his God, to believe his God. There was so much fog and smoke in the way—in my little mind.

"There is no alternative Silas. You have to trust, son. I want you to understand me, son. I love you."

I jumped from my deep chair and ran to him, burying my face on his shoulder, crying out loud. Mommy put her hand on my back and kept rubbing, patting.

Justin rose and left. He left with the same painful dispatch that he bolted with back in September when I was being taken from their home. After a few minutes he returned, having dried his eyes.

We embraced like were a family. I now see that their input into my life was done—besides their praying for me. They parted, leaving me a promise that they'd visit regularly—weekly—until they had to go, which was a month away.

As I'd mentioned, I looked for opportunities to get away from being stuck with Mommy in the big stone residence house. School was an adequate diversion, but when school was out and we had vacation weeks, I made sure I was out as much as was permitted. Tyrone, Kyle, and I spent a lot of time around the channel, mostly fishing. All we caught were snappers, sea robins, once in a while blowfish, eels, and only once I caught a big weakfish. We never had much luck bottom fishing for flounders or fluke in the channel, at least not as much as I had back at Justin's house near the ocean, but we did catch some. We caught a lot of crabs for a couple of weeks late in the summer, but then it just died. Our moms packed us a lunch a few times, and we stayed out all day in the sun.

We could fish only when the locks were closed actually. When the locks were opened, the current surged and rushed too swiftly, pushing all the fish out into the bay. The locks were built to regulate the tide waters' passage through, opening for short spells every six hours. Boats came through then: tugs, fishing boats, cargo ships, rarely pleasure boats, skiffs, and yachts; sometimes big barges crept sluggishly through, and sometimes they docked along the bulkhead for consecutive days.

One day during spring recess a barge was tied up directly across the avenue in front of the residence. It was a cloudy, windy, April day—the kind of day that teased, threatening rain but never delivering any; a raw, tumultuous day that allowed momentary flashes, glimpses, peeks of sunlight; a day full of damp, airy dalliance. Tyrone and I lay our poles on the dock and jumped onto the flat, deserted barge to explore. We guessed this was probably forbidden, but we didn't inquire to know for sure. We were impressed with the rigging, the heavy tackle and rope, all the rusty apparatus. We passed time throwing some rusty bolts, nuts, and other corroded pieces of metal that lay strewn on the deck into the channel. Tyrone spotted a drum: "A drum!" he said. "Look, a half a drum!"

I immediately pictured in my mind a percussion instrument. "A drum? What drum?"

He pointed. Several fifty gallon drums filled with some kind of cleaning fluid stood against the cabin at the front of the barge. We walked. There was an empty, cleft in half drum lying on its side, rocking slightly, dry inside.

"Why's it in half?" I said.

"Who knows."

"How do they cut it like that?"

"I don't know. Big cutter I guess."

"Wonder what for."

"Who cares. What a neat little boat this could be," Tyrone said.

"Yeah."

"This is so cool."

We were quiet a moment, rocking this thing back and forth.

"Let's take it in the channel!" Tyrone said.

I said nothing.

"Let's see if it floats."

"What's it made of?"

"Plastic I guess."

"I guess seein's okay."

"We could sit in it. It's big." He had that same, commanding, autocratic tone in his voice he had back in December when he'd said, "Let's get off the bus at Joey's stop." His sudden expression-filled quest to breach boundaries, my quick penchant to follow, our blended aspirational thirst for thrills, all seemed to just drive us to move heedlessly. Without a word we each took an end and lifted, walking sideways toward the water, placing it down again.

We looked around, simply standing before this thing, beside the channel, on this big flat barge a moment. No one was watching—only one seagull on the barge.

"Go get that wood! That plank thing!" Tyrone said, pointing to a weathered, four-foot-long one-by-six.

I walked, picked it up.

"We can paddle around with it."

"Good idea," I said.

We lifted the hard, cleft, plastic drum again, over the inch high gunwale, down three feet into the water. "I'll hold it. You get in first," Tyrone directed.

He leaned over, holding. I stepped down carefully—one foot, then the other. I stood a moment, rocking gently, testing its stability. I strained to balance.

"Sit! Sit down!"

I sat. "Gimme the board," I said. He reached down with it, and I gripped. He stepped down carefully—one foot, the other—and he sat facing me.

We pushed off from the barge, and our little tottery bark drifted out into the channel. A gust pushed us some, making surface ripples on the water. We looked at each other's tremulous, wide-eyed grimaces. I remember feeling that ecstatic rapture taking my breath away a moment. I wanted to scream with this excitement. This all happened so suddenly, almost thoughtlessly.

"Gimme the board," Tyrone said. His white teeth shone within his dark complexion, the inside of his smiling mouth like a fence. He paddled, intent on crossing to the Jersey side. The flat, untapered ends of the drum made steering troublesome, and we kept twirling. Even though the locks were closed there was a slight drift toward Newark Bay as gusts kept blowing. I looked across, into the water's murky cinnamon color which seemed, under the overcast sky, to have no translucence whatsoever.

We were out for about five minutes when we realized we had very little control directing our little bark. We had to be very careful to remain seated and still in the center of the drum, because any shift of weight gave us the feeling like we'd roll and tip. It was less stable than even the narrowest of canoes.

We bobbed in the middle of the channel, and we drifted maybe a couple hundred yards down the channel. There were two men on the Jersey side pointing at us. One shouted, "Hey you kids! You wanna get killed or something?"

It reminded me of the voice from the passing car when we'd crossed the bridge in December. It struck me funny again as I wondered whether I was supposed to answer the question or not. As I felt invincible in this drum, untouchable out there in the center of the channel, I boldly responded: "Yeah!"

We both started laughing. We were such wise guys. We didn't know what we were doing. Neither one of us could swim either. It must have seemed we had a death wish, but we really were just hoodwinked, thinking we were invulnerable. We were both afraid to die.

After about twenty minutes of slow drifting, about halfway to the bridge, we realized the locks had opened. A strong current pushed us, advancing by our mini, heavy bark. We looked at each other with fear and excitement.

"Locks open!" I said.

"I think you're right! Uh-oh!"

"Here we go!"

"Cool! Awesome!"

It's all so tragically comical as I recall now. There we were, wards of the state, afloat in this drum, precariously endangered, heavily invested in by uninformed taxpayers—tens of thousands of dollars—while psychological and sociological "professionals" back at Crossings House sat "watching" and "counseling" and aiming to help our messed-up "mothers" become mothers, sitting around a table maybe—discussing us, having meetings, hearings, conferences, discussing our mothers, talking "goals," planning our well-being and futures, picking up their paychecks, talking textbook terminology, tossing around imposing terms like *disintegrating consociation* with staid expressions on their faces, savoring their own self-esteem and reaching self-actualization and convincing themselves they were making mighty contributions to humanity, while Tyrone and I were afloat at that very hour, drifting one wrong tilt away from drowning death, careless, filthy, ridiculously neglected, coarse on the exterior—like Huck and Jim—moving further into degeneration. This was so tragically comical!

We spun even more, caught in swirling eddies, and we were quickly passing under the bridge. It was from this point southward to where the residence where we'd launched and the locks—slightly farther—were that the channel was the narrowest and closest to New

Jersey; but from this point northward it gradually widened, flowing eventually into Newark Bay.

Tyrone stuck the one-by-six into the current, thinking maybe we could steer or slow down. It only made us twirl more hectically, causing the drum to reel, wobble, almost tip, giving us a panicky frantic feeling. "Whooee!" We both shouted, giggling nervously.

"What a we gonna do?" I said.

"Maybe we could drift by the shore."

On the banks of the hastily dilating channel we could see three more people pointing and shouting to us, but we couldn't hear their words. We waved—not for help—but just to be genial. I still laugh when I think of this. We had only a small idea that our lives were seriously in danger.

Soon we bobbed into this small gulf called Newark Bay where, because of the width, the current no longer drove us along; however, waves were no longer only ripples, but choppy rollers that slapped against our little half-canister. This was new scope to us: Bayonne, Elizabeth, industry, cargo ships, access to New York Harbor, the stench of chemicals and paper products being manufactured.

With this excitement and dismay, I had this subliminal pleasure of escaping Mommy with this instinctive craving of drifting farther from her. At age nine now, in the spring semester of third grade, the actuality that this was not permanent still didn't link in my immature mindfulness. I had no fear of "getting in trouble" as I simply lived for gratification of the moment. I imagined I could breakout. I imagined Mommy and Daddy Sparks were watching me. I looked up. The clouds were charcoal chalk, gorgeous undulations, impressions of heaven. Off to the east I could see the rising pinnacles of the twin towers peaking silvery, brilliantly like prongs of a tuning fork, above trees and houses and their other nearby buildings. The towers shone, glossy, proud. I felt the wind on my face, moving my tight, tangled hair. Feeling cold, I pushed down the sleeves of my sweat-shirt. I imagine we looked primitively curious out there.

After about ten minutes in the currents of the widening body of water, a fast, snow-white, twenty-five-foot craft came racing toward us from the Cary Island side. Large black letters on the hull told us it was the bay constable. The vessel stopped and turned broadside before us. One officer steered, standing; one stood with his fists on his hips and sunglasses on; and the other held out a speakerphone. All wearing their authority-blue windbreakers with white Police let-tering, we could hear the loud electronic command: "Unauthorized, unregistered small crafts are prohibited in these waters!"

We didn't know what this meant. We looked at each other, half grinning, halfway to tears. When they realized we were kids much younger than what was probably reported from those adults beside the channel, they lowered a dinghy. The men that weren't steering got in and rowed toward us. The one black man said, "What are you rascals doin' out here? You want to drown or something?"

"We just floatin' around." Tyrone said.

"Well you just better be floatin' around in the swimming pool. This is treacherous waters."

We mostly kept quiet. The concerned, amazed scolding continued as one man clamped our drum tightly and rigidly against the dinghy—which seemed huge compared to our drum—and the other man lifted us in, one by one. They rowed us to the big police boat; we got a won-derfully exciting, fast ride back to Cary Island, and were taken back to the residence. All along our mothers and the house directors had been thinking we were fishing in the channel. The director of the residence, old Mrs. Blamel, was asked to resign because of that.

A couple of days after this affair something awful happened to Mommy. My half-brother she'd been carrying was about to be born, early. She was hurried to the Cary County Hospital, where I'd been born. She went through labor in the same fashion she'd gone through with me and with my older half-brother whose name I've never come to know, who'd lived somewhere in Connecticut.

It was a rainy April morning, in fact a deluge. I watched from our second story window—the one Mommy always smoked out of—as one of the workers helped her into the car, as another held an umbrella over her.

My half-brother was born dead by noon. She gave birth to this still-born whom she named Nicholas. Jesse, one of the young black workers at the residence, took me to see Mommy that afternoon. That nice nurse who'd helped Mommy give birth to me nine years earlier was still there. She was the supervisor now.

The county paid for Nicholas's little interment. This made me cry a lot for a couple of days. I was sort of looking forward to having a baby brother.

At once Mommy descended into a deep depression. She wouldn't talk or eat, couldn't sleep or carry out everyday duties. She didn't even shower. A lot of people at the house gave her a lot of attention, and then after about ten days or so, she snapped out of it. In fact she seemed to become especially happy, almost ecstatic. She was crazy, way off balance. I didn't feel right around her. Her overflowing elation was not honest, was scary.

Later that spring—in May—Mommy was given some extra freedom. The new head program director Ms. Harris—an overweight, middle-aged black woman—rewarded her with this because Mommy seemed to have made some progress. It was largely because Mommy implored and argued for it a lot. This was a mistake. Mommy was not ready. Their giving her a few inches of freedom, sort of testing her with time on her own, induced her to take a few yards. She stayed out on two occasions for four or five hours, and on one occasion she stayed out all day. Because she'd returned apparently intact, unbroken, and equipped with distinctive alibis, her absence was overlooked and their too lenient trust in her continued. Their observance of her interaction with me was suspended for a while.

The relapse came one Friday in early June. Mommy put me on the school bus like other mornings. The bus rolled down Channel Turnpike, making stops and detaining cars and clogging traffic like other mornings. I spent a normal day in school like a hundred and sixty other days, and I returned at two to discover that the residence administration was in dismay at Mommy's not having returned. The afternoon moved into dusk, and then into darkness. I was sent to bed. I slept. I awoke. Morning. Mommy still hadn't returned. It wasn't until that afternoon after school that I was informed that Mommy was in the hospital recovering from an overdose of heroin. She'd been discovered by the police who'd received an anonymous call, and she'd been rescued in some apartment building hallway, unconscious, near death, covered in vomit and urine.

That evening Molly tried to talk her supervisor out of assigning her to bring me to the hospital to visit Mommy, but there was no dissuasion from this because it was a law. I had to be taken to see my mother.

This visit certainly didn't do me any good. Fortunately Molly made sure it was a short one. We parked, walked, and stepped inside the busy lobby, then onto the waxed, gray tiled floors of the Cary County Hospital corridors. I was instantly reminded of my last visit back in November when I'd had my bad asthma attack. It had that distinctive, antibacterial smell. We stopped at the elevators. Molly pressed the up button, and we waited. I could hear it ascending, arriving. The door opened. We stepped after some strangers and moved swiftly upward.

"I don't want to be here."

"In the elevator?"

"No."

"You mean the hospital, honey?"

"Yeah."

"Me neither, Silas." Molly grabbed my cheeks, scrunching my lips together. Then she rubbed her pretty white fingers through my crimped hair, smiling. I didn't know what to expect with Mommy— what she'd look like, what all this meant. I had a presentiment that another change was coming my way again, but I wasn't sure. I had a secret hope I'd go back to the Sparks', but I also had a doubt that that would happen since they'd moved away to Ohio.

The elevator door opened; we stepped out onto the shiny gray again, and then walked, making turns at the ends of brief corridors. Molly found the room. We stepped into the yellow, semi-glossed, soapy smelling room where Mommy lay. I felt a heavy, gloomy disgust in my soul. It was nauseating. It was like I was fighting hatred—for my mother, for the whole world. I wanted to curse out loud. I cursed loudly in my head.

She lay slightly propped up with a tube in her nose, an intravenous tube bandaged into her arm, the plastic bottle dripping cloudless drugs from the slender stand which erected itself plumb above her like a mortal watcher. Mommy turned her head from looking out the sunny window, strangely searching for us, for some focus, with vacant eyes.

"Hello Maureen. How are you feeling?" I could hear a slant of disappointment and even disgust in Molly's voice.

"Silas," was all Mommy said, delayed, looking at me, looking away again, then shaking her head. She raised her intravenous bound arm twice. She looked at her hand, clenched a fist, let her arm fall. Her legs lay inert.

"Hi Mommy. You feel better?"

Mommy didn't answer me. She shut her eyes tightly. She gnashed her teeth, emitting a sort of growl. She shook her head back and forth, up and down, almost violently. She said some things that were totally senseless. She seemed lost, so far away, so completely mindless.

I quickly walked to the big window and looked out. The sky was huge and blue, the island full and green as the crowns of the leaf bearing trees smothered lower roofs and colors of the streets, obscuring the darker blending evergreens which are always so embossed in winter. An uninterrupted horizon line of the Atlantic cut across this picture of the world like a deep blue slice. The underside beneath was a ragged, irregular ruffling; The ocean's profundity of cerulean cut a trenchant sliver, separating land, earth, Cary Island life from vacant bare sky, somewhat like the way the channel did from New Jersey. It was as if the sharper shapes of structures denoting life on this island broke its formerly smooth, pristine, naturally-structured continuity. The world looked so creatively beautiful from up here.

I turned and looked back at Mommy. The thought that I'd emerged from her womb here in this hospital nine and a half years earlier crossed my mind, baffling me. The skin on her face looked shiny, oily, almost transparent. Her hair was dirty, matted. From across this yellow room I could see the contour of her skull. It was as if I could see through her sweating skin and behold her skull. Her veins in her forehead were greenish, perceptible; her eyes sunken, dark. I had a bad, unhappy feeling. I wanted to cry, but not there, not then.

Molly watched me.

Mommy began to shake her head again. She was so ugly.

"Silas I think it's time we left. This is not good," Molly said.

I walked toward Molly, reaching out my half-grown, brown hand. Her pretty white hand covered mine, squeezing. I took one last glance at Mommy. She stared vacuously at me with her sunken organs of sight which at one time were lovely eyes of blue, like the Atlantic on that same blue June day. I didn't know then that this here visit in my ninth year of life was to be the last time I'd see Mommy Maureen, my birth mother. It makes me oddly sad to think of it now, but I don't think it would have then, if I'd known it was to be the last.

TEN

THE HOLLOW

If I could have scaled ten feet of the craggy trunk, the first crotch of the big swamp maple would have furnished me with a limb that reached parallel with the ground—some footing I could stand on—and then, not far above, tributaries of limbs and smaller forks, occasions for climbing higher; or outward onto buoyant, thinner ends of limbs; uncertain springy regions, just for the thrill. This tree was a colossal shell of green, with still leaves full of vigor, no dead branches. It was a place where the cerulean-blue, gray, white, or starry sky of that June was hidden by shadows and green, totally.

I kept trying to scale this trunk. I tried repeatedly, clutching the gnarly ridges; hugging; squeezing with my knees and thighs; pressing the insteps of my new, county provided, white sneakers against it; plastering all of me—even my cheek and temple—attempting to walk, mount, pull, shimmy my thin frame up like a caterpillar—upward—two, three, four feet up—upward. I then slid suddenly, repeatedly, down to the ground. Three steps up, three steps down—over and over. Opposing spirits of spite and failure seemed to toil against me. Frustration. I tried—typically boyishly—for an hour, never able to really get off the ground, never able to ascend.

This scene metaphorically sketched my nine years of life. "I'll try this again tomorrow," I said to myself, backing away from the trunk, looking up into its wonderful green canopy.

I thought about what Mr. Kemp my gym teacher had said to me on the last day of school, his hand on my shoulder: "Sometimes we get flat tires in life Silas. We just have to fix em!"

"Okay Mr. Kemp."

He'd heard that I would have to repeat third grade because of my poor progress. He'd come to me, thinking maybe this had bothered me. It hadn't. I'd understood what he meant.

I wonder now if he perceived the general attitude among some teachers toward types like me, the attitude that I was a "case," a lost cause, one whom a teacher with so many other students with potential shouldn't go too far out of the way for, since I didn't hold as much hope. I'm sure he'd noticed that some other teachers often redirected attention to kids who had more potentiality.

"It's just a reality of living," he'd said, his lips lifting and spreading with eye-catching elasticity—all over his open face—with his serious yet friendly stare. He'd always been profoundly philosophical in such an uncomplicated way, I remember. "Expect flat tires in life son!"

"Okay Mr. Kemp." I did expect them, but felt that I had too many, and I had them in the rain and snow, and I rode with worn treads, and I grew suspicious that worse and longer breakdowns were coming.

"You have a lot of talent kid. You're a good athlete. Stay involved Silas. I'm sure we'll be readin about you in the city papers in seven or eight years."

"Okay Mr. Kemp. Thanks Mr. Kemp."

Looking up into this tree I thought of Mr. Kemp. The thought alone somehow brought me a sentiment of security. His recent influence was something I could lean on, even knowing I wouldn't be going back to Channel Elementary anymore. As I struggled to climb this tree, I imagined Mr. Kemp watched, impressed.

This new place dipped a couple of miles away from the Atlantic, enclosed in the island's interior; yet no sector on this island lay far enough away that smells of tides or cries of gulls couldn't perforate. This was Horse Hollow, near Cary Island's center, slightly below sea level, a place where horses had traipsed, slept, and been tended on farms only seventy years earlier, before these suburbs had chased them away. Old black and white photos within glass preserving frames in the public library galloped residents into the past. Of course, the hollow had once been rural, picturesque; but now it was common and clangorous like most of the island. This shallow hollow provided for tarns and ponds, made ground more sodden, a haven for tupelos, swamp cedars, and these swamp maples. Rainy days made streets streams, basements flood, and pumps pump. This condition had never kept the builders from building; however, and never dissuaded the gaping urban sprawl from swallowing the fields, digesting the stables, and settling in the low mud.

I stepped away from the tree, exhausted, and I sat on the bottom step of the stoop. This was where I lived now, on Mare Trail, a people-noisy lane, with a small tarn across the street where peepers choired all night, where cattails hid the view of water, where litter, old tires, rusted shopping carts, and other junk were strewn. I lived behind this big swamp maple in a slender seventy-year-old townhouse which looked too much like all the others on the street and neighboring streets. I lived with the O'Neils, Kevin and Martha, who were in their fifties; and their twenty-eight-year-old unmarried daughter Karen; with her two children, five-year-old Edwin and his four-year-old half-sister Rosie. Neither of these kids knew his or her father.

"What are you doing Silas?" Mrs. O'Neil said from behind the screen door, behind me.

"Just climbin."

"Don't get hurt."

"I won't." I looked back quickly. Her thin little frame, heavy eyes, and short gray hair all seemed smudged by the blurring screen. This is how her personality always seemed to me—indistinct, blurry. She kept her distance, avoiding nearness and knowing me.

I slept downstairs in the bottom bunk beneath Edwin, and I kept my clothes in the bottom three drawers of his big bureau. This was my settlement for now. I felt like a bottom dwelling flounder now, especially this blue June day, having strived to ascend this trunk.

This arrangement was understood to be temporary, until the agency found a "permanent" place for me—maybe even a family who'd adopt me. Sometime in the summer they were going to have an adoption party, an affair where a bunch of us older kids got dressed up and had a dinner while potential parents came to observe, sort of shop for a child, and then pick one they liked.

My mother's rights were being terminated at this point. Imagine, it took nine and a half years, and now finally the system began to get things going. Besides this, Mommy and Daddy Sparks were communicating with the agency at this time, trying to adopt me. I'd received a letter from Mommy Lucinda which I always kept with me in my pocket, and often took out, unfolded, read, folded again. In just a week it had softened like a tissue and become gray and soiled from crumpling.

Dear Silas,

We all miss you so much, and we pray for you every day! We're still working on getting you here with us. We don't know what will happen, but we have to trust Jesus, Silas. He knows best. The court in New York there is not permitting this adoption because things are still technically unsettled with Mommy Maureen, and besides that, you are the property of New York State, not Ohio. That makes things tricky. They say laws are laws, and they are to be complied with. Let's just keep praying.

*He has a wonderful plan, no matter what. Right? We are so
busy with the new church. Justin has made a couple of new
friends, and they are very nice boys. He will write to you soon.
We love you, Silas.*

Love, Mommy Lucinda

It was quite ironic. I loved to read this, even though I didn't
know what a couple of the words meant, and even though it made
my heart ache every time.

These O'Neils did a lot of this temporary housing for foster kids.
It seemed like they were running a sort of hotel rather than a home.
The bed, the bath, the meals, the drawers, and the rules were the
extent of bonding. No hugs, no kisses, no pats on the back, no yells,
and no lessons. All temporary dealings, no tent stakes hammered.

I felt so contiguously alone, unloved, and angry in those days
that summer. I was partly afraid and partly tired of making new
friends in a new neighborhood. At night time I had a hard time
falling asleep, especially since it was hot down there in the hollow.
It was like the nice ocean breezes blew above, and I was down in
this valley-like hole where the air was stagnant and summer-thick.
I'd move around into varied positions on the bed, trying to find cool
spots on the sheets, listening to peepers and crickets. My asthma was
acting up, and so was my eczema. I wheezed and chafed. I regressed
back to thumb sucking, and it became more of a compulsion the
more I felt lonely and scared. Boy, was I a case. There I lay, nine and
a half years old, in a strange place where the people barely talked to
me, sucking my thumb; scratching my chapped, crusty skin; trying
to breathe, night after night.

I made some halfhearted attempts at befriending five-year-old
Edwin, but he was just a little kid, often out with his mother, and he
really was sort of too young for me. In fact, I found that he was sort

of babyish, even for a five-year-old. He was an annoying little kid, the kind who'd make me repeat myself two or three times whenever I said something to him.

"Wanna go to the tarn Edwin?"

"What?"

"Wanna go play at the tarn?"

"Ha?"

"Wanna go to the tarn? Wanna go to the tarn?" I got loud.

"No!" He got loud.

This sort of thing was exasperating. Sometimes he'd mumble for minutes and I didn't even realize he was talking to me. I thought he was talking to himself. I didn't really like being around him. He was dull, and a bit of a brat. It wasn't his fault, but he was just that way. He loved television, science fiction stuff, and toys. What really bothered me was that he always helped himself to my things, looking around in my drawers and stuff. But if I ever touched his stuff, he'd have a fit, crying; and I'd get spoken to about it by Mrs. O'Neil who, by the way, didn't want me to call her Mom or Mommy. I didn't care much about that. Whenever Edwin was out with his mother Karen (That's what I called her), Mrs. O'Neil would watch me.

I spent a lot of time just hanging around the front yard under that tree, venting my anger by trying to climb the stupid thing, sometimes for hours. I was an enraged little person, and I was a lonesome little person too. I spent a lot of time talking to imaginary friends, imaginary brothers, sisters, an imaginary dad, an imaginary mom. As I look back I can realize that I really started to go a little crazy that summer. I'd talk to my hands, talk to the tree, and once I talked to a baloon, as though it had a personality. I never gave these friends names though. I remember sitting on the front porch one very oppressive day, feeling the heavy, cranky grief of confusion and loneliness in my chest. I smothered my crusty, itchy, eczema blotched face into my hands and cried, and cried, and cried; and that must have gone on for fifteen minutes. No one noticed. But rather than talking to these imaginary beings, I talked to God; and I talked without an iota of resentment. I simply cried for help. I referred to Him as the God that Mommy and Daddy Sparks believed. That was quite a desperate cry I spilled out that hazy afternoon, with a very simple monologue. It really did help me get through that day.

Halfway through that summer I discovered big Staten Park just ten blocks east. There were ten basketball courts, the kind with steel backboards; chain nets; modern green and red asphalt. There were baseball fields and soccer fields too. A lot of kids, especially in the evening and into dusk, hung out there and played ball. I got really acquainted with basketball that summer there. It didn't take me long to get neat-handed at it either. I improved a pretty good shot, fast. Those older junior high kids invited me to play often, knowing I could handle the ball—bring it up court even with a press. I could dribble, slithering in and out of guys with some speed and deception. I was quite smaller, but that didn't matter. In fact, in some areas it helped me. It seems like I often got connected with older kids in my childhood, and that was good for developing skills in sports.

Sometimes we played baseball. Some of those kids were really into baseball. They brought bases, catcher's equipment, everything. I was fascinated with the catcher's equipment, and always volunteered to play catcher, confused as to why no one else really liked it. I mean I was involved with every play, with every pitch. Why would someone choose to play third base, or worse—outfield—where he might not even make contact with the ball even once in an inning? Playing catcher guaranteed action, and I just loved all the equipment.

For one short span—three consecutive nights—we played soccer. It was cool enough those nights, and it was a change from baseball and basketball. I loved to play goal keeper, partly because it required less sweating and running, and partly because I felt I was pretty good at it, having quick reflexes, daring recklessness, and somewhat of a protective instinct—like a catcher in baseball. No one ever wanted to play goal keeper either. I liked playing those different, separated positions. I don't know why.

Whenever Mrs. O'Neil said it was okay—which was usual—I went to the park. I took my bike, looping my mit on the handlebars, threading my bat through the loop, and holding my basketball with a free arm, bouncing it as I stopped at a traffic light.

The one obstacle, almost without fail, came a few blocks down. This black dog always came out of nowhere, it seemed, barking, sprinting, growling. I'd speed up, racing, evading. It became a nightly challenge, a regular vexing nuisance. He'd get his wild looking white teeth right up to my circling, peddling sneakers. I could feel this animal's breath. He ran directly beside me. I almost ran him over once. I sort enjoyed taunting this dog that taunted me. I felt a strange pleasure in watching him give up his devilish pursuit of me, wearied in the heat with his long tongue swinging down. I looked back with my angry, smiling momentum as he'd finally surrender. The only nice thing about this speedy flight from this crazed canine was that I'd get to Staten Park quicker.

I'm still amazed at how quickly this big group of kids could organize, choosing sides, getting games started. We loved it, as evening temperatures were almost comfortable. The competition was thrilling. Oh, sure we had arguments over plays, even some fights—who's out, safe, out of bounds, who fouled. That goes with the terrain of kids, competition, and no umpiring supervision.

One of those muggy evenings stands out in my mind. It was August, one of the last nights I lived at the O'Neils'. I had a sad, lonely, full of rage day. Roy, one of the twelve-year-olds, had initiated a nick name for me: Scuzzy. He'd been calling me Scuzzy for two or three nights because of my very visible eczema, and it started to catch on with the other kids. All of them began calling me Scuzzy on this night. It sort of climaxed, connecting with a lot of laughter too. Well, this was getting me furious, in a dangerously quiet way.

We had a close baseball game going. In the fifth inning, this kid Doug hit one into the outfield. Patrick, on second base, took off, rounded third, and headed home while I was behind the plate catching. When the throw home came, I stepped in front of the plate. It was a decent throw—one bounce, right to my waist. I caught it, turned quickly, and tagged Patrick a few feet before he crossed the plate. He should have slid. He was clearly out. "Out!" I hollered. "You're out!"

"Safe!" Patrick yelled. "I'm safe! You missed me! I'm safe."

"No way! I tagged you right on the shoulder. You know it!" In the tension of the competition I forgot how young I was, how new to this part of the island I was.

"Safe! He's safe, Scuzzy!" Roy stood there shouting. I looked over at his fat, white, concave legs. He was on deck.

"He is not, you fat liar! You're a liar. You can't see you fat blind bat!"

"He's safe, Scuzzy, you filthy punk!"

"What did you call me?"

"You heard me. You're a scuzzy half—nigger punk. What are you gonna do about it?"

This made me furious. I looked at Roy's eyes. I lunged at him. He was three years older, thirty pounds heavier, and five inches taller; but I lunged at him anyway—punching, raging, screaming, feeling that same angry knot in my chest I'd felt when I'd tried to vent my anger climbing that unconquerable swamp maple. It was insane. He was bigger, but I didn't think about it. I did hurt him. I felt my punches connect, surprising him. I was completely padded, with all the catcher's equipment on, including the mask. Big Roy just grabbed me, lifted me, and threw me down like I was some clawing cat or something. I landed on my back, squarely, and all the wind was just knocked out of me instantly. I felt I couldn't breathe, or even move. I rolled to my side, still furious, more furious now in my humiliation and gasping. I lay there, gnashing my teeth in a depth of fury that I could not understand, that scared me, that brought me to tears. I felt like the loneliest person in all the world. I could hear the sounds of the muggy dusk. Kids surrounded me, standing over me, waiting to see what would happen. No one knelt down, or even bent down, to see if I was okay. A fight was entertainment to a bunch of kids. They just stood, watching—black kids, white kids, a couple of Hispanic kids.

After a long time I stood to my feet, walked to the fence, removed the equipment, took my own glove and bat and left the field. I was shaking, stunned, queasy. No one talked to me, as far as I can remember. They talked about me in the third person, as though I were not present.

"I think he's going home."

"He's quittin'."

"Now somebody else has to catch."

"Ah this game is over."

"I don't want to play anymore. You wanna keep goin'?"

"Scuzzy's leavin'!"

"Is he all right?"

What made matters worse was my bike got stolen. At first I couldn't remember where I'd left it, and I walked around the park in this stunned, pained, shaky condition, searching. I stopped, looked, stood in disbelief. I returned to the baseball field feeling panicked. A few kids were there. "You guys see my bike? I can't find my bike."

"Nope."

"Didn't see it. Sorry."

After a while I began to walk back to the O'Neils'. After about five blocks that night I noticed how quickly the dusk was descending into night. I had a strict nine o'clock curfew from Mrs. O'Neil, and

I didn't want to blow it, so I started to run. I didn't know what the time was, but I didn't want to take any chances. I wanted to be permitted to come back to the park in the evenings. I kept a nice pace— better than a jog—down that familiar city street, Mare Trail, ignoring the pain in my back from Roy slamming me.

When I was a few blocks away, sure enough that dog came out barking, running at me. I dropped to a saunter but kept moving. This horrible dog wouldn't stop. It seemed he got madder and madder, with his bared teeth, heated panting, and viscous saliva against my sneakers. "Get outa here!" I screamed. "Get! Get away!" Who owns this horrible, belligerent dog, I wondered.

This dog's stature reached my waist: it was not a small dog. His barking decreased as the growling fury increased. I grew nervous as I got angry. I stopped, and as soon as I did, he snapped at my foot— not penetrating, but affrighting me in any case. In reflex and rage I swung my bat, instantly cracking the top of his skull. The dog went down, yelping, sort of spinning in the dusty sidewalk, flopping. A man in a doorway across the street watched. I felt swallowed up in unmanageable rage. Something took over me. I felt it. I disregarded the world around me. I swung the bat again, and again, and again.... bringing it high above my head, like an axe, then down, pounding, pulverizing. I felt inside of me this horrifying, insatiate, ravenous quest—something like an urging craving brought near a summit, a brink, just short of gratification. After about the sixth mad thrash of the bat, the dog lay still, motionless, soundless. But that didn't stop me. As I raved, I kept slamming this dead, black animal, and as I did with all my vigor, I cried, releasing a grunting furious screech with each slam of the bat, until my breath was lost, panting.

Finally this man from the doorway ran across the street, and from behind he grabbed me, holding me, holding my bat, shouting, "Stop! Stop! Calm down, son! Stop!"

I did, and my tension relaxed in his arms. After a half-minute he released me. Some other people came out of their city corridors, stood around, watched.

I sat on the curb and cried, uttering moans and even howls—howls the dog might have emitted had he still lived. I repeatedly threw my head back, then down again, between my knees. Up and down, back and forth, crying, scared, horrified. I became aware of the dog's blood sprayed over my sneakers, socks, and bare legs. I rubbed my legs and looked at the dog's blood on my hands. I wiped them on my shorts. I sat there on that curb, rocking. Somehow that song Molly had taught me so many years earlier beneath those April apple boughs returned to my ears. "Jesus Loves Me": it kept tolling in my ears, in my mind; and in a mysterious, lullaby-like way it gradually calmed me down.

After a few long minutes, I wanted to go back to the O'Neils'. I picked up my mitt and bat. It was late and I didn't want to get in any trouble, but the man wouldn't let me. "You just wait here, son. Be still." He was kind.

The owner of the dog, a big, soiled, laboring man, finally surfaced, along with the police. The kind man who witnessed the whole thing explained everything. They listened. The policeman wrote out a report.

"This dog is never contained officer—"

"He's always contained. He breaks loose," the owner said.

"The boy come running down the street and the dog chases him, barking, and he did bite the boy, officer. I saw it. The dog can get vicious. I've seen it. So the boy threw a fit, and I don't blame him. Poor kid was scared, and now he's all upset as you see. He was protecting himself."

So I got off the hook. Even though I became more vicious than that dog, I was exonerated—even though I went beyond destroying him.

The policeman took me home. This was now my second ride with the police, and my fourth encounter with them. Imagine, I wasn't even ten and I was no longer awed by the police. We stopped in front of the O'Neils' where in the early darkness the car's colored resplendence and beaming radio utterances attracted a lot of attention with the neighbors.

We walked under the swamp maple and met Mr. O'Neil at the door where the police officer explained everything, where I kept interjecting my little additions here and there: "He chased me every night. He bit me. I didn't want to kill him."

Small, bald Mr. O'Neil leaned his small frame on his arm which rested on the stoop railing. His small pot belly bulged forward in his white tee-shirt as he nervously scratched his forehead with one finger, repeatedly nodding to the policeman's explanation. When I interjected, he ignored me. I could tell he was angry, embarrassed. "Well, he's not my boy. We're just fostering him for a spell," he said twice in the discussion, making sure the policeman understood that he was not connected to such a boy.

I kept wondering what was to be done with the dog. Would I see him there tomorrow night like so many cats, raccoons, opossums, and sometimes dogs I'd seen by the side of the Cary Island roads? Did somebody bury him? I was afraid to ask.

"I'd say he might need some counseling after an episode like that," was the last statement the policeman made as he tapped my head and walked to the car. Mr. O'Neil made no response.

In my memory Mr. O'Neil is like a statue, an entirely disconnected detached figurine. His human touch, as far as he'd touched me goes, was nonexistent. Strangers were warmer. He was living, yet he wasn't living; he wasn't dead, yet he was dead.

That was the third to last day I spent there.

"We're not going to have any more of this!" I heard Mr. O'Neil say from the other room, within his discourse with his wife that night, as I lay sleepless in the bottom bunk, as I lay wondering, alone.

"That's the kind of kid that'll wind up in and out of the Cary County jail! That's the kind a kid that is!" he prophesied.

I can still hear his mean, mewling voice. It still haunts me.

The day before I left I began in the morning by striving to ascend that swamp maple again. It took three tries, and I made it. I was able to fasten my forearm around that first parallel limb I'd told you about, then reach one foot over, and lug the rest of me up. This had been a chief ambition of mine that summer, and I'd succeeded, and it felt good. It felt good to just climb around, swing, look through the green muddle out at the street and into the sky. I stayed up in the canopy of that great tree for about an hour.

When Mr. O'Neil came home from work that night I said, "I climbed around the big tree Mr. O'Neil! I reached the big limb!" "Terrific kid," was all he responded, without looking at me, and I think those were the last two words he said to me.

ELEVEN

THE ASCENT

Molly arrived in her typical way: smiling, encouraging, trying so hard to pour hope on me. My trunk was all packed, and it seemed like the accumulation of my belongings diminished rather than multiplied each time I moved. All I know is that this time I didn't have a bike, and that bothered me.

She came with the fifteen-passenger New Blossom Children Services van, driving it herself. I was going to a new household.

"Someone stealed my bike." I was mad. I was mad at Molly. I don't even really know why. That happened now and then. I directed my steam vent at her. She seemed to understand though, never returning anger back at me.

"Someone stole your bike? Oh no. Where?"

"At the park." Folding my arms, I stared straight ahead.

"Well that's not your fault, honey—"

"So!"

"So? What's 'So!' mean? Uh-oh, Silas is mad!"

"So of course it's not my fault! I didn't steal my own bike! That's stupid!"

Angry tears filled the shallow pools of my lower eyelids. I was so furious, at everything. Molly was my outlet.

"Well we'll just have to get you a new one Silas. That's all. That's not your fault."

That was relieving news. I'd been worried that maybe I'd have to suffer without one because I'd been careless or something. "Really?" I said, hearing my own tone's delight.

"Really," Molly said.

Mr. O'Neil was at work this morning, and Mrs. O'Neil didn't even walk us out or anything. It was another sunny, late August day, with that 'almost school' sensation in the breeze. Cicadas screamed in the trees just like a year ago when I was headed to Mommy Maureen at Crossings House. "I think you're going to really like living with your new foster parents Silas. The Roccos have a big beautiful home with two other foster kids!" She said this as she slammed the back hatch after lifting my trunk in.

"Any of 'em my age?"

"Yep. Anthony's ten, maybe eleven."

"Does he play sports?"

"Yep I think he does."

I felt a little at peace. Molly opened the door for me. I climbed in, buckled, and she closed it. She walked around and got into the driver's seat, buckled her belt, and started the engine. She looked so amusing to me seated in that big van like a man. She waved at the front door where I could see Mrs. O'Neil's thin little frame blurred by the screen as usual, waving. I waved, and we drove away.

"Is it near the water?" I had to tilt my head back a little as I looked at her face because I liked to wear my Yankee cap down low over my brows, like the other kids did.

"No, not near, but you can see it. That's for sure."

"Where is it?"

"Only a few miles. It's in a new development—new houses—way up on Stony Hill. Wait till ya see it, Silas. You're gonna love it. Boy was this ever a find! I'm so glad for you, kiddo!"

Molly's big pretty smile always made me smile. I believed her. I could tell by the way she spoke that she really worked hard to get me into a decent place. They were hard to come by, but they were out there. I hoped this would be permanent, at least for more years. I trusted her, and I really loved her. Sometimes I prayed that she'd become my mom, and I prayed especially after hours that I'd spent with her. As far as I was concerned, she and Mommy Lucinda were the nicest people in the whole world.

"Stony Hill's the highest elevation on Cary Island. You know that? Three hundred feet above sea level—not a mountain—but it's nice up there in that community. Get a great vista, and lots a breezes, you know, kiddo?"

"Whatsa vista?"

"A vista's a big broad view."

"Oh good." This didn't matter to me much; although the idea of breezes sounded nice after a long summer down in hot Horse Hollow.

"Next week the agency's going to have their second adoption party Silas."

"Where parents come pick out a kid?"

"Yeah, that's how it works, in a way. It worked out pretty good last summer, so we're doing it again—advertising a lot and all. Maybe it will be an annual thing—you know—every year."

"Where?"

"At the orphanage."

"Where all the flies are?"

"You remember that?"

"Yeah, I remember that."

"That's a long time ago, kiddo. You have a great memory, know that? You're a sharp cookie!" She reached and pulled my hat further down, over my eyes.

I smiled.

"You don't have to go Silas. You know that. No one is forcing you, but if you want to you can. The only thing is that not all the kids get picked. It's got to be just right, for each family, and we're never sure who's coming, and we're never in a hurry. You see what I mean, kiddo."

"I guess I'll go."

"Good. I'm glad. I'll come and get ya. It's next Saturday."

"Guess I can try it."

"That's all. It can't hurt seeing, right?" She looked at me. "And if nothing happens, then that just means God has a different plan, right?"

"I guess so."

I looked out the window. Morning traffic made driving a drowsy, stop and go cadence. The suburban streets of Cary County were congested, busy, with just too many cars. I became a little pensive about things. I really didn't want to hear about Mommy Maureen, but in an adult sort of way I felt I was supposed to inquire, so I asked: "How's my mom?"

Molly hesitated. It seemed like she was surprised I asked. "No one has heard from her, honey. No one knows where she is, or how she's doing."

My guess was that she wasn't well. "I'm not gonna have to go back to her again ever, am I?" This was one of my big fears.

Molly shook her head as she looked forward into the traffic. "No, Silas. That's over. That's not going to happen."

There were a couple of minutes of silence.

"The courts have terminated her rights to you, and that's really the best thing. It took a long, long time, but finally it's done, and it's the best." She paused, glanced at me. "Don't you agree?"

"Yeah," I said, looking out my side window, beyond a black iron fence, at rows and rows of tightly aligned headstones in one of the big county cemeteries. I felt nothing at hearing this—no sadness, no joy, maybe a dull grain of relief, but mostly nothing.

Molly eventually made a left turn, and I could see ahead that there was a gradually ascending hill. This was a district of Cary Island I wasn't sure I'd visited before, and I liked new territory.

"I have some news to tell you, Silas."

"What?"

"Don't worry—good news."

"What?"

"I'm getting married."

I didn't know what to say. I didn't know she had a boyfriend. "How can ya?"

"What do you mean 'How can' I?" She giggled.

"Who ya marryin'?"

"A very nice man by the name of Robert McNeil."

"McNeil. Sounds like O'Neil." I looked out the window to my side again.

"I want you to meet him soon—you and just a few of the other kids—because you're special to me."

"Where'd you get him?"

"Where'd I get him?" She laughed. "That's funny."

I didn't laugh.

"I met him in court. He's a nice man. He's an attorney."

"An Ernie? I thought he was Robert."

Molly made a baffled face, and then she laughed harder, again. "No silly, he's an attorney!" she annunciated, pronouncing slowly. "He's a lawyer—in court, in family court—and we've been together for almost a year now. I call him Bob, and you can call him Bob too. You can meet him soon." She kept giggling at me.

"What's so funny?"

"You're silly. And don't you call him Ernie! Hear me?"

I laughed, then after a few seconds I said, "Oh, I thought you were too young to marry."

Molly laughed again. "Well, I'm not, really, Silas. In fact, I'm getting older, and I don't want to get too old when nobody will want me. See?"

"How old are ya?"

"I'm twenty-nine. Can you believe it?"

"Yeah." I guess I knew it, could figure it mathematically, having her as my social worker since I was two; but she'd just always seemed like she was around twenty-one to me. "You seem twenty-one."

She just laughed again. She really thought I was funny, or cute, or something.

"I thought you would marry a judge."

"A judge? What? Why?" She was really laughing hard now. "You are the funniest kid. You know that Silas Dillon. You make me laugh!"

I don't know why I said I thought she'd marry a judge. It was just right there, connected with a lawyer and court and her world; and it just came out—probably because I really just didn't want her getting married.

"Judges are old Silas!"

"Yeah, I guess so. They have white hair."

"So you think I'm twenty and I should marry an old judge ha?" She continued to laugh at my comments.

"How old is he?"

"He's thirty, a little older than me. Is that okay with you Silas?" She laughed again.

I wondered why she asked me if it was okay with me; but now, recalling, I know why. To be quite honest, as I sat in that van looking out my side window, inquiring, I had some serious sadness. I'll have to admit that I thought Molly was all mine. Sure, I knew she had some other foster kids whom she over-sought in her social work; but as far as I'd always experienced Molly, it was almost always alone— just her with me—alone together. When together, I got her undi- vided attention, and secretly loved it. She could tell that this both- ered me some. I really was jealous. As I look back now, I can see that I had one of those little-boy crushes on Molly. She was pretty, sweet, and she liked me. I was jealous but didn't understand it, and there- fore wouldn't admit it. I felt an anger. I felt that maybe I now began losing Molly, who I thought belonged to me, even though it was an periodic sort of belonging. I was jealous of this Bob. I understand now that some little boys have crushes on their moms, some on their elementary school teachers; with me, it was my social worker. I loved Molly. She was mine and I was about to lose her.

"Are ya still gonna be my worker?" I looked at her, tilting my head back. Her eyes made contact with mine in the shadow of my cap. I noticed tears in hers. She really loved me. "What's the matter?" I said, confused.

She couldn't talk as she choked back her tears. "You, Silas. You're the matter."

"What a ya mean?"

She hesitated, wiping her eyes. "In a good way, honey."

"Oh."

After a minute or so she said, "Yes I'm going to be your social worker. Don't you worry. I'll be around awhile, kiddo."

"How long?"

"As long as I can, honey. I love my work."

"Are ya gonna have a baby after ya get married?"

"I hope so—sometime soon. We want children, a family."

A long minute lapsed again. We were cresting this hill, which was really like an upland table or plateau or something like it. The homes up there were bigger, more exquisite than the rest of the island. They weren't quite like the mansions down by the ocean, but they were obviously nicer than most of the others on the island.

"What day ya gettin' married?"

She thought. "Two months. Pretty soon. October 29, a Saturday. And guess what."

"What."

"You are invited."

"Oh yeah! Oh, I wanna come."

"And we want you to be the ring bearer."

"The ringbear?"

"The ring bearer. At weddings they usually have a boy bring up the rings on like a little pillow. It's part of the ceremony—in the church."

"Oh."

"Okay?"

"Yeah I guess so. That's not hard, right?"

"It's an honor, Silas. It means I think highly of you."

"Oh. Okay." I smiled. "Is it hard?"

"Not at all. We'll practice. Don't you worry."

Recalling now, I realize that she had more suitable, younger family members who could have done this. She chose me. She wanted me in her wedding. Back then I wasn't as touched by the honor as she hoped I'd be, but she understood it was because I didn't know much about it. She wanted me nevertheless, knowing that someday I'd understand her love and care by inviting me.

We were at the top of this hill now, near the big house where the Roccos lived, where I was to reside. We could see a spectacular view of Cary Island, the ocean; and on the other side we could see Manhattan, the two shining towers of the world trade center towering over the other structures, upright like fingers above a fist of knuckles; and we could see Brooklyn. It was awesome. Because it was rocky and high, trees that tend to block the panoramic view were sparse and small. It looked so nice up there, and I was beginning to get excited as I looked. It was hard to believe that this was part of Cary Island, New York City. The properties were larger up there too; not as large as plots on Long Island or Westchester; but much more spacious than the limited, little, swimming pool sized plots on most of Cary Island.

"Here we are," Molly said as she pulled the van into the driveway—a long, S-shaped, asphalt alley. The house stood tall—two-storied, with a steep roof above. It seemed to climb into the clouds, light gray, vinyl sided, white trimmed, and red shuttered, with a long porch and landscaped foundation. It stood so aristocratically. I noticed a little shrine, a statue of the virgin Mary within a little shell on the lawn, with nice landscaping all around it, concluding that these people were Roman Catholic.

She stopped the car and turned off the engine. "Ready, kiddo?"

"Yeah," I said, yet could feel that old, secluded ache of despair stippled with nervousness and hope as I opened that van door, ready to enter another world, another chapter of my multi-chaptered life. I just followed Molly's lead—to the back of the van, to the big porch, to the front door of the Roccos, with my head down and my eyes on the ground and my shoes.

TWELVE

THE HILLCREST

Mr. Rocco wanted me to call him Papa, and Mrs. Rocco wanted me to call her Mama. They both had faint Italian accents, having come by separate boats from Italy to Ellis Island forty years earlier as children. They owned a fine Italian restaurant by the beach resorts called Palermo House. It had an excellent reputation, and it was managed mostly by their only son, thirty-three-year-old Peter Rocco, who lived in as fine a house next door with his wife and two boys, little Peter (my age) and younger Joey.

Mama had a very big heart. Her having lost her ability to bear children after Peter's birth is what moved her to open her home to foster kids, once Peter married and left their home. They've been foster parents for almost ten years. Papa has been content in this outreach toward us disenfranchised ones mostly because it seemed to make Mama happy to remain at home. For some reason they never adopted.

I had a whole room to myself, and it was a big one, so comfortably spacious, furnished, carpeted, wallpapered. The view from my window was vast. I could see the ocean, the hospital, steeples, rooftops. I could sit and daydream for hours. Erin, a very quiet thirteen-year-old, was also in care here. She had the room next door; but she was looking eagerly forward to going back home with her mother, once her parents' messy divorce was settled. Besides Erin, there was Anthony, that eleven-year-old Molly had mentioned to me, who'd been here at the Roccos' since he was eight. He had his own room on the other side of mine.

Mama was quite a cook, and it seemed like every night was one of feasting. There was pasta, sauce, wine, garlic—all sorts of dishes with Italian names we all know. Even though Papa could have regularly brought a lot of food home from the restaurant, Mama insisted on cooking for her family. She loved doing it, and it gave her a sense of worth, I guess.

Both of them were big: Mama was plump and cute; and Papa was tremendous, not so cute. He was three hundred and fifty pounds, and only about five feet ten inches tall. His shape had a lot of disparity: his legs were sort of thin, and it was hard to imagine—looking at him—how he kept his balance. He had no waist, but always made sure his pants were belted high, just under his chest. What was funny about Papa was how he always insisted on artificial sweeteners, diet soft drinks, and the like; while he never restrained himself from consuming large portions. I remember watching him one Sunday after Mass as he ingested fourteen slices of French toast, swamping them all with diet syrup.

Sundays were big days at the Roccos': Peter, his wife Angela, and little Peter and Joey came over after Mass—traditionally—to eat and spend the day. My first Sunday was not different; in fact, it was a bigger day than most, because they had a welcoming party for me, with cake, balloons, and everything. We barbecued steaks out back on the enormous concrete patio in the hot, early September sun. The thick humidity was nothing their sparkling in-ground pool, shady awning, iced tea, hillcrest breezes, or centrally air-conditioned house couldn't assuage. This place, slightly closer to heaven on this hillcrest, was like paradise to me—so far out of the league I'd been accustomed to. The marvel of all its stunning sensation really had a way of causing me to temporarily misremember my disturbing past, and of anesthetizing my wounds; and I think it helped heal me in some ways.

Well this first Sunday was quite absorbing and fascinating to me, while it seemed everything was ordinary to everyone else there. The most stirring, imposing spectacle was Papa in a swimsuit. He sauntered out from behind the sliding glass doors that afternoon with white trunks pulled high over his navel, with a pink towel dangling like a scarf around his neck, and orange flipflops at the heels of those spare (by comparison with the rest of him) legs I'd told you about. He somewhat resembled a flamingo or some other long-legged fowl like it. What a sight! Papa was the hairiest man I'd ever seen also. I can still envision his black, woolly back as he moved his wobbling, bouncing, gelatinous mass eagerly toward the pool. He was in a happy mood, smiling. He dropped his towel on a chair, and lifted himself up onto the diving board. I had a profile view of this this first time, and I immediately covered my mouth with my hand as my eyes widened. I didn't know if I would laugh or shout "Stop!" I did neither. I just shouted, "Be careful," and immediately wondered if I should have.

"Okay, Silas," he responded, laughing.

What really had me concerned was the diving board. Papa kept smiling, springing up and down from the end of it without letting his feet lift off the board into the air. It was at this point I realized that this was pretty much a summer routine at the Roccos'. Recalling, I suppose he had simple confidence in the strength of the fiberglass board; but I really thought the thing would snap in two that day as I watched the tip nearly immersed in the water's surface. Its bending curve made a half-circumference, like a fishing pole pulling in a large one. After six or seven smiling springs, which made me wonder with amazement at his balance, he launched his massive substance into the pool.

What a splash! Waves, bubbles, silence—until he surfaced, yelling, "Whooooo! Whoooo!" laughing as he swam around, bobbing like a buoy. His mass in that pool was like an ice cube dropped into a full glass, lifting the water level. Papa's baldness was now made very apparent: the tuft of hair on one side of his head—which had been raked over his capacious scalp to veil the baldness—lowered to his shoulder, while the tuft on the other side scantly scraped his ear. What blatant, comic incongruity! I'll never forget that first exhibition!

After this he climbed the ladder of the slide, with little Joey behind him. He lay down at the slide's summit, his flesh enveloping and bulging around and over the slide itself. He was smiling, saying, "Come on Joey. Get ona my back. Be a careful Joey. That's it. Here a we go! Whhoooo!" as little Joey courageously shouted with him, smiling, lying on his Papa's hairy back and clutching his neck all the way down until they plopped like a walrus with her young into the water.

I really enjoyed that pool, especially that first Sunday. I slid right in immediately after them, down the slide, delighted; and I did it repeatedly. I must have stayed in the pool swimming and playing with little Peter and Anthony for two hours, all the way until it was time to eat. But beforehand, while I was in there with the boys after Papa had climbed his way out, I beheld yet another very memorable spectacle. It was the show of a lifetime. Papa sat down on one of those older poolside chairs, the kind with the light aluminum frames and bands of flexible vinyl. Well, his flesh barely neatly fit between the chair's arms, and after a minute or two something happened to the chair. The vinyl bands just sort of surrendered, abandoning themselves to the pressure of Papa's wet, dripping heft. His bottom collapsed through, sinking; and as his thicker, looser waist caved in and down, his bulk became wedged, stuck. Impulsively he tried to stand, but could not straighten his back or legs since he was so snugly trapped into the frame of this flimsy chair. There was this look of jolly panic on his face.

"Rosa!" he shouted to his wife, remaining on his feet and leaning forward with this chair binding him, sticking in the air behind him.

"What happened, Papa?" Anthony shouted from where we were in the pool.

"I'm-a stuck, Anthony. Where's a-Mama? Where's a-Rosa?"

Peter and I looked at each other and could not help but begin to laugh, and hide our laughter. This was just too much.

Mama came over. "Jesus a Mary, and a Joseph! What are you-a doin' in the chair, Nunzio?" Mama said.

"What does it a look like, a-Rosa? I'm-a dancing. I'm-a dancing in the chair, Rosa. I thought-a I do a dance in the chair, Rosa Rocco! Only I need-a the Lawrence Welk on. What-a you think I do in the chair? The chair a-broke on me and now I'm-a stuck." He pulled and pried, and he couldn't free himself from the chair. It seemed like his flesh just swallowed up the frame, concealing it, bulging shapelessly all around it.

Mama walked behind him, and with a very serious, unamused expression she pulled the chair, yanking, twisting. Papa's big body was yanked back, shoved forward, back, forward... in unison. They twirled around three times. Peter, Anthony, and I saw his rear and his head three times as Mama tried to free him, as they spun. We were mesmerized in alarming, silent, hysterical laughter in the pool.

"What-a you do, Rosa! Stop! Stop!" he shouted. Suddenly, with one final yank from Mama behind him, Papa stumbled and fell, shouting as he fell to his side on the grass. Now he couldn't get up, still stuck in this position. He began to laugh uproariously with a loud coughing and gasping. It wasn't until he laughed that we felt free to laugh out loud as well.

Peter their son came out now. "What is going on out here?"

Mama said something in Italian, exasperated. Peter (Mr. Rocco) began to laugh too now. He dropped to his knees beside his gigantic father to see how he might be freed, looking, shaking his head in disbelief. "What if we just turn you up and let you stay in the chair until after you eat Pop. Then we'll get you out," he said jokingly.

"I'll be fat more, Peter. No!" He laughed loudly again.

Well, after thinking awhile, scratching his head and looking down at his hairy father on the grass, Mr. Peter Rocco got an idea. He went into the house and returned with a bottle of olive oil. Once he and Mama got Papa to his feet again, he poured the oil all about Papa's flesh and the immersed, hidden frame of the chair. All the while laughing together as they wriggled, writhed, tugged, and twisted this flimsy chair from Papa's loose corpulence. After about ten minutes of this contest, the chair that was now bent and crooked, slid free, defeated; and everyone with laughter applauded. We talked about this all the next week, and all that joviality made me feel like I belonged here, in a lonesome sort of way.

The next Saturday came and Molly arrived in the morning to pick me up for that adoption party. I had my best clothes on as she'd told me to, but I couldn't get too excited about this; I guess because I was feeling so comfortable at the Roccos'. School had begun on Wednesday (I was in third grade again) and everything was going fine so far in the classroom. The work was coming easy, probably because it was the second time around for me.

When we got to the orphanage I had this sad recollection from when I was two, that day with all the flies. It was bizarre the way some of it came back to me, and still sticks with me. Anyhow, tables were all set for a dinner; and there were toys and games in the adjoining room where all of us different aged kids could play and socialize while these possible parents would be observing us.

This all took a couple of hours. I didn't know what to expect, having this inner fear that as these adults spent time with all of us, they'd pick the kids they wanted and take them, immediately departing with them, leaving a small residue, of which I'd be a part of. I imagined I'd feel like the kid at the park or in gym class who was of the last to be picked by the choosing captains, left standing isolated and fatigued with that lonely sense of incompetence and rejection, leaning against the chain-link fence or the matted gymnasium wall, looking down at his sneakers, working hard to conceal any of the enormous pain he was feeling. I'll have to admit that as some of those people observed me, I felt like a piece of merchandise or animal on display—like a car, stereo, clothes, puppy, appliance or something to be rated for value.

When Molly drove me back home (to the Roccos') we had another one of our talks.

"Well I guess no one wanted any of us this year."

"What makes you say so Silas?"

"Well I didn't see no one pick no one."

"How do you know that?"

"Well no one left or nothin.'"

"Oh well that's not how it works Silas. It's not like they're getting a pair of shoes at the store. That's not the way it works."

"It doesn't?"

"No. It doesn't work that way, kiddo."

"How's it work then?"

"Well, if someone thinks a child would be right in his home, he inquires. They investigate a little, you know—find out a little about the child and see if the child would be right with them or not. Then they spend a little more time with the child, maybe take him, if he's available—you know—in between foster homes, without a foster home, into their home. You know it has to be right. It's hard Silas. This is hard business—not that it's business—but it's hard. A lot of these kids are hoping to find parents that will love them and be committed to them, and I'm the first to admit that these sorts of people are the hard ones to find out there in the world."

"Why?" I asked, looking down at my chafed, red, eczema irritated arms, wondering, actually somewhat assured, about people not wanting a kid with nasty skin.

"Why?"

"Yeah, why? Why are no people worried about no kids Molly?"

Molly thought hard as she drove late that cloudy September evening. She thought hard about my question, and about how she could answer me so I could go on with some strength.

"Why don't grown-ups help kids like me too much? They care about stuff that's not so important all the time." I intently stared at Molly's face. It seemed to me that she strained, and then, as she watched the road that stretched with is starts and stops before her, I could perceive a glimmering, faint light of resolution cross her expressive, beautiful face. It was an expression of decisiveness, as though she decided to just tell me the truth plainly, even if it hurt me, understanding that its pain would at length—finally free me.

"The reason is because people are selfish, Silas. People are concerned about their own pursuits and concerns."

"What's pursuits?"

"What they want. What makes them happy. Things they go after and want in life. A lot of people in our country here believe other things matter, when they really don't. I don't want you believing that you're not going to get into a nice home Silas. God really has a plan for your life, even if people don't. Someday things are going to turn for you. I just know it. But people really need to hear about boys like you. And for now, as far as you go you just have to trust. I know he cares about you. Hold on, kiddo, you hear me?" Molly reached her pretty hand and touched my encrusted face; then she patted my leg.

"Yeah."

The Roccos had a certain tremendous 'living room.' It was the first room by the front entrance foyer at the landing of the exquisite, split staircase. This room had some beautiful Mediterranean furniture; and some other fine things like lamps, figurines incased in glass cabinets, and vases. We weren't allowed in this museum-like room; in fact, it was roped off, and even the rope was plushy and velvety! Well one afternoon that first week when Papa was at the restaurant and Mama was in the basement doing laundry, I sneaked under the rope and went inside this room that no one, except for Mama when she dusted, ever entered; and I looked around at the neat sacred things, opened some empty forbidden drawers and cabinet doors, walked around on the soft pink carpeting, and sat on the silken sofa which was protectively enclosed in durable transparent plastic.

During that brief exploration, Anthony came down the stairs; and before fully descending, noticing me, he stopped and watched in disbelief. As soon as I noticed him as he sat on a step gaping between two white rails with his hands over his head on the banister and his big face between his arms, and as soon as our eyes met, he continued descending and on his way. A few minutes later Mama came up. Seeing me exiting the room under the rope, she began to holler— in Italian—pointing at the room, at my face, with her finger nearly touching my nose. I didn't understand a single word she said, but I fully seized the message.

I had been suspecting that Anthony, this chubby eleven-year-old foster child, was moderately jealous of me, especially since the Roccos had given me that little welcoming party; and now I was sure of it: he was a tattletale, a rat fink. To him, I was someone who'd crept in and perhaps stolen some attention and whatever else (in his mind) away from him in this household. He was a year older, about six inches taller, and thirty pounds heavier than I, and he could have been more of a bully, but he wasn't; in fact he was sometimes peculiarly afraid of me, or if not afraid of me, just afraid—generally fearful. He was always squealing on me for little stupid things, like the way I'd leave the bathroom, or for not making my bed, or for not putting my bike away in the garage (the Roccos bought me a nice new bike to replace the one that got stolen in the park that evening) and leaving it on the driveway. Always after he squealed, he stayed far away from me, didn't talk to me, avoided me; and I'm certain now that it was because of fear. Like all of us foster kids, he had his baggage that he carried around and didn't know what to do with. His biological father was in the state prison for murdering someone, and his mother got remarried, discarding him.

Anyway, these "scandals" he snitched about were little transgressions that the Roccos didn't bother me about, but they never dissuaded Anthony from being the informant. They probably had a history of my mischiefs, like my crossing the bridge into New Jersey, the floating adrift down the channel in the drum, the horrible slaying of that dog, the crashing of the bathroom wall tiles and towel rack (maybe not), and the array of things that happened in school. Maybe they were on the lookout for potential hazards; I don't know, but I do know that Anthony was very insecure, probably as insecure as I was; but he unleashed his insecurities in mean, treacherous ways.

My own anxious insecurity aroused me toward this perpetual quest for acceptance, almost at any cost. Because Anthony was a year older and had been established in the Rocco home longer, and even though he made his furtive opposition toward me seeable, his acceptance was something I recurrently trailed. I wanted to be his pal!

Two months expired. Whatever leaves hadn't fallen from the trees were no longer green, but were yellow and brown and fading. It was October 29, Saturday, and Mr. Rocco drove me to a very pleasing, high-ceilinged, varnished church where Robert McNeil was marrying Molly Fresh, where I was going to be a ringbearer. I was all dressed up, and I was excited. Because I was small for a ten-year-old, my bearing the rings to the altar appeared not that unusual. Molly's dad, Mr. Fresh, showed me what to do. When he signaled, I simply walked, balancing these rings on this shiny rayon pillow, and I smiled at smiling strangers as I made my direct course toward Molly and Bob.

After the church ceremony, I got to ride in one of the limousines to the catering hall. What a fancy car, and what an elegant place! I was seated at a table with two other foster kids (older girls) and some old school friends of Bob's. There was nothing enthralling happening there, so except for when I ate, I spent all my time behind the long bride's table beside Molly where the big cake stood. I kept trying to talk with her, and she seemed not to mind. I found it fascinating watching up close when after everyone clinked their glasses every once in a while, Molly and Bob kissed very seriously and passionately. After they kissed, they smiled, because people kept taking their picture. I got in a lot of pictures, even the professional photographer's shots. Molly sent me a few of them too. There they were, smooching away with their eyes shut, with me behind them, staring.

We looked great together, the three of us—me and Bob with our deluxe black tuxedos, and Molly in her angelic white. It sort of looked like I was their kid or something. To be perfectly honest, I imagined that I was their kid all that day. I imagined that they were my steady parents—that Bob was my dad, Molly was my mom, and we were a happy family. The thought of having a mother like Molly had always been a fine way for me to escape the pains of those foster care years. Mama Rocco got me a little frame to put one of the pictures in. I kept it right by my bedside and always looked at it—Bob, Molly, and me all smiling and centered and looking right at the camera.

A few weeks later, on the day after Thanksgiving, Anthony, Peter, and I spent the afternoon playing football in the yard. It was a frigid windy day, the kind where the sun tries to pry through packed clouds, piercing through fissures now and then with blazing brightness. Layers of undulating clouds swept over the island, soaring out over the thin strip of the Atlantic's distant horizon which spun its color from sapphire to charcoal as the sun fluttered in and out. The high autumnal suburb was full of hue and motion: Flocking clusters of starlings and red-winged black birds, seemingly aimless in their wandering and playful touring—like lost souls—kept gathering and forming their shifting shapes, lifting from trees to air, then falling to trees again. Big geese squawked and honked across the island like sent spirits brimming with mission. Tree limbs whipped one another, uttering, whispering.

The tips of our ears and fingers grew cold; so we went inside the big shed beside the cedars in the corner of the deep yard. The things inside, especially where Papa's work bench was, lured us boys. We plugged in his drill motors, inserting bits, and boring holes through wood scraps. We plugged in his circular saw and pulled its trigger, titillated by the power and the whining sound. We tried in vain to light the welding torch. We thoroughly perused a musty, fifteen year old pornographic magazine that Papa thought was well hidden, or forgot about. We opened and sampled cans of beer from his mini refrigerator.

"Hey, let's light the grill; that'll get us warm," Anthony said.

Peter and I looked at it buried under garden hoses and leave rakes.

"We don't got no charcoal," Peter said.

"Yes we do. Right there."

"Where?"

"Right under it, see? What're ya, blind?"

I leaned, looking, seeing.

"Get it out," Anthony commanded.

I pulled the bag out, shaking it, opening, looking in.

"Get those hoses off," Anthony said.

Peter removed the rakes, standing them up in a corner as I shoved the entangled, heavy hoses back behind the barbecue. Anthony lifted the grill cover with one hand, then the grid with the other.

"Pour 'em in! Go ahead Silas! Pour 'em in! Pour the bag in!" Anthony said this with his typically demanding, impatient manner, looking at me with his depressed brown eyes, with his nose running, with the cover and grid aloft in his fleshy hands like they were cymbals and he were ready to play and march right there in his thick new coat in the shed.

As he said this, something like a governor in my conscience urged me, telling me not to; but the dense pressure of Anthony was just too much. I poured, emptying the pillow shaped chunks of dark, dusty charcoal, its dusty scent filling the chilly air of the shed with a smell of summer.

"Don't worry Silas. It's just a barbecue. People do it all the time. Here's the fluid."

I took the bottle, looked at it, saw the word flammable in red, looked at Anthony's face which demanded, "Do it!" without using words. His impatient, unquiet glare made me hesitate.

Peter had climbed onto the bench, kneeling and poking around on a shelf where he found a box of matches. He kept shaking them like they were candies or something. "Here. Here," he said, reaching, handing them to me.

"I put the box on the bench."

There was silence.

"Come on, my hands 're cold, Silas. Pour that stuff on the coals! Just flip up that top there. Come on!" Anthony stood there in his width, rubbing his pudgy hands and fingers together. He was so lazy, and so pushy.

I flipped the top up and turned the container over, squeezing, squirting, dousing. They both had grins in their excitement while I began to feel both recklessness and fear in the pit of my gut. I kept squirting until half the contents were emptied. "That's good. That's enough! That's good, Silas!" Anthony instructed. The smell was as fixed as turpentine. The coals were saturated. I looked at both Anthony and Peter, and I was quiet. Peter again handed me the box of matches. Whatever made us think we wouldn't be smoked out of there with such a low ceiling and without vents is beyond my comprehension now. I had this thrilled, terrified grin on my face. I struck a match, threw it onto the little black pillows of coal. The fire spread, slowly.

"Put more on. More fluid!" Anthony said.

I raised the container and squirted again. Suddenly an inferno blazed. Instinct sent the three of us backward. The inside of the shed remained luminous as the igniting, consuming sound of fire swarmed our ears. Heat gusted onto our faces like wind. We all hollered "Whoa!" At once flames singed and scorched the low plywood ceiling and the wall. We looked for water. There was none. The hose that in season is connected to the outdoor faucet was now out of reach, abreast of the blaze. Small flares sprang on the wall, the mower, shovel and rake handles, stains where I carelessly splashed fluid as I doused the coals. We all coughed in our panic as inky smoke fumes charred our throats and lungs. Within moments flames attached themselves like tentacles onto the dry adjacent wall. Before long we could hear the distinct, familiar sound of crackling wood as we exited, choking.

For a minute we didn't know what to do as we just stood hacking, watching the window panes glowing orange-yellow and puffs of smoke venting from the open door and slender gaps. We backed away.

Anthony ran to the house, and Peter and I watched as his big slow bulk pushed forward. I began to get nervous. Soon Mama came out, running, screaming in Italian, pulling Peter and me farther from the shed, commanding us to move up to the house. She assaulted her way back inside for the phone.

From behind the sliding glass doors we all watched. Within ten or fifteen minutes, flames and blasts of smoke bathed the whole shed. The sure sound of the fire department's sirens and the creeping advance of fire trucks screamed. This was all so fabulously beyond belief to me. It was like television. The fire kept burning, wasting Papa's tools, devices, lusts, everything. We could hear what sounded like small explosions from within the consuming shed—the sounds of igniting cans of paints and solvents. A sudden sunburst brought dark color to the leaning, wind-chopped column of smoke which, at this windy hillcrest, I presumed could be seen from all of Cary Island, even Bay Ridge, Brooklyn; South Street in Manhattan; and Jersey. All the while the brown football hunkered alone on the autumn lawn like a witness.

The sight of this vehement rage of nature mesmerized me into a trance, a wonderment of the spectacle and of the power of one sulfur match. As I reflect now, I regard that conflagration as an expression of my own rage. The incendiary explosiveness that had lain latent within the dry wood and contents of the cabinets of that shed paralleled my own veiled, verdant volatility. There were things inside of me—destructive and constructive—that only needed a catalyst, a simple spark.

THIRTEEN

THE DESCENT

"Awright, I did it," I finally confessed, yielding to Anthony's swift witness: "Silas did it! Silas burned the shed! We saw 'im do it! Peter and me saw 'im!"

Though Anthony tried to disown any part in the fire, Peter's tremulous pity for me owned up: "Anthony told him to! Anthony told Silas to light the barbecue! He told 'im to do it cause he was cold. He didn't wanna get in trouble. He wanted Silas to do it! That's why he—"

"Yeah, but Peter gave him the matches! Peter got the matches in the cabinet and gave 'em to Silas! If Peter didn't give 'im the matches he couldn't start the fire even! And Silas is the one who did it!" Anthony, in fear, began to cry out loud, boisterously. "I was just kiddin'! I didn't think he'd really do it! I was just kiddin' around! I didn't want him to burn down the shed!" Anthony was loud, spraying saliva, pointing at Peter who also started to cry.

There were Mr. and Mrs. Peter Rocco, Mama, and Papa standing elbow to elbow in the kitchen like an impervious wall. Erin stood behind them, curious, arms folded, leaning against the entrance way trim. Little Joey stood behind her, leaning in fear so he could see us during our trial. The firemen had finished and left, and the three of us were seated at the kitchen nook, breaking. Only Peter cried. I felt some grave hatred for Anthony, the big stool pigeon, and I wanted to bash him. The feeling was so strong that it deadened any feeling of remorse for lighting the coals. I still wonder what Anthony felt then, besides fear. I didn't cry. I just sat there, mad. I really looked like the culprit.

Once the grilling indoors seemed to settle, the wind outdoors stilled as dusk closed the daylight. I stood at that sliding glass door, taking another look. What had been a fine shed was now a crumbled structure, a charred skeleton, blackened cinders, a scorched riding lawnmower, wheelbarrow, metal tool box, and grill. Like a grave after a funeral when the mourners first drift away, that area which had been a focus of human commotion an hour ago was now dead emptiness. The hardy cedars were burned black on one side. That corner of the pretty, curved yard looked like a messy wound. The clouds were gone and the peach-colored glow of the set sun released its grip, giving way to Venus, blue darkness, and stars.

Peter was taken home next door, and Anthony and I were sent to bed early without supper. It took a long time for me to descend into sleep. I kept turning on my light and picking up the framed photo of me, Molly, and Bob at their wedding. Finally falling to sleep, I woke up once, early on, dreaming of surrealistic images from that whole afternoon in the yard, having mixed visions and distorted drifting thoughts. I dreamed I saw the ocean's horizon with its unencumbered blue, the silvery city skyline in a kaleidoscopic distance, magnified ships in New York Bay with the exaggerated sounds of their electric horns on the wind. I saw manifold clusters—colossal in this fuzzy obscurity of my mind—of red-winged blackbirds and starlings with their ever-changing shapes transforming into dead leaves in the wind, then into the changing shapes of the shed's blazing fire and billows of smoke in the broken blue sky. I saw in my dreaming all the twisted images of that windy day, twice dreaming of falling and reaching for a football. These blended, blurry mental forms in my slumbering mind awakened me, only to recall what was real, and then to fall asleep again, soundly, somehow peacefully.

In the morning, Papa woke me up. "Get in-a the shower and get dressed!" he said with that Italian trace in his English, with hardness.

"Okay, Papa."

I was having a hard time breathing this morning. The sound of my high-pitched wheezing moved me to taking deep breaths, listening, fascinated with the echo-like delay of sound. I took my inhaler, shook it, inserted it into my mouth, pressing, inhaling, waiting. This had become perfunctory, like tying my laces. I was itching as well, and could see the flaring red of eczema on my skin. It disgusted me.

When I came out of the bathroom I saw Papa carrying my packed trunk down the stairs. It took me about two minutes to figure out, with all the cold silence, that I was being removed from this home. My clothes were on the now bare mattress of my bed. I peeked out the window and saw him placing my trunk in the trunk of his car, slamming it shut. I hoped, wondering if my bike, scooter, and skateboard they'd bought me were coming too. I was a little scared, sensing their revulsion of me that gray Saturday morning. That thick rejection felt the way silence sounded, like the cold hush following the slammed door of Papa's luxury car's trunk. There was this sudden vacancy, a feeling of nakedness. I didn't want to go. I felt so dead inside. I watched as Papa trudged like a beast from the car to the front door, hearing his entrance. He went into the kitchen, and I could hear him and Mama talking in Italian. I could sense his hugeness even from upstairs. It made me feel puny.

"Silas!" he shouted up the stairs.

"Yeah."

"Down-a the stairs."

I descended, pulling my Yankee hat low over my eyes, hearing another slamming door as Mama entered the cellar with my sheets, descending into the laundry room. She didn't want to look at me. I walked into the kitchen.

"Sit. Eat." Papa said, pouring milk onto cornflakes.

I obeyed, hungry. Not having supper, I could have eaten more, but was afraid to ask. This was so strange. I was so used to eating a lot here—even too much. I knew I'd gained weight at the Roccos'. Papa left the kitchen. When I finished, I put my spoon and bowl into the sink and sat back down.

Papa reentered. "Into the car," he said.

I went to the front door, took my coat from the closet, zipped, opened the door, stepped out, descended the imposing stoop and entered the car, buckling. I looked at the house, its gray, its white trim, its red shutters, its palatial facade. Anthony stared out his window at me. He remained there, looking. I don't know if he could see me looking at him. There probably was some bleary glare on the car window. Neither of us waved. I remained enraged at him.

Papa came out the door, walking, balancing that enormous torso on those awkwardly thin legs, jingling keys and patting his long tuft of hair which fastened across his scalp, showing its snowy streaks of baldness, hiding the rest. He entered, inserted the key, ignited the engine, made a brusque three-point turn, then descended swiftly down the long S-shaped driveway.

"Where am I going?" I said carefully.

Papa hesitated. "Far from here," he said, burping.

I made sure I sat still, looking out my window—not a word. Papa was hard, like a stone. The big fancy car made the long gradual descent until the vista dissolved. I took one look back. The black asphalt in the November gray seemed so impeccably straight, dividing the rear window.

We passed my school, the mall, the graffiti-ridden embankments and factory walls, the gas stations, convenience stores, all the businesses, the railroad. We descended, rolling silently and comfortably under the traffic lights, finally making a turn, and then another, and then another, into the lot of the agency's orphanage where Papa drove audaciously right up to the front door. "Get out," he said.

I obeyed, shut the door, waited. He removed my trunk from his and carried it up the steps, expecting me to follow, saying nothing. Inside he dropped the trunk before the receptionist's desk.

"I called a Mrs. McNeil about bringing back-a Silas. Tell her I need-a to go now." Papa turned, bobbing his heaviness away, stepping past me in my puniness, descending, entering his car, not looking back. I stood beside my trunk, wondering about my bike, my scooter, my skateboard; wondering about Molly, who was now married and probably aiming to begin her own family; barely wondering about Mommy Maureen, who had her rights to me terminated, severed completely; wondering about Papa's ferocious anger about his shed and everything in it; wondering what was to be coming in my direction now.

F O U R T E E N

TIDINGS

This orphanage was the same place where I'd stayed for a while back when I was two, that time after Mommy Maureen got caught leaving me alone on Bay Street. Only now it was winter, and there were no flies. While I stayed here everyone was careful to keep matches away from me since I'd burned down Papa's shed. I guess they all thought I might be a pyromaniac or something. I could hear them talking, saying things like, "Don't let the Dillon boy in the kitchen," or "make sure the matches are in the security cabinet."

About a week after I'd been brought here, a letter from Mommy Sparks was handed to me. This had been sent to the Roccos where they thought I still lived. I opened the letter eagerly and read:

Dear Silas,

We hope you are doing well. We have some news we've been meaning to tell you. Justin is very sick. He has been diagnosed with leukemia. It's a terrible disease in his blood, a cancer. We are spending much time at the hospital here with him. We wanted you to know about this because we know you will pray very hard for him. He sends his love to you and wants you to know that he misses you very much. We will write to you again soon to let you know how things are going.

We all love you very much.

Love, Mommy Sparks

After reading this I strangely felt very far removed from them all. My life in their house suddenly seemed like such a long time in my past. Blemished retrospections, fleeting glimpses, sounds, even smells flashed back in my skull. I smelled their home, my room, Mommy Lucinda's paints and cooking; I saw Justin at the docks fishing, on the street playing; I heard glitters of his laughter, resonances of Daddy's exhortations in church, all in a transient few seconds. These came back to me like a splash. I promised myself I'd pray. For some reason I didn't cry, but I felt an ache in my chest. I did consciously know that whatever they might have been doing to fight for me, to try to get custody of me from all the way out there in Ohio, had now ended. It didn't take a lot for me to understand, even at ten, that their energies would not be expended in the courts as much as they would be at that hospital where Justin was being treated.

I placed this letter securely in my old trunk.

Since things were going well at the school I'd attended while living at the Roccos', Molly thought it was best for me to remain there. So that's why I had to stay here at the orphanage for three months, waiting while Molly worked very hard at finding me an appropriately suited home within the margins of that school district.

Every weekday morning Molly arrived and drove me to school. I was the only child of the thirty at the orphanage who wasn't tutored in the orphanage. I guess I was privileged. After school either Molly or some other worker picked me up to take me back. Bus service was not for students outside the district. That was policy.

The drive between school and the orphanage took about fifteen minutes, and the numerous and notable laughs and conversations Molly and I had together each trip made that part of each day the most meaningful for me. Two of those trips are ones I remember especially. One was on a cold January morning, a Monday. I'd eaten my cereal and was seated in the lobby—the one where Papa had dumped me—waiting for Molly. When she entered, I could immediately tell that her mind was preoccupied with something.

"Ready for school, kiddo?"

"Ready." I stood with my backpack of books already strapped to my shoulders over my coat, and I fixed my woolen cap on my head.

The biting cold of that morning briskly touched my face like a cold hand. I jumped into Molly's car which was warmer than the lobby. Once Molly was buckled in I said, "What's the matter Molly?"

She took a deep breath.

I waited.

"How can you tell something's the matter, kiddo?"

I shrugged my shoulders, hearing the sound of all my winter fabrics rubbing together, watching her. I was getting used to bracing myself for all the varied tidings that can come in the direction of a kid like me.

"I have some news to tell you Silas. I'm not sure how to tell you, but I know I have to, and I think I'm the best person to do it." She looked at me. I trusted her. My head tilted back. I still loved wearing my hats down far over my eyebrows.

"What?"

"I don't know how you're going to take this, but here it goes: Honey, Mommy Maureen died on Friday."

"She did?" was all I could initially, instinctually say.

"Yes she did Silas."

I could comprehend immediately. I looked frontward over the dashboard as Molly glanced at me. The news was not something that

I could not accept. I accepted it immediately after I comprehended, and there was no feeling, no emotion, none.

"I've been praying for you this weekend about this, kiddo, about how to tell you and everything."

"How?" I said, returning my vision toward her as she drove. My question was impulse, a reflex. I felt I had to further understand. "How did she die? Drugs? Too much drugs again?"

"She died of AIDS, honey, that sickness in her blood she had for a long time, that I told you about... remember?"

I looked away again. "Where?"

"County Hospital."

"Where I was born?"

She nodded.

Silence.

"She wasn't taking very good care of herself... for a long time now. You know that, right Silas."

"Yeah."

The car's engine ran quietly as the heat blew delicately from the floor. There was a self pitying temptation to challenge about why I wasn't told that she had lately been very sick, but the honesty in my awareness that I would prefer to have not known prevailed, and I kept my tongue, withholding my anger. Molly may not have known that Mommy was that sick anyway.

"There's going to be a small funeral Silas."

"There is?"

"Yes honey, and others at the agency thought it be best to leave it up to you."

"What?"

"Whether you want to go or not."

I shrugged.

"You don't have to answer now, kiddo." She touched my shoulder, then my head.

"When is it?"

"Tomorrow."

I shook my head.

Molly watched me. "No, you don't want to go?"

I kept shaking my head. "No, I don't want to go."

"Sure?"

"I don't want to go." I felt certain of this.

"That's fine, honey. That's okay. I think that's fine, and I think if you feel that way that it's probablåy better, honey."

Silence and the sound of warm heat emitting kept breaking our words. I leaned back against my books, again hearing the sound of my fabrics.

"Are you going?"

She nodded. "Yes. Okay with you?"

"Yes." Okay with me."

"You don't have to go to school today Silas, if you feel you can't, you know."

"No I want to go. I want to go to school."

"That's okay. Then you can go. I think it's good. I think it's better you go too."

When we arrived at school, Molly got out with me. She wanted to explain to elderly Mrs. James, my teacher, about Mommy and all. Molly figured this might be a difficult day for me. It really wasn't, as far as I remember. I didn't cry. In fact, the activity of the day had me so absorbed that I didn't even think of it, except maybe once after I was finished doing some seat work, looking out the window. It was two weeks before my tenth birthday, and the weather outside was the same bitter cold as the day I was born. "Ten years is long," I said to myself. Then it was time to go to gym, which I loved, and I forgot about Mommy dying until the end of the school day when Molly came for me. I knew Molly would come for me that afternoon. She cared about my feelings.

I never cried, as a child, for missing Mommy Maureen. The big problem was the aversion I had for her. I was so disappointed in her. It was a paradox. My disappointment in my mother was, in a way, like a parent's disappointment might be with a child. I was actually strangely angry at her, rather than grieved for her. I was angry she'd never pulled herself together, and even more angry now that she was dead, since nothing could ever been done about it. It's inexplicable.

I also felt relieved that I'd never again be coerced into being one of the system's guinea pigs, an experiment, by being the big part of their allowing her another try at raising me. If a Sparks' family came along again, I'd be free for adoption, unchained to a pacifistic, detached system that bent too far to a vagrant mother's sin and selfishness. The only problem now was that I was older, and the older one of us orphans grew, the more baggage we accumulated, and the less people were willing to come forth to adopt. One thing that I'm sure about anyhow is that Mommy's death meant emancipation, moving me one step deeper into freedom, yet at the same time one step deeper into the slavery of anger. There was a fury swelling in my interior.

Our conversation that afternoon on the way back to the orphanage concentrated on my day at school. I guess Molly, avoiding discussion of Mommy Maureen, just wanted to see if I was doing okay.

That night I couldn't sleep, feeling guilty as I thought about my decision to not go to Mommy Maureen's paltry funeral the next day. So first thing in the morning I got one of the orderlies to call Molly for me. "Hello, Molly? I want to go. Can I still go?"

"Of course, Silas honey," she said with all her friendly warmth directly into my ear, immediately making me feel better. "I'll be there in about an hour or so. You just be dressed nice and be ready. Comb your hair, okay, kiddo?"

"Okay Molly." I hung up the receiver.

Besides Molly and her minister and her attorney-husband Robert McNeil, who turned out to be a slender, fair-haired, fair-skinned man with a broad face, who seemed to either like or pity me since he kept rubbing the top of my head and sort of hugging me by pulling me against his side by my shoulder; no one else came to give respects. No one from Mommy's (my) family, wherever they were and whoever they were, and none of her drug addict friends were there. Just me, Molly, Robert, Molly's pastor, Mommy's long casket with a few flowers, and Mommy's little stone.

I can remember that hour of that twenty-fifth day of January distinctly. A warm front had moved in overnight. It was one of those January thaws, with wind and clouds and dampness, but no rain. City sounds—horns, trains, trade—seemed muffled, far. The ashen hardwoods and the emerald evergreens kept shivering, waving, moving, and snapping limbs as the soft roaring of warm wind bent against them: it was very much like the way gentle pleasant words in whispers lean against cold icy silences, shaking them, breaking them. The typically tight tall houses of Cary Island seemed taciturn through and beyond the perimeter trees of that dilating cemetery. They seemed like watchers—an array of motley cubes and triangular roofs and colorful other obtuse angles of dormers and porches, watching—and it seemed to me the four of us were like performers among those rows of stones, alone in the center of that silent graveyard, standing and pensive, with audience. I was a numb statue there among the rows, as an unfeeling scarecrow among rows of corn. An infrequent vehicle passed on the nearby street, made a turn, watching us—I tried to imagine—as well. It was all in my mind. No one cared. Death had come, preceded with numerous emails and lettergrams, warning; but like the rest of humanity, my mom just deleted and discarded them like they were junk mail. Death had come to my crazy mother, but the world just went about its business, unfeeling.

Looking up, I could see the swift motion of colorless clouds and shadows of clouds crossing before those of higher clouds. I could see in the blended gray, the motion. The sky was all a flurry of fog, a crowd of clouds rushing to who knows where, as we stood still. I couldn't help but keep gazing upward at the massive vapors moving, shrouding, sweeping swiftly overhead in the invisible wind. I didn't know where the sun shone from beyond those vapors, but I knew it was there, somewhere.

"And they found the stone rolled back from the tomb, but when they went inside they did not find the body of the Lord Jesus." I remember this was read aloud. Bits and pieces of a sermon about hope beyond the grave, hope for even the hopeless, founded in the emptiness of that old tomb, are what I recall about his sermon that hour. But for the most part, while he read and preached I let my mind remain in this life, in this vapor clouded world where Cary Island's humanity hid in those tight narrow dwellings shaped like these tombstones. I thought about Mommy and her dead life, about the degenerate cycles of this life. "If only Mommy were adopted!" I thought loudly. If only Mommy were raised in a nice home. If only Mommy could really have known about love at a ripe young age, then maybe I'd get it and be able to live easier. If only injustice wasn't so pervasive in this life, maybe I could have had a better chance, a better start, for sure. I thought these thoughts by my mother's graveside.

When we walked back to the car, I took one last look back. Mommy's casket and flowers among those stones lounged recumbently. I made it my focal point for about ten seconds, then forced myself to look away, until we drove away.

My birthday came on the thirty-first, and the kids and workers at the orphanage were nice enough to celebrate my tenth year of life in this world by singing "Happy Birthday," and by eating portions of the cake that advertised my name in colorful script. Mrs. James also had a party for me with the class. Since it was customary for a parent to provide the cake for the school party, Mrs. James—as busy as she was—provided mine. I was the oldest, the only ten-year-old in that third-grade class, though I looked a little younger. Those ten candles looked very impressive to the other eight- and nine-year-old boys in the class. Ten is an aspired age for young boys. Anyhow, I really did feel special on my tenth birthday, even though I was now a true orphan, no longer an orphan of the living.

The other trip to school I remember came on a gray February morning, a few weeks later. I finished my oatmeal and juice in the usual way, and waited for Molly in the lobby. She entered, saying, "Good morning Silas," in her usual way, but I knew her expressions too well. Again, I could tell something was going on. She had this removed, ruffled, facial cast where she bit her bottom lip and lowered one brow. When we got into the warm car and buckled,

"What's the matter?"

She laughed, looking at me. "You can tell again?"

"Yep."

"Well I do have news," she said with a flimsy smile.

"What?"

"I'm having a baby," she said, patting her tummy through her coat.

"When?"

"Oh six or seven months."

"Cool."

"But the doctor says I have to stop working. I have to rest. I'm having some problems with this—physically." She looked at me to see what I was thinking.

I couldn't imagine what she was experiencing. "Does that mean you're not going to be my worker any more?"

She took a deep breath. "Yes Silas, it does."

Stunned—"Are you still going to see me?"

"Yes Silas, and some of the other too, but not as much. You see, I have to rest, almost all the time, if I want this baby—to live. And I do, of course."

"How about after the baby?"

"Well after the baby's born, he'll need to be cared for—you know, diapers, feedings, all that stuff, kiddo."

"Can't a babysitter?"

"Well, yes, but Bob and I prefer I stay home, you see-"

"Well maybe it's a girl."

"Maybe."

"How much can you see me?"

"As much as I can, kiddo. I love you. You know that. And I love Terry, Bobby, Ashley, and Joey—my other kids too."

The same gentle sounds of her car with its comforts eased the momentary silence between us. I thought of her words, "As much as I can," of their weakness, their ambiguity.

"You know I love you, right Silas?"

"Yes," I nodded. Then, as I wondered, and somehow had this notion, this far fetched hope, I said, "So maybe I can be adopted by you and Bob?" I looked at her, at the same time routinely tucking my hat down just over my eyes, hiding them, at the same time trying to see hers as she responded.

Molly became immediately taken by a stressed, startled look. I could see that she searched to respond. "Well honestly Silas, that's not something—to be perfectly honest with you, honey—that Bob and I have ever discussed. Um, I don't know if that would be best, for any involved." She paused, searching for words, careful with my heart, so carefully searching. "Um, I don't know what to say Silas." She looked at me with this panicked expression, with this desperate hope that she was not letting me down even deeper, with a cover for Bob and his grand expectations of marriage with Molly.

I imagined that maybe she would begin to think about it, and I imagined that she'd try to talk Bob into it. I just imagined. It was all merely my imagination. I hoped I sparked something, and that she'd return to Bob and talk to him about it. I imagined there was something in her expression that challenged her, maybe moving her toward me this way. I imagined that there was something in her expression that spoke of her already considering it, and that there were other kids to consider as well. I knew that adopting a troubled child that's older is something the professionals have confirmed to be not in the best interest of younger children already in the home. But I couldn't let go of this faint hope. I was growing older, and my chances were slimming down.

Molly's reluctance was cemented in statistics and in her devotion to preserving the finest environment to raise her children in. Let's face it; I had problems. Molly knew it; and I know it now. But I refused to surrender this faint hope of getting into a family who would love me.

The image of those apple boughs in bloom we'd sat under after she'd rescued me from that apartment on Bay Street when I was two returned to me. She'd wished she could have adopted me then, saying, "Oh Silas if I were married and didn't have to work I'd take you home with me and make you my boy." I guessed that now might have been a different story, that she'd been idealistic then. And now I was older, prone to getting into trouble, prone to bringing shame and disgrace to my guardians; and perhaps she wanted to start fresh with a family of her own. On the other hand, at times I'd also been quite guilelessly naive, actually assuming the adoption idea might be something she still wished for, even planned for for someday; but I remained mindful that I probably just dreamed, and now simply awoke to the dread of reality.

"Oh," was all I could say right now. I didn't know how to respond to this sudden news. I sank in my seat, in my heart. I felt crushed, like I wanted to die. Molly was abandoning me, and I couldn't take this. She was the only enduring stability in my life. I tried hard to be brave. I now felt like my mother just died. This was killing me. I could feel that old frustration, that rage of defeat growing like a flexing muscle inside of me. I felt like I was pinned down. I burst with a groan, and then just began to sob.

"Oh, Silas honey. Don't cry."

I could tell that my being upset was beginning to upset her, and I didn't want to do that. I wanted to be brave, but my nature caused me to regress, to lapse into fear, this infancy, this terror. I could only cry. I covered my face, leaning forward, restraining. I felt so lost.

Molly pulled to the side of the road. People were near, walking, moving outside the car. I felt her hand on my back, which helped a little. "God help this boy! Help Silas Dillon Jesus," she said. Then she said, "Silas you know you don't have to go to school today."

This suggestion seemed too familiarly recent, only this time I yielded, muttering through my sniffling, "I don't want to go today. Please, I want to go back to the orphanage."

"Of course Silas. Of course."

Molly turned her car around. There was this separation I felt from her for the first time ever. I had this sense that she'd experienced situations like this with other kids numerous times before, and that she was now forcefully preventing herself from over-involvement, maybe even regretting some of the attachment. It was hard to render precisely.

When we got back she settled me in a comfortable chair in the activity room, finding me a book.

"When's your last day?" I asked.

"Today Silas. I'll be in and out a bit for the next week or so, you know, to tie up knots before I go and stuff, but today's really my last full day." She smiled.

"Oh," I smiled back at her. I wondered in my mind, saying, "What do you have to tie knots for?" imagining her tying knots with ropes or strings.

She laughed out loud. "You're so silly kiddo." She pushed my hat down over my face. "Not real knots silly boy! I have to finish business, cases, stuff like that silly!" She kept laughing, and I smiled.

She went to the big kitchen and returned with hot chocolate for me. "I have some other news Silas."

"What?"

"I found a home for you."

"Where?"

"Right near your school."

"Who?"

"With a nice lady named Shironda Todd. She has another foster child."

"How old?"

"Six."

"Oh." I said, disappointed.

"Tammy."

"A dad?"

Molly shook her head. "Shironda doesn't have a husband. She's separated from her husband."

"Oh."

There was not a lot of certainty in Molly's tone about this, but I was somewhat satisfied to be able to get into a home, to stay in my school, and to get out of this orphanage.

"We can only try, right kiddo?"

"I guess," was all I said as I looked at the title of the book she handed me: *Adventure in the Tundra,* and the cover illustration of a young boy before an Alaskan tundra and an alpine backdrop framed in a silhouette of a howling wolf. I then glanced out the window at the dreary street, speculating about the tundra beyond those panes, wondering about my own next adventure.

TWELVE SEASONS

Shironda Todd was a decent black lady who worked very hard. She worked at the Shore Avenue Elementary School, which I attended, doing clerical tasks in the main office, especially in the copy machine room, copying things for the teachers most of each day. As soon as I saw her I could remember I'd seen her from time to time at school. At night she worked part time for an oil company, answering phones and making out bills. She wanted me to call her Shironda, rather than Mom. What did I care!

A few times in that big three story school I saw Anthony. Once when I was in line with my class I could see him down the hall with his. I waved to him, but he didn't wave back. I guessed he didn't see me. A second time I saw him from the window, down on the asphalt playground with his friends, at recess, playing basketball. For the most part he just stood around with his fleshy hands in his pockets. I felt sorry for him, knowing he was just a foster kid like I was, even if he had been mean toward me because of his jealousy. A third time I saw him after school by the buses. I passed right by him and said, "Hi Anthony!" He looked right at me, and then just looked away. That made me feel so angry that I wanted to hit him.

I liked to be out by the buses after school. I was often one of the last kids to get on my bus because I liked to horse around with some of the kids. Mrs. Ong the bus monitor was always out there smiling, helping to keep order. Whenever the sun shone, she held an umbrella over her head. Some of the kids called her the umbrella lady.

One sunny spring day when we all first stepped out of the school, she saw me and said, "Hiro Siras! How was your day today?" Somehow she knew my name, and that flattered me. She had some kind of Asian accent, and I always liked to hear her talk.

"Pretty good," I said.

"Jus pretty good?" she continued with a big smile.

"Yeah, it was good." I smiled back at her, stopping before her, saying, "How you know my name anyhow?"

"Oh I just know you Siras." She paused, smiling.

"Oh you know Shironda right? You know Shironda, my foster mother, right?"

"Yes I know Shironda, but you just a special little ferrow."

Somehow her saying that really did make me feel special, and I liked her more. "How come ya got an umbrella?" I said, looking at her aging face. I always subliminally wondered about this umbrella in the sun. I looked up, squinting. She had an enlarged, bulging, lazy eyeball, with an odd absence of blinking in that eye, which sort of half diverted her Asian looks. Her face was very loose, worn. She really appeared homely, unsightly. It made me think she'd been through war or difficulties or something. I was tempted to ask her, but resisted, understanding that that might be disrespectful. Even with this facial disfigurement there was something lovely about her overall mien; there was something honest and kind about Mrs. Ong.

"How come I got the umbrerra?"

"Yeah, how come? The sun's out today."

"I have neurodermatitis, Siras." she enunciated slowly in her tainted English, smiling, patient with me.

"Hey that rhymes."

"Rhymes?"

"Yeah, sort of."

She laughed, looking a bit bewildered.

"What's neuraderitis?"

"Oh it's a skin condition. I had ever since I was a litter girr."

"Where'd ya come from?"

"Where I from?"

"Yeah?"

"Where I from, I from South Korea, and I come a long time ago. I had this skin since a long time ago."

"Ya did?"

"Yes, my face, my neck, and sometimes my arms, my elbows..." She pointed to her body parts as she told me. "They get red and scary. Terribry itchy! The sun irritates my skin, see."

"They get scary?"

"No, scary, scary—like fish, scary!"

"Oh scaly."

"Yes scary." We both laughed.

"I got eczema," I said, feeling like part of a skin affliction club or something.

"You do? I didn't know that Siras," she said so kindly. I really think she did know. Since she knew my name, seeing me often, she had to perceive that something was wrong with my skin, because sometimes it was just awful, blotchy, ugly, and red.

Kids kept walking, running, passing us, bumping against me and getting on their buses and making a lot of noise, screaming and laughing, dragging and holding their coats.

"How come ya the bus lady then? Why don't ya get another job? How come they don't give ya a different job like a teacher or principal or somethin? Somethin where ya could work inside more."

She laughed, touching my head, squeezing my cheeks. "You are a charming litta one aren't you Siras! How old you are anyway?"

"Ten." My smile and continuing stare told her that I really was curious, wanting to know.

She looked away, then back at me, "Sometime life not make much reason Siras. See? Life not make sense a lot of time. Sometime things jus not the good way." She glanced around for a moment, to make sure everything was okay with the kids, and then she lowered her voice some, getting closer to me. She said, "Sometime Jejus allow us to be where it no make sense, where it seem like it hurt us, see? Where it jus not make sense. But He know. He know it do good, somehow. Life is like that in the earth, see, Siras."

"Jesus?"

She nodded, having a poise in her expression. She watched my reply.

"Oh I know about Jesus."

"You do! That is so good Siras."

"Yeah, Molly my other social worker taught me about Jesus. Mommy and Daddy Sparks—they're my old foster parents—they took me to church and read the Bible with me in their house a lot." I felt a pride that I had some of this in my short history. I felt good about this.

"It so good to know Jejus, Siras. It so so important, not to just know about Jejus, but to really know Jejus. You see Jejus reary love you Siras. He want you to know He reary love you!"

I felt this strange, riveting warmth. I looked fixedly into her one, straight eye which seemed to momentarily peer right into my heart, while her other broken eye seemed to be looking into another direction.

"Jejus love you," she said again.

"Yeah," I said, fascinated, wanting to stay here and talk with Mrs Ong for a long time. I had a strange longing for the Bible again. I felt a homesickness inside for those days at the Sparks' house, and for those days at their church.

At this time, shy little Tammy, my dark-skinned foster sister, stood beside me. She was only in first grade, and she liked to get on the big bus with me. I was her protector. She stood patiently, holding a piece of paper. She always held those papers she was told to bring home, afraid she'd forget about them in her backpack or something. She was so conscientious about doing things right, even in first grade. She wasn't like me.

"This is from the nurse, Silas."

"What is it? What's it say?"

"Some of the kids got lice and the nurse is telling all the moms. All the moms have to know in case we get lice in our heads too. Mommy has to know so she can watch out for lice in my head, for them in my hair."

Mrs. Ong reached to see the notice. "Oh, some kids have the rice," she said.

"No lice!" Tammy said.

"Yes, rice. No one wants the rice!"

"Lice," Tammy insisted.

"No that's how she says it, Tammy. She from Korea. That's how she says lice. She says rice. She knows. She knows its bugs on ya head. That's how she says it."

Mrs. Ong laughed, and she rubbed Tammy's head the way she'd rubbed mine. I laughed, and Tammy smiled.

Mrs. Ong was like an angel to me. I went out of my way several more times (whenever I wasn't with my friends horsing around and stuff) that spring to talk to her because she said nice things to me about Jesus, and about myself.

Before that school year ended Molly came one Sunday to Shironda's to pay me a visit. I was so happy to see her. She knocked on the door of Shironda's cluttered house, and when I opened, I immediately stepped outside onto the porch, hugging her.

"Hello, Silas kiddo, how are you?" She held me, patting my back, squeezing.

"Good."

"I miss you!" she said, griping.

"I miss you too."

Shironda stepped out in her socks onto the porch, blinking in the brightness of the day.

"Hi Shironda. How's it going?"

"Things are good. Things are good. With you?"

"Oh, what can I say, we've been having a tough go of it."

"Oh?"

"Where's your baby, Molly?" I said, jumping in.

"Oh, there isn't going to be a baby, Silas."

"Why not?"

"At least not yet, honey." Molly looked at me, then at Shironda. I stood confused.

"Oh, I'm so sorry, Molly," Shironda said.

"What happened?" I asked.

"I had a miscarriage, Silas."

"Oh." I said, afraid to ask what that was; but I guessed that the baby had died somehow. I kept looking at Molly's pretty face which seemed occupied by grief, at her eyes which paused on the threshold of tears, then at her flattened belly, wondering.

"We're hoping God will send another baby to us though." Molly wiped a teardrop from just beneath her eye, and I thought about how I'd never seen her with sorrow like that. I'd never seen her cry, and it made me love her afresh. I hugged her again. "Oh Silas," she said.

"Oh, I am so so sorry, really I am!" Shironda said again. "I went through that myself. Tst tst," she said, shaking her head. She stepped over and hugged Molly.

"Are ya gonna be my social worker again, Molly?"

"No Silas, no I'm not, honey." She laughed, touching my face. "I'm staying right where I am, at home, Silas. I really think I need to do that for now."

I kept looking at her, smiling.

Molly couldn't stay long that day. In fact, she didn't even come inside. She at once left from standing on the shady porch there, and I watched her descend the steps, collapse into the seat of her car, wave, and drive off. I could feel that old ache again as I cemented my vision to the back of her car until I could no longer detect it, all the way up the street as it diminished into the shining urban sprawl. I thought I could still smell her since our hug.

It was only about seven or eight months after that that Shironda came to tell me that Molly had another miscarriage, and that she wanted Shironda to tell me. Shironda explained to me what it was, and I imagined it must have been hurtful. It was the first time in a long time that I prayed, for Molly.

Things were pretty quiet for the next couple of years. In fact, I really made some progress with my education. I didn't get left back. I made it into fourth grade without a problem, mostly because third was a repeat year. I made it into fifth with some extra reading help and a lot of coaching, coaxing, and firmness from Shironda. "Did you do your homework Mr. Silas?" she'd say from the kitchen while I sat before the television.

"Not yet."

"Well, sit down here at the kitchen table where I can see you and get it done now, mister."

"Okay," I'd say compliantly, slowly shuffling my way there, watching the television screen over my shoulder to the last flash, moving to my books.

"What did you get on that short story you wrote over the weekend Silas?" she might ask, if she saw me in school.

"I got a B+ Shironda!"

"Great, Silas! Thas jus fine!"

Sometimes the conversation went this way: "Mister Silas, have you finished your math homework?"

"Yeah!" I'd moan back."

"Well let me see it, son!"

I'd rise from whatever it was I was doing in the house, retrieve my crumpled, much erased, smudged work from my weighty math text, and bring it to her. She'd pore over. "Let me see the book!"

I'd get the book, and return to her with the page opened. She'd be at the washing machine, for example, and stop her drudgery amid the hot fumes of bleach water and the cadent rumbling of a twirling dryer; she'd look at the book, then at my work, then at the book, then at my work.... After a minute or two of this, as I waited, "Okay mister, go redo number eight and number twelve. Look carefully. Check yo work. Go, come back agin when yo done again, mister. I'll check it again. You got be more mindful with some of these ones mister!" She had a stern expression that in some way grinned at the same time.

Silently frustrated, I'd plod up the basement stairs to search for a pencil that had some eraser left on it, to wear away my paper some more, to first stare into space awhile, and then to try again.

Shironda really cared for me, and she probably loved me, not in an affectionate, cuddly sort of way; but more in an accountable, strict manner—the kind that wouldn't let me slide, slither, or coast; the tough kind that impelled me to become responsible for my own inaction or actions. I'm grateful for Shironda's discipline in my life, for giving me chores, for all of that.

Early in the fifth grade I received another letter from Mommy Lucinda in Ohio. It was addressed to the agency in Brooklyn since my address changed so often. It said this:

Dear Silas,

We hear from Molly that you're in a new home with a very nice foster mother, and we're so happy about that. The past two years have been very difficult for us, as you can imagine. Justin has come through many medical procedures, but God has been very gracious to us. His leukemia is in remission, and the doctors tell us that things look very good, and there is a strong likelihood that he will survive this and live a long life. We look to the Lord and trust Him, and He really has been our help! Our prayer is that you too are remembering the goodness of God.

As soon as things get good and stable here, we want to come to New York for a visit with family, and to come and see you, of course. We will let you know.

It would be good if you would think of Molly in your prayers, as she has been battling with some things.

We love you very much,

Mommy Lucinda

I hadn't received a visit from Molly for about six months when I received this letter, and I had been wondering why, supposing she was busy with her new life, being married, and maybe having some children of her own by now; so I asked Shironda if she could find out Molly's phone number from New Blossom, especially since Mommy Lucinda said she was having troubles. The next day Shironda got her home phone number, and as soon as I got home from school that day I gave her a call. I had to dial a different area code since Molly had moved off Cary Island and now lived in Manhattan, close to the firm where Bob practiced law.

After dialing and uneasily listening to four rings, Molly's answering machine answered. I heard Molly's sweet voice say, "We're sorry but we can't come to the phone right now. Please leave a message and we'll return the call as soon as we can. Thank you and have a great day!"

"Um, this is Silas. I want to know how you are Molly cause Mommy Lucinda said in a note that you were bad and not that good." I paused in nervous silence since I felt graceless talking to these machines. "Okay, goodbye, I'll see you Molly. Bye."

A few minutes later the phone rang. I answered, "Hello?"

"Is this you, Silas?"

"Hi Molly."

"You been well, kiddo? I've been thinking about you!" She sounded tired.

"Yeah. I'm good. Are you?"

"I'm okay."

"Are you tired?"

"I guess I'm a little tired, kiddo. Why, I sound it?"

"Yeah. What happened to you?"

"Oh, Silas honey, I had a miscarriage again."

"You did?"

"Yeah, honey. It's sad for us, you know." Molly was crying a little. I could tell by her shaking voice.

"I'll pray for you tonight Molly."

"Oh, thank you, kiddo. That's so nice." She sniffled. "You're a sweetheart. Is that why you called?" She marveled over my calling. I could tell that this touched her. I wanted to be her gallant knight. I really wanted her to be well, and I wanted to be a part of comforting her. I hated the thought of Molly being sad or sick.

"Can you come and see me sometime?"

"Yes Silas. Yes, I want to. I miss you. I didn't forget about you, kiddo! We live in Manhattan now. Did you know that?"

"Yeah. Shironda said. Do you like it?"

"Well, I like Cary Island better, kiddo. It's sort of dark here, and noisy, you know. These buildings cut off all the sunlight. I don't know. Bob works nearby. And it's easier. I don't know."

Some silence stood like an imposing party between us for some moments. I imagined her face, her gentle fingers wiping tears off her cheek. This hurt me.

"Maybe you will have another chance to have another baby Molly." My awkward, direct way of aiming to comfort Molly made her get choked up with tears again.

"Maybe," she said, pausing, sniffling. "Maybe, kiddo. We're praying. It's hard."

"I'll pray to Jesus to bring you a baby, Molly," I said.

"Thank you, honey."

Silence and awkwardness artlessly suspended again. After a few moments, I said, "Okay bye Molly. I hope I see you soon."

"Yes, you will, Silas. I'll stop by soon, kiddo."

"Okay bye."

"Bye, kiddo."

I hung up the receiver.

A couple of weeks later, on a Saturday afternoon, Molly came and took me out for ice cream. She looked so nice, and I thought about how much I missed having her in my life. She seemed sad and a bit busy in her mind though. She asked me simple questions about school. When she took me home, she stayed in the car, leaving the engine running. That was unlike her. When she had worked with the agency, it seemed she had more time for me, even though she had other children in the system to watch over. Now she seemed distant, different, distressed. It bothered me. I really felt sad for Molly about her losing her babies.

The seasons passed, and then I went robustly into sixth grade with an unusual, intrinsic love of learning, of reading, of determined cerebral stimulation and intellectual enchantment. I was motivated because I'd actually begun to love school. I wasn't as absorbed in getting good grades; but when the good grades appeared, I was pleased. One of my two sixth-grade teachers, Mr. McClarty, held very high expectations of his students, and that helped me.

Shironda was always a little wary about me, having witnessed firsthand my moodiness, my tantrums, having learned of my past adventures like the drum-rafting, the dog slaying, the journeys into New Jersey, and of course the shed torching. She was surprised that I'd never received any formal psychological counseling, which could have been prescribed by my social worker. Now that my social worker was Sandra Jackson again (the worker I had when I was a baby, before Molly) the two of them found occasion to sneer at the fact that I hadn't received any of this professional attention. Having worked for the school district for a few years, and having worthy concern for me, she made arrangements for me to regularly meet with Dr. Rosenpanz the intermediate school psychologist.

Meeting with young Stan (Dr. Rosenpanz felt this first name basis was good for our relationship too.) only proved to be a tiresome burden three times a week for me. He asked a lot of tedious, irrelevant questions in a fake friendly manner, as far as I was concerned. I never felt good leaving his office; I only felt fatigued. I guess he was "diagnosing." Stan Rosenpanz was a very effeminate, sissified man who asked me personal, impertinent questions that made me feel very uncomfortable, and even angry at the time. Although his discussion was never threatening, he certainly had a way of basely directing his fascination on irrelevant, elusively erogenous nonsense that had no support to help me. As I look in retrospect, I'm not convinced Stan Rosenpanz was serious about the study of human behavior in terms of his supposed purpose to assist kids like me.

Anyway, this newfound satisfaction with learning came from a combination of Shironda and my teachers' assistance and steering; and was also generated from my own subconscious will to escape, which suppressed my latent angry depression, which had remained shrouded and deep within; which like a sleeping cat needed only a clang, a reverberating tremor, even just a stirring, to awaken. It was only a matter of one quake.

Besides this love for learning, I was in love with Marissa Mellina, a dark-haired girl with big, brown eyes, snow-white skin, a fragile little nose, full lips, and a reserved, quiet nature that just added to the mystery of her delicate prettiness. Every idle moment I looked at her, at her profile as she sat just one seat forward in the next row over. I sometimes scrambled to get on the lunch line behind her. I just loved being near Marissa Mellina. Her thick, dark curls always smelled so pleasantly clean. I took notice every day of what she wore. I dreamed of her, thought about her on weekends, imagined she was always near and watching me, felt yearning and warmth whenever I thought about her. I dreamed that someday we'd be married, but almost never spoke a word to her. I was so bashful. The thought of talking to Marissa made me panic. I'd never felt this way about a girl before, except of course for Molly when I was younger.

Beautiful Marissa had a head cold once. I was mystified by this. I'd thought she was perfect, like an angel, until this, when her lips were chapped, her nose running and red, and her normally lovely voice became distant, stuffed. So intrigued, I watched her profile from that daily angle as she suffered the whole day with, as she blew her dainty little nose, as she piled her tissues on her desk. This sudden revelation of her imperfection dazed me, stunned me with puerile wonder that whole day; but I remained totally infatuated with her nevertheless.

With the arrival of my thirteenth birthday on January 31, while I was in the sixth grade at Shore Avenue Intermediate School, which adjoined the elementary school that had served me so well, the first percussive signals of my adolescence started tapping. Physical changes and emotional tremors sounded themselves, slowly, like a faint, far drumbeat. I began to spin into that major change of life.

On the ides of March of that year there was a major snowstorm which smothered Cary County. That winter had already been long, cold, snowy; and now this last blast which locked us in for recess for yet another spell made us all fidgety and restless with the bleakness. Kids at school had grown cranky and fatigued with cabin fever. The cafeteria aids were having a hard time keeping us under control. They shouted, blew their whistles brutally, broke up fights, wrote out detention slips, and sometimes called the principal Mr. Young down to awe us. We who'd advanced into that intermediate school were full with fury, intensity, hormones, and noise. The twenty minutes of recess following the actual dining in the cafeteria were very long minutes, especially for the cafeteria aids.

On the first of those snow-in days the school cafeteria served us grapes for dessert after a pizza lunch. What a classic mistake that was! Intermittent flying grapes moved in the air at random, occasional angles. I figured out a way to conceal my launches, by placing a mushy one, or one I made mushy, on my plastic spoon, holding the handle still, refracting, flexing back the spoon, aiming, releasing, then catapulting the grape. On this afternoon Mr. Young was there, standing sergeant-like with his fists on his hips, helping with controlling things in the cafeteria, distrustful, intimidating, with his sleeves rolled up, sort of pivoting around a bit, watching and just generally looking mean, speaking occasionally with one of the aids there. He was about fifty feet away from us, across the cafeteria.

"Watch this," I said to Dennis, a classmate.

"Wait. Mr. Young's here."

"I know. Don't worry."

"Who ya wanna hit?"

"Bobby Marks. Over there, see?" I said, setting my catapult lower than the table so that no one could see. I bit back my prankish grin, forging an innocent expression.

"That's too far. You'll never hit him," Dennis said, daring me, watching.

"Let's see. Here it goes," I said, releasing, feeling the faultless force of that one perfectly forty-five degreed launch, catching its glossy greenness with my vision as it ascended, soaring, way off the mark (Bobby Marks), but dead on toward Mr. Young.

"Wow!" said Dennis, watching with wonderment. "That one's really goin'!"

"Uh-oh!" I said, as we both saw in disbelief as that especially large, intentionally squished, pulpy grape collapsed, smashing onto Mr. Young's mouth—at least unquestionably somewhere between his nose and chin—splattering, avalanching fleetly down to his tie, then his thigh, then to the floor.

"Holy macarolly!" I said, turning my head, restraining nervous laughter.

"Oh my God, you hit Mr. Young! You hit Mr. Young right in the face! You hit him right in the mouth! Holy smokes!" Dennis kept marveling.

So quickly surprised, Mr. Young jerked back, his face forward—sort of like a chicken—his hand immediately wiping as he pivoted, searching, scanning hopelessly across the din of the junior high multitudes. He stomped his foot in fury, said something to the nearby aid. She blew her whistle, steadily, loudly until everyone got quiet.

Mr. Young began shouting, "Not another sound! Everyone! Be quiet! Right now! Sit in your seats!" The meter in his raspy voice made him sound like a poet with a cause. "Are you a bunch of animals, or what!"

Some distant kid's voice shouted, "What!"

Another voice shouted, "Animal!"

"Everyone stay seated, with your hands folded! If one more piece of food is thrown, everyone of you will be in detention!" This exploded from a red face, arteries popping in his neck, fists pinned to hips, hairy forearm sinews flexing.

I didn't know what was going to happen. I could see a slight glistening on his chin. I didn't know if it was his saliva from his fury, or some of the grape.

Just then, Dennis whispered to me, "There's a piece of grape on his shirt. See it? See it on his shirt?"

I could see the green speck stuck on his white shirt. I had a really hard time harnessing my laughter with this, even though I was terrified. I wondered if anyone else had seen that grape strike him. This was like a dream. I couldn't believe I hit the principal with that grape! I kept praying under my breath. My prayer went something like this: "Please God! Please don't let him know." A few minutes of tense endurance lapsed, and I was safe. The pounding of my heart eased. Recess ended. I eluded a capital repercussion.

Well, the next day, still cooped up inside because of all that slow melting snow, exiting the cafeteria with Dennis, I saw Anthony, who was now in eighth grade, who was still living with the Roccos, standing by the exit to the hallway, chubbier than I'd ever seen him. He had this sarcastic, scornful grin on his face. He stood beside one of my classmates, Alex, a big kid who was sometimes a trouble-maker, who now thought he was special because he was hanging out with an older, eighth-grade thug, Anthony. Well Alex said something to Anthony that I couldn't hear. They both looked at me, and then they both laughed. I had this bad feeling. Stepping passed them, I looked at Anthony.

Alex said, "Hey scuzzy skin!"

I looked at him, astonished. He looked at me, giggling, while Anthony laughed obnoxiously. I said nothing.

Before I went to the classroom I stopped at the boys' room to look in the mirror. As I'd expected, my winter eczema blazed red, chafing, ugly. Sometimes my cream worked; sometimes it didn't. I was always revolted and sickened with my skin, especially my face; and the more repulsed I seemed to feel about my skin, the more it acted up. Stress affected my eczema and asthma.

I heard this twice more from Alex that afternoon. I didn't know what to do. I was tempted to just punch Alex, but I really didn't want to get into trouble. I didn't want to disappoint Shironda, and I knew I was supposed to control myself. I wanted some help, but I'd never tell the teacher. I wanted to fight my own battles; but more than fight, I wanted this or them to just go away. It didn't, and they didn't, and I was afraid of getting upset.

The next day three other kids called me scuzzy skin, and I'd begun to sense the dregs of anger surging inside of me. As this anger churned, I felt my asthma also activating. I felt stifled, smothered, hearing a slight wheeze. As I made my way out of the cafeteria, moving into the hallway with the drove, there stood big Anthony and big Alex as usual, like they owned the place or something, commenting about girls, tripping kids as they walked by, just being plainly obnoxious. I cringed, because I really hated confrontation. I didn't trust myself. I wanted to turn the other way, but there was no other permissive way. So I braced myself, and sure enough, just as I thought that perhaps I had eluded their notice, knowing full well that Alex was prodded by Anthony, who'd never said a word to me—good or bad—I heard Alex once again, "Hey, scuzzy skin, burn down any sheds lately?"

I immediately looked at Anthony, saying, "Wadya tell 'im for, Anthony, ya big fat pig?" I saw in his face that guilty look for having his disloyalty discovered. Then this look transformed, became erased by a suddenly defiant, gloomy mien.

I thought at first he might deny saying anything, but instead, abreast with his proud, second facial response, he said, "Cause I felt like it, Dillon!"

Now I was Dillon, I thought. Now that I was just some other kid at the intermediate school, I was Dillon. Back at the Roccos' where we were once foster brothers, I was Silas. What a cheat! I thought, with wrath. "Ya big elephant!" I said, making myself no less perfidious than he, even feeling the poisonous venom of anger inside of me.

I saw his expression battle off injury, contesting against more stabs. His pout always exclaimed the same agony that I'd felt. I saw it flare into fury, into a countenance that declared war. He didn't know what to say. He just shouted, "Yeah, ya twerp! Ya fire maniac!"

I followed the rest of the flock into the hall toward the classrooms.

"What's he wanna fight ya or something?" Dennis said.

"I don't know."

"He looked like he wants ta fight ya!"

"Yeah, he's mad—for sure."

"He wants ta fight!"

"Prob'ly."

"He'll squish ya!"

"Yeah," I said with fear, moving, not looking back. This fear was less about Anthony squishing me than it was of his shouldering his way into my sphere of classmates, instigating things.

I had this eagerness to get back to learning. I wanted to run away, and academics was all I had to run to for escape.

That night I went to bed with a lot of this on my mind. I couldn't seem to focus on my school work since all of this opened up. My sleep was shallow, and I kept waking, worrying, feeling pent-up with anger. I dreamed a vivid dream that I couldn't find a pencil with an erasure—a common daylight hours dilemma.) I searched drawers and floors for one of those school bus-yellow, number two pencils with an erasure. Finding none, I tried to erase some class work mistake with the one discovered pencil that still had a thin, pink bulge of erasure from the base; but it was too thin; and I couldn't hold the pencil perpendicularly enough as the wheat-colored, metal sheath that clasped its rosy softness within and to the putrid pencil scratched and tore my paper, shredding. I tried to bite the clasping sheath to squeeze out the malleable pink, but it all disintegrated, disappeared the way things do in dreams.

Then, somehow in the indistinct, blurry, meshing lacework that often makes up dreams, these pencils became people. They became lives, visually, with compressed faces and frames confined into the slenderness of the pencils, with faces jammed in the wheat-colored, erasure-fastening tops; and legs blended down into the pencils' points. I blearily saw people of my life, mostly kids from school— their faces in smiles and sneers, eyes evil—clustered together. I vaguely heard their utterances. I saw Anthony, Alex, intimidating with glares. In this delirious way these pencils became lives.

As I lay lapsing into alertness, I imagined the architect-God as the plentiful source of semi-diamond shaped, dawn-tinted erasures poised for all the dark flaws of humanity. I then awakened fully, recalling this.

That next day brought more of this ridicule. Alex and Anthony kept calling me scuzzy the dog killer. I guess I'd told Anthony years earlier about my slaying that dog on the way back from Staten Park after my bike had been stolen. I don't know. My asthma got so bad during recess in the cafeteria, I had to go down to the nurse's office for my inhaler. It helped some, and I sat there until recess ended, mostly because I wanted to avoid the constant harassment. I'd somehow become the brunt of jokes, the target of fatuous kids, and I was at my wit's end. I finally went back to class.

For most of the afternoon in social studies we learned about President Andrew Jackson and the Cherokee Indian nation and other stuff around that time in American history. I felt so bad for those native people, chased off their land like that, dying on their way to Oklahoma and all. Then, for the last forty minutes of the day, Mrs. Slack, who taught us in the afternoons after Mr. McClarty in the mornings, allowed us to get started on our social studies home-work early. Only a few kids ever really did concentrate on that at this time of the school day; most of us talked or goofed around or just waited until it was time to leave for the buses. Mrs. Slack was just tired of teaching. Well, this one afternoon, big Alex, who sat in front of Marissa, decided to start in again. He got freckle face Brandon and black Maxwell to start in with me again.

"Scuzzy!" Alex whispered out loud. "Scuzzy!" he said over and over, looking for my stir.

I looked down, pretending I concentrated on my Cherokee Indian questions.

"Hey scuzzy boy!" Maxwell said, deforming his voice, deepening it, making it more nasal to gain more of a giggle from the others.

They laughed.

"Scuzskin. Scuzskin. Scuzskin...." Brandon said rapidly, repeatedly looking over at Alex for his approval. I knew that Brandon, typically a decent kid who minded his own business, felt elevated as he felt a part of big Alex's circle.

I glanced over toward where Alex sat, careful not to make eye contact with him. I could see he had his thick torso swiveled around to focus on me. I could see his bulging, fleshy protoplasm overlapping his belt. I couldn't stand him. I looked at the clock. Twenty minutes remained. That would be eternity. Mrs. Slack stood in her closet, out of touch with what was going on anywhere in the classroom.

"Scuzzy face! Hey scuzzy face! Eczema man!" Alex persisted.

"His skin's fallen off! He's like a lizard. He's sheddin his scuzzy skin," Maxwell said, laughing.

The other two laughed.

"When he itches it starts snowin'!" Brandon added.

I looked at Marissa. She watched me. It was hard to tell, but I think she was waiting for my reaction. I didn't want to look at her long, for fear of disgrace; so I looked back at my book, pretending to write. I just kept writing her name over and over, disguising it, covering it. I was so in love with her.

I felt my asthma averting my breathing, but imagined it may have just been in my mind because of the intensity. I felt pressure to save my dignity, but I didn't know exactly how to do it. I felt so solely isolated, like a feeble herbivore fighting off a pack of wolves.

"Scuzzy face got dandruff! Hey dandruff face, ya better wipe the skin off ya book or else ya can't read it!" Alex said.

Suddenly about five people burst out laughing.

I looked up, locking my eyes directly onto Marissa's, seeing her laugh as she tried to smother her laughter with fingers over her lips so Mrs. Slack wouldn't catch her and exhort her. This made me want to die. I suddenly felt so stupid, imagining that she might have feelings for me, with my skin. I'd been so glowingly infatuated with her, and now she was laughing at Alex's taunting me. I was crushed. Nothing worse could have happened. Why was this happening? I wanted to scream, roar, bark, bite.

Mrs. Slack stopped whatever it was she was doing by her closet, and looked over toward us threateningly, to get us quiet. She said nothing. Everyone looked forward with heads down, muffling giggles. She turned her focus back into her closet, peeking out again seconds later.

What happened next is hard to account. I felt something, like an invisible primate with claws, descend on me. I imagined it was a demon that fastened onto me, injecting me with fury, or stirring my own fury. Dread asphyxiated me. This horrible tangibility seemed to sit upon me, on my shoulders, head, and back. I saw red. I saw beautiful Marissa Mellina, my dream, my escape, my puerile hope, as she continued to struggle at submerging her laughter behind sluggish, vexatious Alex. I felt this sure, definite tug in my conscience toward controlling myself, to be still, to leave it alone; but at the same tempo I felt that driving push of pride, self, and vengeance intoxicating me, envenoming me, urging me. My heart raced. The surrounding giggles lingered. One, two, three seconds expired.

I yielded: my chair slid back. My hands reached into the open slot of my desk, hauling out my bulky math book, squeezing. I could feel the enslaving inebriation of rage radiating in my chest, in my neck, in my face, like heedless heat. My eyes wouldn't blink. I stood. No one seemed to notice; this all happened so fast, so strangely mechanically. My feet took my frame into the isle, four steps forward, behind Alex. Marissa and Brandon noticed, bewildered, saying nothing, wondering. Alex, unaware, faced forward. My eyes beheld the top of his head, pupils fixed on his hair where it parted in the center. Like a mechanical sanitation truck hoisting a dumpster, my red sleeved arms elevated the mammoth math book, up, high, over my head, its red cover facing the ceiling. The book swung down, slammed brutally down, was thrown so much faster than gravity could drop it. It thumped directly onto Alex's head. He hollered. Screams, shouts!

My feet took me back to my desk. My legs bent and brought me to sitting. My hands shoved the book back into its slot. My eyes finally blinked as my face was momentarily covered with those same hands.

Alex's heavy chest pressed against his desk, with his head—face down—upon it. He unwillingly rested. He cried, screamed, labored, unable to move as his large frame convulsed under an apparent seizure. Students gathered around him, touching his shoulder.

"Alex, are you all right?"

"Take it easy Alex."

"I'll get the nurse!" Brandon dashed out the door.

"He's hurt bad! Oh, Alex is hurt bad!"

"Silas hit him with the book!"

"Mrs. Slack! Alex is hurt!"

"Alex was makin' fun a Silas n' Silas got mad and hit him with the book, Mrs. Slack!"

This demented, unforgettable commotion gripped the room; maniacal, unforgettable cries drained from Alex's mouth.

I sat with my palms on my forehead, elbows on the desk, staring at the floor, at my sneakers, at the green-gray V of the chair between my parted thighs. I wanted to crawl away somewhere and curl into a fetal ball and cover myself. I couldn't look up, at anyone, anything. Somewhere in the deep recesses of my core I could feel tears, cryptic sobs that wanted to burst; but couldn't. They were down there, held down somehow by the hard hand of anger. I stared. I didn't blink. A flashback reached me: that hour years earlier when I'd leaped up from the deep soft chair in the residence house, burying my face into Daddy Sparks' shoulder, crying out loud after he'd told me they were moving to Cincinnati.

I sat there in that classroom's commotion that afternoon, feeling neither remorse nor relief, just wishing I could cry like that time I did on Daddy's shoulder, but I was powerless, haunted, stone, temporarily insane.

SIXTEEN

TWELVE NIGHTS

Cary Island's small hills sat idly and wet in April, rolling down gray rain, filling lowland pools and dirty brooks. Bars of sunset light broke in the heavens, shattering shiny, glistening fragments over all that had been gray. Three ducks flitted smoothly and swiftly above the kills that spread like veins in the neighborhoods. They darted through the dampened air in formation, quacking and quacking and quaking a calm silence.

The snow had melted, and like thawing beef the water soaked earth softened, swelled. Like a tired man, the earth, having slipped off that thickness of late winter, that quilt of early spring snow, sliding slowly, as though earth legs, waking, had kicked it to the foot of its bed. Twelve days of mostly gray had come and gone, some with driving rain chasing March's wind into corners, or away. For twelve days and nights grass blots had enlarged through white, disclosing themselves like confessions, like green eyes peeking from frozen sleep through blurry windows of slush.

I walked alone, stopped. It became early night, with stillness and blackness at the edge of black woods beside water, a small pond somewhere in the preserve in the interior of this grand island. I could see swans like angels in white moving beneath the high heavens in the clean, clearing, lavender evening. Saintly, slowly upon a smooth and waveless surface, like ancient ships that once wore masts in white canvas, silent and distant on indolent water they drifted, sailing. Nothing excited; no one spoke in those moments of moving time, until, suddenly their wings widened, slamming upon the air, against water, under forward stretched necks. Their hurried feet ran across the surface of water in that soft twilight, suddenly swallowing silence in turbulence, then launching, lifting, softening their noise, lifting farther upward, rising in gigantic, white flight. As I watched, listening, it was as though all earth was fixed on that moment, with this flock, this sound, this motion, and was still.

I came out there this night to escape my thoughts. These swans helped, but my thoughts had caught up with me. All the alterations, conversations, and sights of the past twelve days had besieged me like swarming bees. I couldn't get that picture of Alex's trunk shaking in immobility at his desk, out of my mind. I could envision the ambulance, could see the dismay in Mrs. Slack's eyes, could still hear Shironda telling me about his fractured neck, and the steel halo he'd have to wear for weeks. Inside, part of me said, "Poor Alex"; while another, angrier, defunct part said, "serves him right!"

I wondered if anyone said, "Poor Silas." Probably not. I guessed that I'd now become just some bad memory. Well, I was history at that school now. Home tutoring was my means for the rest of the school year. I was too violent to be cut loose with kids. Sure, I was provoked some; but the school board wouldn't and couldn't take any chances.

I couldn't get that picture of Marissa laughing at Alex's jokes about my skin out of my mind. God, what a dagger. I still hemorrhaged over that.

Eight days later Sandra Jackson came over and she and Shironda sat me down to talk, to gently throw another grenade. Part of that conversation went like this:

"Silas, we have some information we have to tell you," Sandra said in her affected, practiced, social worker tone.

"Yeah."

Sandra looked at Shironda. They took deep breaths. "Tammy and I are moving down to Florida, Silas," Shironda said. "We're moving where Mr. Todd is, and he's employed with a new company, and we've decided to commit to working our marriage right. It's important for Tammy, and me—both of us. We been talkin', and things are very hard for Tammy and I up here, makin' ends meet and with working two jobs and everything, and well, we just feel it's the best way to go right now."

"Yeah. So I'm goin' too?"

"No, honey, you're not."

"Yeah, that's right. I belong to New York State."

"Uh huh."

"So I'm goin' in a new foster home?" I wouldn't look at them. I just stared down and tapped my feet on the floor and clasped my hands together, weaving my fingers, twisting them, revolving my thumbs around and around, hurried.

"Yes, Silas, we working on finding you a new home here in Cary County, honey."

"It's cause I broke Alex's neck, right? you're afraid for Tammy, right?"

"No, Silas. No, it isn't at all. That's not it at all! Don't you be thinkin' that now, here me?"

"Yeah."

"We know you are gentle with Tammy. Tammy loves you and no one's scared. Hear me, mister?"

"Well, it doesn't matter," I said.

Anyhow, that was pretty much the beef of that conversation. Nothing new under the sun. I verged upon a new foster home, and who knows where.

All this absorbed me these days and nights. All this current junk and all the settled old junk within me haunted me. I'd walked alone in this night, stopping for moments by this pond in the preserve, looking for rest like some fallen spirit, thirsting, barren, yearning, fiercely lonely, wheezing, scratching, thirteen, half white, half black. Nothing new under the sun. Earnest thoughts of suicide for the first time tempted me for the first time in my youth. Three ugly methods swiftly crossed my mind the way the three ducks crossed my vision, the sky. My anger had been lulled into a deep depression, and I just hated life.

Minutes lapsed. The swans' soaring sounds died in the distance, and their wavelets completed their rippling over the pond's surface. I wondered where they'd flown to. I thought about the day's rain, which remained depleted, having poured itself out into the kills that filled the wide pools, like that swollen one I stood beside. Water still dripped and dripped from the still deciduous trees which had no blossoms, no leaves, only small closed buds. White clouds cracked, split apart in the heavens. Night's blackness began to fill the cracks, and higher yet, scintillating stars eased that blackness. A small light from a window through scribbles of limbs seemed to reach out (I imagined) its warm hand toward me, toward my aloneness. This reminds me of what I'd mentioned early on, "I was placed 'into' homes, near other fires. I never really caught though. I wasn't allowed to get too close, actually." This was my life: I was the frizzy-haired furor always on the outside, looking in; always alone, reading thoroughly the friendly communion.

As I turned to walk back to Shironda's house, I became freshly aware of the sounds that lived within that darkening stillness: peepers making their music in the pool; scarce half-quacks of weary ducks; the dull hum of the mile removed, roaring Atlantic; remote barks of dogs; car wheels on a far, rain-soaked street; this dripping; my footsteps; my laboring lungs. Walking, I also became freshly aware of the sounds that lived within the darkened stillness of myself: my isolation, my desolation, my musing, my fears.

It's in these pauses where I struggle to keep from reflecting too much into the past, where I struggle to accept what might be a tomorrow without a promise.

TWELVE MOONS

One might superstitiously believe that the balmy, breezy, sunny day in May when I was delivered to my new foster home was a bright sign of the same sort of future; but it certainly wasn't one for my immediate future. I was delivered in a typical way, in the county agency's vehicle, with my worker Sandra doing the delivery—promptly, assiduously—along with my trunk. An old "retired" policeman named George was the chauffeur.

"Do you know where the new home is George?" Sandra said respectfully, conscious of my presence.

"Yeah. Off Verrazano Boulevard. Not far from the old Armory. Lousy section. Lotta blacks!"

"I beg your pardon!" Sandra said, with her erudite, social worker's style, somewhat challenging.

Old George turned his seasoned face momentarily around, to look at Sandra with his yellowed eyes. Having overlooked Sandra's color, realizing, he grinned, winking apologetically. "Bad area," he said. "Lotta problems in the area! You know what I'm talkin' about." He snorted, hacked, opened the window, spat out into the passing street.

I sat belted in the front passenger seat of the van, wearing a brand-new Yankee cap which Molly had brought me, reading lyrics from the Christian music CD that I could still hear singing in my head, that she'd also brought me, that I had listened to repeatedly the night before. I turned to look at Sandra's face in the back seat. At age thirteen, these adult tensions in conversations now rarely eluded me.

Sandra shook her head, wearing an angry, disgusted look, sighing deeply, long, exasperated. She wouldn't look at me, resisting from combatively rebutting George. Unsure of whether it would be proper to dispute him on his racial illiteracy in my presence, she wisely refrained.

Being a black and white blend, I sometimes felt safe, but sometimes more vulnerable to these tensions. I wasn't sure. In this case, I felt favored by Sandra, and most of the African-American community. I'm convinced my being bi-racial put me in the category of being black, as far as both the black community and the white community categorized me. I had that Shakespearean "dram of evil," so to speak. I now felt warmly rejected by George, and felt that very same rebuff from some white people, especially those in their autumn years. Maybe some of it was all in my head. I didn't care, really.

George turned on the radio, now grinning sardonically to himself. His deep-seated inflexibility, made inveterate probably from years on the streets of New York, took pleasure in striking a nerve in Sandra. That was not hard to see.

I went back to reading the lyrics on my lap, and could hear the echo in my inner ear, in the darkness of my skull, the sweet voice of the female vocalist who I liked to imagine was Molly herself, and the mellifluent acoustics beside her:

My lips will praise You
For You are holy
My voice will ever

Rise before Your throne
My heart will love You
For you are lovely
And You have called me
To become Your own
I am Your own
and I will worship You alone
I am Your child
And I will worship at Your throne
I am Your own
And I will love You.

How I wished that I could sing that! How I wished that I could say that! That I could cry! How I wished on that sparkling May morning that I could make some sort of breakthrough into some real clearing, and not just in the weather! Nevertheless, the heavenly lyrics kept visiting, and something inside me kept listening, and something kept pulling me toward a certain fire that, for most of my brief life, I had been removed from.

When Molly had found out about my moving again, she came to see me the evening beforehand. We sat on Shironda's porch, hearing the singing of the many returned birds, scenting the fragrance of white and lavender lilacs in the breezes, watching the lengthening shadows as dusk had begun to encompass us. She'd divulged to me about how she'd miscarried a third time, and she told me very directly, like I was her friend whom she could confide in or something, and she'd spoken with tears: "I don't know Silas. Maybe we're not supposed to have our own children." She shrugged her shoulders.

"Yeah, but you'd be the best mom, Molly."

"Thank you, kiddo!"

"It's nothin'."

"I don't know. For some reason we're sent into these storms sometimes. You know? It's like there's some reason for the grief we endure, and it's part of a big plan."

I nodded. There was long silence among the songs of birds.

"I've learned, Silas, that the dentist often hurts, but that his hurts are really helps. I guess there's a force very often works like the dentist. What do you think, kiddo? You know what I mean?"

I nodded again, smiling.

"I don't even know if having my own biological babies is all that important anymore, at least not as much as it is to Bob." She looked at me. "Bob really wants me to bear him a son."

I just listened.

"You know that story about how Jesus sent His disciples out into that storm?"

"Yeah," I nodded.

She nodded. "And it seems He sometimes deprives us of what's most dear to us!" she said, not with complaint, but with injury of heart, and with discovery.

I nodded again, doubtful.

We gazed onto the street where straight shadows wove through the straight lines of this sprawling city's suburbs. I didn't understand her pain then, but I did know that she was feeling it; and that insight alone was enough for me to feel for her, while in a curious way it was a comfort for me as I plainly understood that others suffer too. As I recall, I think Molly may have been indirectly teaching me this, by telling me of her hurt. Hearing her, seeing her eyes shine with tears, somehow removed me from my own unsteady, depressing whereabouts. It really was nice of her to come all the way from Manhattan, across the bridge, to see me on the night before I was to be moved again.

"Could you bring me to the Hellers' tomorrow?" I entreated her because I was scared.

Molly's expression told me she was confused.

"The Hellers is the new people taking me."

"Oh I see." She paused. "I'm afraid Sandra has to do that Silas. It's official, you see. She's the worker on your case, you know. It's just the way it's done. Well, I could come along I suppose. Oh, no, I can't, I just remembered Bob and I have to take care of something tomorrow."

"Okay."

"I'm thinking of you Silas—all the time!"

"I think of you too Molly," I said.

We were quiet for a while again, staring at the street. Traces of sunlight perceptibly diminished. We could hear a piano across the street, its tranquil sound seeping and twining out through a screen onto the street, mingling with the lilacs, reaching us onto that porch. Molly kept singing to herself in this serenity. She obviously knew this hymn. I could hear her sweet voice as I strained to listen, pretending not to: "Be thou my vision, oh Lord of my heart...." and then she hummed, so sweetly. It came from the depths of the sweetest person in the whole world, as far as I was concerned. I loved just listening.

"I read a really great chapter last night, Silas."

"Ya did?"

"Yeah. I read about Peter. Well, there's a lot about him."

My fixed eyes told her that I wanted to hear about it.

"Jesus told Peter some things in advance, you know, Silas. He said, 'Peter, when you were young you were allowed to choose and do and go wherever you wanted; but when you become old you'll have to be brought to a place or situation you won't like.'" Molly paused. "God does sometimes send us into tough spots and sad times. You know what I mean Silas?"

I could only nod. "Yeah," I said, unready at that green age of thirteen to seriously venture into daring Molly's sad certainties.

"God really does allow us to fall, and fail, and get disappointed. I think it's a preparation period, for us, for our lives, for eternity! You see Silas?" Her pretty, earnest eyes remained fixed on mine.

I kept nodding, listening, adoring.

She looked out onto the street, finishing: "Some of us just go through longer periods. We go through hotter fires I guess." She looked at me again. "Some of the very bad things that happen to people can be used for good you know. I think we gotta believe that!" Again she looked out at the street. "We gotta believe it, Silas. Otherwise there's just nothing, nothing at all!"

Molly left me again, and drove off into Manhattan. I'd watched her drive down the street with her headlights beaming into the shadowy dusk.

Anyhow, on this next day the van pulled over beside the curb on Staten Street, at the Hellers'. Their home was a typical, tall one, very much like the one the Maddens owned, and very near that same neighborhood. Mrs. Heller sat on a white wicker chair, on her very small porch. The sun shone brightly against her. Her gray hair and squinting eyes made her look as though she were older, in pain. She was only fifty. She wore a yellow and white checkered house dress, and before the white siding and white wicker, she appeared brilliant.

Each of these houses had little patches of lawn in the front, very much like the backyards; and her twenty-three-year-old son Simon had just begun to mow. But when he saw us pull up, he shut the mower off and stepped toward the car.

Simon Heller was short, thin-legged, with a broad and muscular torso. He seemed to have long, orangutan-like arms which swung as he walked, hanging huge paw-like hands, hands with very long, thick fingers. He walked with his elbows bent out, pushed out by the thick brawn at his sides, elbowing as though he elbowed his way through a crowd, as though he moved through sellers and buyers on wall street, or in a merchandise market, or something. He kept smiling, wearing a blue and white checkered shirt, buttoned and tucked neatly, concealing his bulk, very much like his mother's yellow and white pattern.

As I stepped out of the car, seeing him, I immediately felt smothered, somewhat revolted. His round head held colorless eyes, hairy brows, thin black hair, a prematurely receding hairline. He was only twenty-three, yet he smoked a cigar, something I'd only seen older men smoke. What remained of this thick, crammed cigar was about two inches of length, and it seemed fixed to his rubbery mouth, oozing tobacco juice which he wiped from his chin with his naked wrist. As he approached he momentarily removed this filthy thing to shake my hand, and turning his head slightly, he vigorously spat amber, tar colored saliva into the grass. He looked at his cigar butt, hesitated, then decided, flinging it into the gutter. His tremendous hands wore long untrimmed nails; and his manner was very forward, close, bold, aiming at what I'd hoped was friendliness. He reached out his hand to shake, and I limply offered mine.

"Hey buddy, how ya doin!" he said with a loud, nasal-cramped voice.

I forced a smile. His hands were clammy, or sweaty, or just wet. I wiped my hand on the back of my pants.

He then lifted his immense, moist paw and grabbed my cheeks, squeezing like I were two years old or something, bunching my lips together. He himself was just above boyhood. This short, stocky, elbowing, big-pawed human moved about like a bulky monkey. His little gray eyes peered into me, then quickly all over me, as though I were an auctioned item or something. I felt uncomfortable, but was desperate to try to feel comfortable.

Sandra opened the back of the van. I grabbed my two plastic bags which were filled with my things. "Is this the boy's?" Simon said, handling my trunk.

"Yes, that belongs to Silas," Sandra said in her social worker tone.

Simon lifted it with ease, carrying it toward the house, passing the idle mower, muscling his way up the steps with its unwieldy weight, passing his smiling mother who then greeted me, saying, "Welcome." She then stood in a stance of domination, shaking her head, saying firmly, "Simon, wait for the boy! What's your hurry? My goodness!" She had a controlling manner, even though her expression suggested that somewhere, sometime she'd been vanquished. She had a story too, I knew.

"I am. This thing is heavy! I'm takin it to his room! Give me a break!"

"Oh, go ahead," she said, pent-up, sitting down again, faltering off into the backdrop of this whole opening volley. As I entered through the entrance sideways with my bags, looking at her, making eye contact, she said, "Oh, he's just a good for nothin'!" impetuously wanting to fill me in for some reason.

"Mom be quiet!" Simon shouted from within, muffled. "Silas, come on! Up here!" he shouted, excited, acting like a child who was having a friend sleep over. This was all so odd. I followed him into the first bedroom.

"This is your room."

I stepped inside.

"Like it?"

I looked around. Freshly painted walls enlivened with white. Posters of Yankee players hung underneath Yankee pennants. "Yankees!" I said, grinning.

"Yep. Heard you like 'em."

"Yeah."

"I like 'em too."

"Ya do?"

"Yeah."

"Who's your favorite?"

Simon searched his mind. There was alarm in his eyes, silence in the air. He looked at the wall, pointed at a photo of Tino Martinez straining power in mid-swing.

"I like Jeter."

"How come?"

"I don't know. He's the best, I guess. Jeter's awesome!"

"You're right. Hey, my room's right there." He nodded into the hallway where his door hung open.

I put my stuff down and sat on the bed. Simon darted into his room, and returned quickly, leaning against the door jam, smiling, holding up two Yankee tickets.

"Yankee tickets?"

"You bet."

"When?"

"Tomorrow night!"

"Toronto?"

"You got it!"

"Awesome!"

"Ever been to the stadium?"

"No. I always wanted to!"

"Well, you're gonna get ya chance, buddy!" Simon nodded, smiling, staring at me. I began to think that maybe this wasn't going to be too bad. This grown foster brother went out of his way for me, it seemed. He seemed to like the Yankees. He made the room comfortable for me. He wanted me to feel at home.

"And the day after we're going to Great Adventure! Ever been there?"

"No. I heard about it."

"Well, we're gonna have a blast!" He had this big smile, like he was a kid.

"Awesome."

"You can put your stuff away if you like."

I dumped my things from my bags onto the bed. Simon stood there watching me. I felt uneasy. "You got a job or anything?"

"Not right now."

"Ya had one?"

"Of course!"

"Where?"

"Auto parts store. A parts warehouse too. Before that I was a mechanic—a tire place—changing tires and stuff."

"How come no more?"

"Laid off."

"All of 'em?"

"Yep. I'm workin' on getting' another one soon. You're a smart kid. Know it?"

"Guess."

"Hey, we'll get the subway tomorrow night. Get off at Yankee Stadium. We'll go early—get some signatures maybe."

"Autographs?"

"Yeah, autographs."

"You collect cards?"

"Baseball cards?"

"Well yeah, what else?"

Simon paused. "Used to."

"Oh."

"Hey, wanna see my room?"

"Sure."

We stepped across the hallway, entering. Simon's room was clean, ordered, fastidiously neat—much like his dress habits. Besides the disgustingly wet cigar smoking, his appearance was exact, tight, pinched. Similarly, besides his weightlifting apparatus strewn on the carpeted floor, his room was neat, minimally decorated, stingy, pictureless, off-white. There was a bed made in the corner, a computer in another, a bureau in another, and a closet in the fourth.

The cause of his muscle-bulk now opened to me. "You lift weights a lot?"

"Yeah, enough. You know, I like to keep myself fit."

"How much can you lift over ya head?" I said, wondering.

"Not much really. I'm working upper body mostly. A lot of curling and bench pressing for the most part actually. I bench three hundred!"

"Wow," I said, not remarkably abreast with the weightlifter's world, but saying it because I sensed that that's what he wanted. I didn't even know what "bench" meant.

He smiled, satisfied at impressing me.

At this moment Sandra intruded: "Okay, Silas, I'm leaving now. It looks like you're already at home here, and that's good. That's very good."

"Oh yeah. He's gonna do just fine here, for sure!" Simon cut in.

"Well, we hope so, Simon. Silas really is a fine boy. I've come to know that. He just needs the right nurturing environment and he'll do just fine. We know that. Right, Silas?"

"Yep, I guess so." I bent to lift the weight stacked bar, unable to budge it, barely attentive to Sandra.

"Oh, we'll take some of that weight off for ya, Silas. Get you started, if you want," Simon said proudly. "We'll make you the strongest in the junior high this year!"

I really liked that idea. In fact, I did work on making myself strong there at the Hellers'. It proved to be a great outlet for my anger and frustration, providing me something to aim for.

"I'll stop in or call in a couple of days, Silas." Sandra was already descending the narrow staircase.

"See ya."

"Here. Just pull this pin out here, like this." Simon was kneeling beside me, rubbing his frame against mine. "Then slide off or on however much weight you want. Then take off the same amount on the other side. See? Let's start with fifty for you, then we'll move up from there. See what you can do. Go easy like, you know? Lay down on the floor!"

I lay with my hands by my neck, waiting for him to place the bar across my chest.

"Hands at your shoulders. Hands at your shoulders!" he said, and the weight training began.

Simon really overworked himself to bond with me. And it didn't take long for me to realize he was a bit of a social misfit—having no adult friends, in and out of menial jobs, forever avoiding, shunning, or bickering with his assertive mother, defending himself with shouts to cloud out her brutal accusations and demeaning deflations: "You're worthless! You're just like your father! You'll never amount to anything! Go to hell! Drop dead! Can't you do anything right!" These were some of her assaults.

"Shut up! I'm not listening!" he'd shout over her, curse, slam a door, retreat.

Mrs. Heller once told me about how Mr. Heller, a drunken, abusive, frenzied man, finally left and never returned. It all happened when Simon was about ten years old. Mrs. Heller had acquired a court order of protection, and that was the end of Mr. Heller. Simon supposed his father was either dead, or drunk and derelict, probably somewhere in New York. She'd had to face him once in family court, and Simon thought that he'd seen him once, just standing across the street one winter evening, hands in coat pockets, staring at the house. Other than that, he was no longer a ravager in their home, and was somewhat forgotten. There's an involved, dragging plot around this family, but that's another story.

Anyway, the day finally came when I could visit Yankee Stadium, something I'd always longed for, but for some reason—probably my own diffidence—never felt the liberty to ask anyone for. It's funny— all these years living in New York City, and never getting over to the Bronx to see my team until now! It was a clear bright night in July.

Simon and I crossed the bridge into Brooklyn, zipped through on 4th Street, into downtown, and crossed the Brooklyn Bridge. We connected with FDR Drive and East River Drive, crossed the Willis Avenue Bridge, then fastened onto Major Deegan Expressway, hugging and paralleling the Harlem River, exiting onto the Grand Concourse, driving until we could see it—that historic pearl, that beautiful jewel of the Bronx, the radiant pill-shaped temple of the gods, of the modern idols blazing well lighted and waving its high flags. The rows of seats, like those hoed in a spring field, bare, with sprouts of fans here and there, could be seen, polished and lustered and deep blue from the high hill of the Grand Concourse.

I imagined to myself that in times to come, eons into the future, after this great American civilization inevitably crumbles, that people will visit from all over the world (if Jesus Christ's second coming should tarry) the ruins of this great stadium, the same way people do today in Greece, Rome, and the Middle East. Planet-exalted Yankee Stadium—where nearly a billion visits had been paid by human souls on pilgrimages to applaud, acclaim, worship, and adore—and all in one century—was now in my sight for the first time. The stadium of stadiums! The great mosque of the sports world. Yankee Stadium!

We arrived an hour early. We parked, strolled, bought soft pretzels, Pepsis, tee-shirts, and programs from memorabilia loaded merchandisers who barked on the sidewalks, clutching money, giving change—grasping, noisy, greedy, desperate.

We entered the stadium, ascending ramps that take us to our place in the mezzanine, following the circular corridor until finding our gate. We then entered the rectangular entry, stepping out into the Elysian fields of evening daylight, of lengthening shadows as the sun had begun its setting, of traces of breezes, bands of flocking fans, pulse of music, noises of voices, passing glimpses of conversations. There were smells—smells of popcorn, beer, burning tobacco, peanuts, hotdogs, mustard. And most appealing of all there was

this sudden vista of magnificent green—grains and tinges of emerald-green in geometric rows patterned by the mower, with this suddenness of pink raked earth in the infield, with quadratic pillow-like
white bases. Yankee Stadium. Grand. Majestic. And the Yankees
warming up—throwing, catching, stretching in dazzling pin stripes.
Another game.

We found our seats, shouted for two hours, listened to the cracks
of bats, witnessed three home runs, a Joe Torre fray with an umpire, a
proximal scramble for a foul ball, and finally a 8-6 Yankee victory. It
was one of the best days of my life. I was on cloud nine!

Anyway, that summer was neatly packed with varied amuse-
ments, like more visits to Yankee Stadium, amusement parks, and
the beach; it was full of looking on fights between Mrs. and Simon
Heller, watching Simon gnaw and drool on his fat cigars, and weight
lifting. Usually while I watched the Yankees or other stuff on the
sports channels, Simon spent time in his room sitting at his computer. I don't know what he was doing, but he wasn't really interested
in sports. He just pretended for me.

We went for a lot of drives in Simon's ten-year-old Ford, and I
got to revisit places from my past, like the Sparks' old neighborhood,
the docks, the channel, the Roccos', and Staten Park. Once we passed
the cemetery where Mom was buried, but I didn't say anything to
Simon about that. Simon and I never had any deep conversations.
He never had any counsel for me, or advice, or wisdom. It was like we
were just friends, and he was just a kid, and everything was just peculiarly superficial between us. He was always patronizing me.

Finally, in July he found a new auto parts job, and that gave me
some rest from his persistent quest to show me a good time and get
me to like him. His constant "Do you want some ice cream? Here's
some candy! Are you comfortable? Are you sure you're not bored?
Are you sure? Are you sure? It's not too much trouble. I can do it

for you" sort of doting drove me crazy sometimes. I felt like a pauper-prince or something. While he was at the store working, I would take walks to the library. I just loved the appearance of the colorful patterns of slender books on shelves, and walking the aisles, absorbed with the smells and magnetic draw of infinite books, winnowing out a pile and finding a soft and deep window chair where I could just read, and read, and read, and get lost in other worlds of fiction, and real worlds of information. I got myself quite an education all those hours that summer. This reading was a superb outlet for escape from my sorrow and disappointment. It was good for my mind too.

I also continued to work out with Simon's weights with some regular serious-mindedness. As my body physically matured that summer, I determined to increase the weight I curled, benched, and lifted in Simon's room and forced myself to drink half a gallon of milk a day. (What did the Hellers care! The county paid for all my needs, plus more.) Anyway, by the time summer ended, I was bench pressing a hundred and fifty pounds. Not bad for a hundred-and-twenty-pound thirteen-year-old! This weightlifting was a superb outlet for venting my rage at disappointment. And like the books for my mind, it was good for my anatomy.

On one particular morning, after Simon had left for work, I entered his room to work out. He didn't have a bench, so all the "bench" pressing was actually done on the floor. I did ten presses with a hundred pounds and then lay there, catching my breath, resting, glancing with my head to the side, looking unintentionally under Simon's bed. I saw a magazine, so I reached for it. Little Pets. The cover featured a shadowy photograph of a ten- or eleven-year-old girl, smiling, naked from the waist up. I leafed through, aghast. Pornography! Child pornography! Assorted photographs of children—mostly male—of all ages wove through page after page like a slithering snake. I felt appalled, dumbfounded, dropping the thing, yet at the same time strangely intrigued with the photographs of the girls, the older girls. I picked it up again, leafed through, staring mesmerized at the teenage girls, feeling from the cryptic underground of my physiology that sure, awakening ache. Suddenly the thought of bizarre Simon Heller leafing through these pages horrified me. I dropped it as though it were grime, quickly sliding it back underneath his neat bed. I felt a chill slither down my spine. I stood, exited.

That same night, when Simon came home it was evident that he'd been drinking. He was especially jovial, loud, odd, uninhibited with his stinking cigar. I stayed far away from him, closing my door. I lay on my bed. Once he entered, barging in. "Hey kid, wanna take a ride?"

"No."

"What's the matter?"

"I don't feel too good."

"What hurts?"

"My head." I was lying.

"I'll give you some aspirin."

"I already did. I just want to sleep awhile."

"All right. Relax. See ya later." He went downstairs.

I felt relieved.

An hour later I opened my door to go downstairs to watch the Yankee game. Simon was in his room with his door opened, seated at his computer, leafing through the Internet, assuming I was sleeping. He was startled by me, shifting over to try to casually block his screen. "Hey, what's up?" he said, nervously.

"Nothin'." I focused my vision. I could clearly see half the screen, the body of a naked boy. I pretended I didn't notice. "What ya doin'?" I said, looking ignorant.

He quickly reached for his button and simply, ashamedly turned off the computer. "Oh, nothing. Just looking for some transmission stuff for my job and stuff." His tone was full of jittery concealment.

He stood, blushing, trying unsuccessfully to steer from his embarrassment. "What did ya see?"

"Nothin'," I said, becoming nervous myself. "I'm gonna watch the game. See ya later." I moved downstairs and supposed the strain of Simon's shame and uncertainty of what I may have seen kept him in his room that night. In my youthful naiveté I became fearful, politely withdrawing from that time onward.

That summer was also neatly packed with thoughtful anticipation of seventh grade and a new middle school. My educational authorities, looking into my records, thought it would be right for me to give another try at mainstreaming again, rather than learning in some alternative school, or with tutors. The county's hope was that my outburst of wrath on Alex's neck would be an isolated freak. I know that I was determined to control myself, if I could. I was a bit unusual for a foster child in that, unlike most other foster kids, I had some alternating years, and brief lapses of success at school. School and academic work had their momentums as a homelike refuge for me.

Finally September came and school began, and I didn't have any problem fitting in and being accepted with the other kids, or with the teachers. A lot of the kids at this school were unmotivated. Many of them came from fatherless households. Many of them were black or Hispanic. Yeah, to some degree it was that kind of a district; but there was another percentage of kids who came from an affluent section as well. It was pretty much an even mix socially and economically. My teachers were a bit impressed with my eagerness to learn and participate, compared with the apathy of many of the others.

"Excellent! Very excellent, Silas!" Mrs. Sifer, my math teacher, liked to say.

"You know you're quite an able writer, Mr. Dillon!" Mr. Booker, my English teacher, told me once.

"Good job!" Mrs. McAnnals, my social studies teacher, said, handing back my tests.

"Now that's art!" Mrs. Curry laughed, holding up my work. "Where'd you learn to draw and paint like that, Silas?"

I shrugged my shoulders, smiling, thinking of Mommy Lucinda.

"Soberbio!" said Mr. Colmer, my Spanish teacher.

And then in early September, after the first two sessions of football in gym class, in the locker room Mr. Palladine, my gym teacher, said, "We gotta get you in a slot on the football squad, Dillon! You can't let this ability go to waste! You wanna play football?"

"Sure."

"Guys already started practice, but that shouldn't be a problem. How old are ya?"

"Thirteen."

"When you fourteen?"

"January thirty-first."

"You're old enough. Start school late or get left back?"

"Yeah, I got left back."

Mr. Palladine kept looking me over, chewing his gum, removing his cap, scratching his middle-aged, blotchy bald head. I was bulkier than most of the other seventh-grade boys because most of them hadn't yet reached puberty. "You might be a little smaller than a lot of the ninth graders, but you're certainly tough enough! Make a good defensive back! Wanna play defensive back? Linebacker?"

"Sure. I don't care where."

"That's the spirit! Gotta be a little mean and angry to play back there! Think you're mean enough?" He laughed.

"Sure," I said, amicably. "I get mad a lot!" I could hear my deepening voice cracking, pulling back for intermittent syllables into the high pitches, back for fleeting revisits to pre-pubescence.

Tall Mr. Palladine rubbed my fleecy head, laughing. I watched his whistle swinging, strung from his brawny neck at my eye level, bouncing against his chest. I think he could tell that I was the angry type.

I grinned.

"Maybe we'll try you at tight end, or split end. You got good hands!" He blew a bubble with his pink gum, snapping it quickly back into his mouth. "Show up for practice after school today?"

"Sure. I'll come today." I felt a wallop of excitement, and kept grinning.

"Can't practice till ya get a physical. Doc'll be in the health office tomorra. But we'll suit ya up with some shoulder guards and jersey and helmet. You can meet the guys—mostly ninth graders, a few eighth. You'll be the only seventh-grader. Got a problem with that?"

"Nope."

"Good. Prob'ly got some used cleats for ya too. What size are ya?"

"I think eight."

"No problem. Need a late bus?"

"No. I walk. Three blocks."

"Good. I'll go call your mother—make sure it's okay with her. Think she'll let ya play?"

"Yeah. I think so." I envisioned Mrs. Heller's face.

Mr. Palladine turned, walking back toward his office with other things on his mind. "See ya in the downstairs lockers at three, kid!"

I got my gear and a football locker after school, and Mr. Palladine introduced me to all those older, mostly bigger kids. I watched the whole practice, wishing that that school physician could have been there that day to give me my required physical. I was so thrilled. "This is the best setup I ever had," I thought to myself. I just loved this school, my teachers, everything, except for strange Simon. My doubtful settlement around the Hellers was the only thorn in my flesh, my only disconcerting insecurity.

When I got home that night, after I did my homework and ate, excited about football, I immediately went into Simon's room to work with the weights. While I was up there, Simon came home. He had been drinking again. I didn't know who he was hanging out with, and

I didn't care to know either. As soon as I was done I went to take a shower. While I washed my hair, I heard the door open. It was Simon, with a wiry rod in his hand, letting himself in through my locked door. He pulled the shower curtains apart, looking at me with that glazed, feeling-no-pain look in his eyes. He had residue from his filthy cigar juice around his lips. "Hey, I hear ya playin' football, guy!"

"Yeah," I said, stupefied over his entrance, assuming his mother told him. "How'd ya get in here?"

"Easy," he said, smiling, nodding to his wire, licensing his eyes to pore over my frame. He had this demeanor of authority, like he could do whatever he wanted in his house.

"Do ya mind?" I said, half grinning, careful not to have an attitude, careful to preserve my residence here since my stead at school was so agreeable.

"What?"

"I'm takin' a shower!"

"So."

I didn't know what to say. Water spattered—over my face, swashing my speech some. I stood sideward, trying in vain to cover as much view from him as I could. He kept looking. There was a tense, bad feeling in the air. I began to hate him, feeling that old anger rise inside me.

"So I wanna take a shower alone like everybody else. Ya mind?" I laughed, disguising my disgust. I cupped my hands, catching water, then threw it onto him, dousing him, laughing artificially.

He looked angry for a moment, jumping back. "So what a ya, bashful? What's the big deal?"

I just let out a long, diffident groan. "So if it's no big deal, then leave me alone if I want!"

"Hey, look what I got." He held up two Yankee tickets, safeguarding his relationship with me. He now felt awkward.

"When?"

"Next Wednesday."

"But it's a school night."

"So."

"I'll have homework. Be over too late too!"

"Ah, you'll be all right."

"Who they playin'?"

He had to turn a ticket around to read it. He didn't even know, and probably didn't care. "Minnesota. The Twins!"

I really wanted to go, but not so much with him. "Maybe ya can go with a friend. I'm really trying to do good in school," I said, knowing he probably didn't have any friends.

For some reason this really annoyed him, and I could see it in his drunken eyes. "No," he demanded, pointing. "It's you and me, dude! We're going! You're just thirteen! I'm twenty-three! Get me?"

I wasn't too sure what he meant by this, but it was threatening in a way. I think he was saying that he was boss. I don't know. I was nervously angry, and I was terrified. "Aright! Aright!" I said. "Can I take a shower now?"

Simon shut the curtain abruptly, in a huff. Then I heard the door slam. I was relieved, but at the same time disturbed, to say the least.

Time ran its course. I achieved above-average rank with my grades the first quarter, and then the second quarter also. I received accolades in football, playing safety, making tackles, making two interceptions. I was very fast. And then when basketball season rolled around, I made the freshman team. I didn't start but got a lot of playing time on second string. Naturally, this athletic success made me pretty popular in the Richmond Avenue Middle School. Everything was going well for me. Even my asthma and my eczema quieted down a lot. I scarcely had a problem with either of them those months. I don't know if it was because my hormones were kicking in in my adolescence and all, or if it was because stress was at a minimum. All I know is I was well, and I liked being well.

Some of the girls at school were giving me a lot of attention also, even eighth- and ninth-grade girls. I was pretty popular for a new seventh-grader who'd gotten left back. One eighth-grade girl named Abby Fineman caught my fondness. She was a curly black-haired, brown-eyed, fair-complexioned doll with a big laughing smile. She was a cheerleader—so pretty—and I had the feeling that I caught her fancy as well, especially by the way she always wanted to sit by me in the cafeteria, and more so by the way she waited for me after her cheerleading practice, to walk home with me after my football practice, and even walk out of her way two blocks. There's something about a pretty girl who likes you. You just can't help liking that girl!

In January the school held a winter formal—a dance where kids got all dressed up and adult-like for a night. A lot of the kids were pairing up: boys were asking girls and girls were yielding, feeling grown-up and flattered, even though—as I recall—most of the girls were taller than their partners. (What's funny about that early adolescent level is that the girls are often more physically mature than the boys.) Well, that wasn't the case with me and Abby, though. I got some valiant audacity up a couple of weeks beforehand and called Abby on the phone. "Hello, can I speak with Abby, please?"

"Who is this?"

"This is Silas Dillon, from school."

"This is Abby."

"Oh, hi Abby. I didn't know. Abby, will you go with me to the winter formal?" It just spilled out—clumsily, inexpertly.

"Okay. Let me go ask my mother," she said.

I could hear murmuring, the phone fumbling, banging. Half a minute straggled by in uncertain suspense. I breathed, crossed my fingers, clenched my eyes, waiting.

She returned. "Silas?"

"Yeah?"

"I can go!"

I could just picture her pretty smile. I was ecstatic. My heart beat vigorously.

"Okay. I'll see you tomorrow. Bye."

"Bye," she said. We parted, and all I could do was think about her that night. I could barely get my homework done.

The next day I told Mrs. Heller that I needed a suit, and then later on when Simon came home I could hear her telling him that I needed a suit for this formal. He seemed annoyed about it. (He was such an oddball.) The two of them got into a little argument about it, about who would take me shopping. I didn't know what was going to happen until three days later. Sandra came on Saturday, and she took me to a men's store, had me fitted, and bought me a nice blue suit with Cary County's taxpayers' money. I was all set.

Sandra spoke with Mr. and Mrs. Fineman about my foster care situation and all, and she arranged it so that Abby's dad would pick me up on that night and take the two of us to the formal, and then pick us up afterward. When Abby came to the door with her dad, Simon seemed very annoyed. I could tell because he went into the kitchen and pretended to be aloof about it all. What did I care.

After this, it was understood that Abby and I were "going steady." I bought her a stainless-steel ID bracelet with my name engraved on it in capital letters, SILAS. I gave it proudly. She wore it proudly. We talked—in school, on the phone—and walked home together. Sometimes we were together and just didn't talk. It was all so ungraceful, and we were inept. Sometimes we held hands. I felt like the most significant person in the world! I really did. I was nearly fourteen, in seventh grade, and I was the prince of Richmond Avenue Junior High. I was madly "in love" with Abby Fineman, and I respected her. I was feeling so good that it scared me. I subconsciously feared losing all of this, but I just kept shoving that insecurity down into a dark corner of my head, refusing to surmise it. Nothing mattered except basketball, my grades, my classes, my popularity, and Abby. My past pains were out of my mind. Molly was out of my mind. Jesus was out of my mind. I was giving my heart carelessly away. I was king.

Winter skidded into spring. My days remained pleasantly full with school work, Abby, and now baseball. (My positions were pitcher and a catcher, and I was batting over 500!) Simon's days seemed to be full as well, with work, overtime, and visits to his favorite bar somewhere near his job. When we crossed paths, I spoke respectfully politely. On two more occasions since the first, he boldly intruded into my privacy, finding me naked, seemingly aiming to find me that way. I tried my best to regulate my shower times when he was out of the picture, but sometimes I was just surprised by the creep.

Sometime in April Simon lost his job. He came home drunk at about eight o'clock that Friday, and all I remember is the screaming and cursing between him and his mother. Boy, did they hate each other. So now Simon was back to the lifestyle I remember him living in when I first arrived that last summer. He was lifting weights, drinking, and probably viewing his pornography on the Internet and in his hidden magazines. I stayed out as often as I could.

In early May we had a home game against some team from Brooklyn. I pitched, allowing only six hits, and leading our Richmond Avenue Middle School to a 5-0 shutout. Sometime in the sixth inning, while I was warming up on the mound, I noticed in the small bleachers amid the parents Simon, sitting alone, wearing sunglasses, a Yankee cap, and the grisly thick goatee he'd grown, sucking on one of his stinking cigars. I felt a strange, sudden panic, but then just dismissed it, focusing on my pitching. I wondered how he knew about this game, my schedule. I hadn't told him. It was all so weird. I just figured he probably called the school and had nothing better to do, being unemployed and all. But still, it bothered me. I just didn't like him around.

He left the field before the last out, and when I arrived home that evening, he wasn't there. I didn't ask Mrs. Heller. I first took a quick shower, then grabbed some chicken and cake from the refrigerator, and went up to my room to do my math homework and study. I finished at about 8:30, feeling prepared for a social studies and a science test. Before I went to bed I gave Abby a call. This had become routine. We never really talked about much; we just liked to hear each other's voices.

"I wish ya could a seen the game today!"

"I know. Ya won?"

"Yep. Five nothin'."

"Wow. The Brooklyn teams are usually really good too!"

"I know."

"When's ya next game?"

"Wednesday."

"Maybe I can come."

"Yeah."

"What position did ya play today?"

This was what I waited for. I didn't want to just come out and brag. I waited eagerly for this open-door moment. Thank goodness it came. "Ah, pitcha," I said, changing my tone, vain.

"Really?"

"Yep. All seven innings."

There stood a moment of silence. "Ya must a did good, Silas!"

"Yeah, pretty good. Shut out! Five nothin'!" This came out in rapid succession.

"Wow. That's great. Well, I gotta go now, Silas."

"Bye, Abby. See ya tomorra."

"Bye, Silas."

We hung up.

I went to bed about nine o'clock, feeling so content and so tired, immediately falling asleep. Simon still didn't come home. Two hours later, while I was in a deep state of rest, dreaming of Abby, I dreamed in my obsessive infatuation that we were married and living in a big beautiful house somewhere in the windy heights near where the Roccos lived. In the strange jumble of the dream, the house was the inside of the school—enormous, many roomed—where there was an indoor baseball game going on, and I was pitching, on the gym floor, only the gym floor was rows of green grass, like Yankee Stadium. Abby watched me, along with Mr. Palladine, some other teachers, Molly, Daddy Sparks, and kids from school. People applauded. I felt good. Then, in the strange fantasy of this dream, it seemed like the sky, the rafters, something black from the hazy heights above fell, crumbled. Ending the triumph, the joy, the unreality, the dream. I awoke.

It was nearly eleven. I didn't hear Simon enter my room, but I awoke, discovering him sitting on my mattress, right there in my room in the dark. I was instantly wide-eyed, fully alert. He smelled like alcohol, cigars, sweat. His brawny, orangutan-like, long-nailed hand was on my shoulder. I could hear him breathing, and I tightened my shoulder, resisting.

"Silas," his voice uttered.

"Yeah." I wouldn't look at him.

"How's it going?" He began to rub my back, with pressure.

"Fine."

"Fine?"

"Yeah, why? What are ya doin?"

"Sayin' hello." His tone was slurred, bossy, with an "I can do whatever I want" sort of domination in it, or a "you owe me a lot" demand.

"I'm tryin' to sleep."

Silence. He kept rubbing, and hiccupping. "You like living here, Silas?"

I thought of Abby, school, baseball, this year, my dream. "Yeah, why?"

"Ya like school?"

"Yeah."

"Ya girlfriend?"

"Yeah."

"How about—" The involuntary spasm of a loud, open-mouthed hiccup broke into his sentence, forced him to begin this fourth impish inquiry again. He tried in his drunkenness to sound sophisticated, confident. Boy, did I hate him. "How about baseball?"

"Yes, what a ya askin' me for?" I wouldn't dare look at him. I just lay there with my head on my arm, on the pillow.

He had this self-serving, brutish, diabolic distance about him. I felt frightened.

"And what about me, Silas? Do ya like me? Ya like me, don't ya, Silas?" He continued to rub, down my back, and he continued to include my name in each of his quiz questions this way, instead of just asking the questions. This repetition suggested each question was loaded with expectation of a conceding response.

I was stumped. "I guess."

"You guess? What do you mean you 'guess,' Silas? I mean, come on buddy, Simon your friend takes ya places and gets ya things, doesn't he?" The greasy softness in his subdued voice was paradoxically harsh, sarcastic, sick. His referring to himself in the third person made this all the more fiendish.

"I don't know. I wanna sleep."

Silence. I heard my breathing, his breathing, a car passing on the street. "I'm tired," I said. "I wanna sleep." Three-quarters of my tone conveyed a submissive plea; the other quarter held a faint attempt to govern in this uneven situation, but my lack of assurance was evident.

Hiccup. "Ya wanna keep livin' here don't ya, Silas? Simon lets ya stay here and use his stuff, right?"

"Yeah, what—"

"Ya wanna keep going to ya school don't ya? And bein' with ya girlfriend?"

"It's ya mom's place. Isn't it?"

After this his other hand joined in, and like some kind of a quadruped he began kneading me—my whole frame, thoroughly.

In raging anger and fear and worry about my future I tightened every muscle in my body. Every sinew flexed, resistant.

"And playin' baseball and football and basketball? Ya wanna keep playin don't ya? And liftin' my weights?"

I wanted to spew out curses. I didn't. I didn't respond, except with more bodily tautness; but that didn't foil or frustrate him. He persisted more firmly. His musclebound arms and torso subdued me. He was as strong as a monkey. The pressure was on. I was confined, confused. He kept talking. With each advance, I yielded, afraid, furious. The next fifteen minutes were the worst in my fourteen years, ones I survived by thinking forward, by compartmentalizing each instant aside, out of my mental absorption, forcing my mind away, into counting, into organizing school responsibilities, somehow anticipating relief as though I sat in a dentist's chair. He was a filthy anthropoid ape, I thought. He needed to be caged. He needed to be dead, I thought.

I loved my arrangement at school. I didn't want to lose any of it. I felt I had no alternative but to let this baboon assault me. I understood that if I snitched, I'd be removed, and to who knows where. I was not ready for any of this. His march forward was determined. He had his forceful way, and I felt pain, infuriating pain. He poisoned me with the venom of hatred.

The following day I couldn't help but notice my physical pain. It was glaring, dull, drawing my conscious attention throughout the day, as I walked, as I did everything. I kept silent about what had happened, about Simon's violence. I pretended well. I was paranoid. No one suspected anything. I felt shame. I felt the maddening shame of helplessness and defenselessness. It burdened me with isolated rage. I began imagining killing him, and myself. The violation held me in such shame that in self-awareness and embarrassment I retreated, building higher the wall of dishonest non-transparency between me and other human beings. I had to fake it, to hide, to conceal myself, to smile. At first I felt a strong inducement to tell Abby, because I trusted her; but I just couldn't, wouldn't, because of the shame. I wanted to be able to cry on her friendly, gentle shoulder. Shame, that ugly, mean-eyed, nocturnal creature caught unawares in the daylight—desperate, restless, alone—kept me searching for a hiding place.

For the first time since all the esteem-building jubilation of activity had come to me when school started in September, I seriously prayed, "God, I wanna live in a normal home! God, I wanna stay at this school! Please, God! Please, God! Please, God..." I screamed within myself with frantic, half demanding, half pleading cries, louder than I had in all my fourteen years. I gnashed my teeth with rabid anguish. "Please, God!"

There was no reply.

May was plagued with two more hairy, smelly, inebriated, late-night visitations from Simon Heller. I grew hateful. I felt trapped, owned, blackmailed. Somehow I mentally, physically, and emotionally seemed to endure this torture, to survive, to emerge seemingly unimpaired, "safe." Like a primate's stone, he held the persuasive threat of taking away my wonderful world of friends, popularity, Abby, and success quietly above me, and he did it with calm, demented muteness. I'm persuaded that his violence was at least half motivated by jealousy. He was jealous of me for some reason, and jealousy, when aimed from a position of control, always cages its mark, depriving it of liberty.

On one rainy May Saturday morning, I believe some fear had gotten the best of him. "I got two Yankee tickets, Silas," he said from the kitchen, the way he'd spoken to me months earlier.

I was surprised that he spoke to me. There had been absolutely no conversation since that first monstrous violation. "No thanks," was all I said, turning on the TV in the adjoining living room.

He walked in, approaching, arms swinging from elbows. I hadn't looked at his face in weeks, and still refused to. He held out a fifty-dollar bill. I looked at it, at his hairy hand, his filthy long fingernails. "Here's some spending money, kid. You must need some spending money these days," he said.

I didn't know what to do. I clicked the remote control, stared at the television. Deafening volume exploded out as the weather reporter stood before a map of New York City, Cary Island, New Jersey, and Long Island, forecasting clearing skies. I clicked the volume down.

"Take it. Go ahead. Take it."

I grabbed it, because I did need it. I wanted it. It was apportioned by the county as mine anyhow, but it was supposed to be through Mrs. Heller, the county-certified foster parent. The county "took care" of me. But Simon acted as if it were he who did me a favor. Somehow I sensed I had some power now, though. I wasn't aware of it enough to define it at the time. For some time he'd had this psychological stronghold on me, but now I felt I escaped some. Now I suddenly and strangely felt strong. It was I who now had some inexplicable psychological lift. This fifty-dollar bill wasn't payment for my abandoning to his three lewd intrusions, I felt, but was more of a bribe. Somehow some demon of fear began triumphing over him. I could smell fear, coupled maybe with guilt, in his voice. Of course,

I still couldn't report him because I'd be moved, and because of that repressive shame; but he didn't know what I was about. He manifested this cowering obsequiousness. Something had him scared. I felt he was breaking open.

"Why don't ya stop acting so giving! I'm supposed to get some money anyhow!" I said.

He just stood there, then stepped away. He didn't know what to say to that.

The freshman league's baseball season ended, and on that first Saturday, late in the afternoon in early June, Molly paid me a visit. She'd called the night before. It was so nice to see her. I didn't realize how much I'd missed her until I saw her face and hugged her. She was the only one who had actually stuck with me, who seemed to understand me, who didn't recoil from me because of my outbursts, my repellent skin, my biracial-ness, or any of my other many flaws or quirks. I was entirely inoffensive to Molly, ever since I'd been two when we'd first met, when she'd first been assigned to me and picked me up at the Maddens'. She continued being a friend to me, and it was twelve years now.

I stood with her on that little patch of grass in the front of the house. I hated the thought of her setting foot inside where Simon inhabited, where Simon was probably browsing into the dregs in his computer. It was like inviting an angel into hell, I thought. The whole day had been a gorgeous, dazzling, breezy one. Petals from towering blossoms of locust trees kept falling like snow with each delicate gust, their fragrance robust and luscious in the air. I noticed a few white petals settle into Molly's lovely locks of brown hair.

"Guess what, Silas."

"What?"

"Bob and I put a deposit on a house here on Cary Island."

"Ya did?"

"Yep!"

"Ya buyin' a house here?"

"Yeah, we did, kiddo."

"Ya mean ya movin' outa Manhattan? Ya movin' back here again?"

"We are. In fact, it's only nine or ten blocks from here. Right on Providence Road." She smiled, obviously happy about it all. "Isn't that great!"

"I'll say it's great!" I smiled. I suddenly felt inexplicably secure. Molly would be right by me, right in the more affluent section around this west end of the island, close enough for me to walk and see her. "Can I see it?"

"Yeah, why not. We can't go in now, but I'll show you the outside."

"Awright!" I shouted.

We moved toward her new car. "You better first go tell Mrs. Heller. Tell her you'll be right back."

I ran up the stoop. "Mrs. Heller!" I shouted with only my head in the door. "I'm going with Molly to see her new house! Be right back!"

I could hear from the muffled upstairs her faint "Okay."

I vaulted off the stoop, excited, dashing to Molly's car. I opened, got seated, fastening my belt, glancing out the window at the Hellers' house, up at Simon's window. Sure enough, there was Simon's balding, goateed face snooping, meddlesome, peering out sinisterly, like Dickens' Uriah Heep peering out at David Copperfield, like Stowe's Legree staring down Uncle Tom. I looked ahead, disgusted. Molly drove.

The house was exquisite, charming, well groomed. It stood three stories tall, with a dormered garret, primly in white-painted brick on a corner lot. It stood so admirably and shaded. Two tremendous elm trees like angelic beings stretched their arms above it, their trunks planted like massive pillars, rooted immovably in the stony Cary Island ground. I could recall having noticed that house in the past, passing it from time to time in my back-seat travels, in my treks from foster home to foster home. I gazed in wonder. Its antique, high-glossed, forest-green door and old-fashioned, hinged shutters against the glossy white brick made the whole setting shine, enchanting. High, courtly stockade crowned with lattice enclosed the backyard. I tried to see. "Is there a pool back there?"

"Yes, Mister Silas. In-ground, with more lawn to spare too."

I looked at her with excited eyes. We both grinned. I thought of the Roccos' yard and their pool. "Man, this is so nice! You're lucky!"

Molly laughed. She seemed so happy, having been melancholy for so long because of her miscarriages.

"Lawyers must make lots a money! This is a mansion!"

Molly laughed again. "Not quite, Silas! Plenty of room though." She kept laughing, looking at the place with me, at the fastidious landscaping, the property that lolled more spaciously than others in that refined neighborhood, onto the emerald-green turf that seemed to rouse as the shade kept shifting, as the bluster of air gently gusted through the elms. "Bob does do good, kiddo!"

"He sure does!"

"He pays a price for it though—a lot of hard work and hours. I never see him."

"I can come over sometimes?"

"Of course, silly!"

I was so happy for Molly, and for me. "I got a girlfriend, Molly! Abby! Can I bring her to meet you?"

"A girlfriend, ha? How sweet! But I thought I was your girlfriend, kiddo?" She laughed.

"No, you got Bob. When I was little you were my girlfriend, right?" I laughed. I felt momentarily happy, closing off my existence at the Hellers'.

"Yep, those were the days, Silas."

"Yeah, now we're just regular friends, right? Now you're my big sister."

"That sounds right, kiddo!"

Silence lasted a few moments.

"Aren't you a little young for girlfriends, Silas?"

"You're too old for me anyway," I smiled.

"Hey!" she laughed, hitting my arm playfully with the back of her hand.

I hit her back, and we both laughed.

"I'm only thirty-four, mister! That's not old!"

"Well, I'm just fourteen!" I laughed. "Why you think I'm too young for a girlfriend?"

She smiled. "Oh, you don't want to rush these things, kiddo. I don't wanna see you give your heart away and get hurt."

"Abby won't hurt me," I said, assured in my naiveté.

"I don't know. Girls can be heartbreakers you know."

"Sandra thinks Abby's good for me for a girlfriend!"

"Well, Abby must be an awfully nice girl. She certainly has good taste!" Molly pushed my Yankee cap down over my eyes the same way she used to when I was younger.

I smiled, resetting it on my head the way I liked it. "When ya gonna get to move in the house, Moll?"

"Oh, I think maybe a month. Closing's in a month. Everything seems to going along smoothly."

"That's good."

We drove back to the Hellers' and parked out front and talked some more in Molly's car, and then we separated. I was so electrified about Molly moving close. This was the best news in a long time.

When I stepped out of the car I glanced up again, and sure enough, Simon was peeking out at us. I don't think he knew I noticed. Boy, he annoyed me. When I entered the house I turned on the television and surfed through the channels. Nothing much was on. Immediately Simon came down the stairs. It sounded like a gorilla coming down. I wouldn't look at him.

"Hey, who was that female you were talkin' to and drove off with?"

I hated his nosiness. "Molly." I hated the way he referred to her as "that female," like she was an animal.

"Well who's Molly?"

I shrugged my shoulder, pretending to be completely detached from his inquiring and disinterested in informing him. "Molly's Molly." I kept standing there, surfing through the channels with the remote control, totally removed from my attention to what was on television that morning, yet pretending to be interested, and pretending to be removed from Simon, while actually I was absorbed with despising him, with wanting to snub him. I really hated him.

"Molly's Molly, ha? And Silas is Silas, right?"

"And Simon is Simon." I shrugged, making no eye contact with him. I felt so strongly secure since I knew Molly was moving nearby. He stood in front of me, between me and the television. I looked at his big animal hands as they hung from his wrists and elbows, their long claw-like nails. I sat, clicked off the television, and grabbed a magazine. Mrs. Heller came down the stairs carrying her handbag, wearing lipstick, jingling keys.

"Where ya goin'?" Simon asked.

"Shopping. To the mall, then the supermarket." She spoke matter-of-factly, hurriedly, opening the front door, her loose and wrinkled skin bouncing.

"I gotta go too—got an interview—a shop in Brooklyn."

"Well, that's good," she said. "Maybe you'll get back to doing something with your time—make something of your life. Gotta do something!"

"Gotta shut your mouth, that's for sure."

The icy meanness between them was so usual that both of them rarely reacted with shock to these noxious comments. She withdrew, drove away. Moments later he found his keys, stepped out, and drove away. I assumed he was off to Brooklyn for that job interview. I was relieved. I went into the kitchen and helped myself to some cold cuts and olives and ice cream. Then I decided to take advantage of an empty house and take a shower. I went upstairs and did just that.

When I finished I went into my room to dry. Unexpectedly I found Simon standing there in the open doorway. My heart dropped, startled. I yelled. "God, you scared me! Don't do that! Why ya gotta creep around like that?" I said, with my towel wrapped around my waist, dripping.

He kept gawking at me, not responding. Finally, he said, "I can creep around however I want, pal. You seem to forget it's my house, right?" He shrugged his shoulders, bobbing his heavy head, wearing this taunting grin, and then he stepped in.

"Don't come in here," I said.

"I guess you didn't hear me right, did ya, Silas ol' boy! This is my place. It's not your place!" He pointed at me with two extended, hairy, primate fingers, with an incensed, insulted look on his unshaven face.

"No! I guess you didn't hear me right! I said don't come in here!" I shouted now.

"Hey, take it easy!"

"I'm gettin' dressed. Get outa my room!"

Seconds passed. I looked into his depraved eyes. He said nothing.

"Please!" I stepped back toward my window. Shower water continued dripping.

He took another step, looking at my frame—up, down. "Hey, you're gettin' bigger up on your chest and shoulders, bud. Them weights a mine must be workin'!"

"Get outa here, Simon, I mean it! I don't want you in here! I'm getting' dressed! Look, I said please!"

"Hey, why are you gonna get all bent outa shape, bud?"

"I don't care if it's your house. It's your mother's house anyway. Get outa here!" I was louder. I was desperate. My tone was tinged with rage, my heart was filled with rage.

Simon looked even madder now. Somehow he still held that insulted look, that phony 'after all I did for you,' look, cognizant that he didn't own the place, and that his mother whom he hated owned it, and that he was his mother's twenty-four-year-old boy who still lived home with her, unemployed, and that I was just some fourteen year old foster kid who countered him, challenging and defying him, one he wanted to have his degenerate animal way with. He concentrated about how to react. We both waited, suspended in his dazed indecision. After a long time he finally took two more steps toward me. I was not going to put up with this. I lunged back, nearly stumbling, clasping more tightly my towel at my waist in my closed fist. Looking, I noticed that my thirty-two-inch bat, my Louisville Slugger, stood in the corner, leaning upside-down against the wall, with all its marks and nicks from hits and fouls, with its fat end upright, with handsome, inanimate personality. Like my baseball glove, it had become a comrade. For days now, since baseball had ended, it just stood there somewhat providentially, that way, intact. I grabbed it, held it up, gripping the thick end.

"You gotta be kiddin' me, kid!"

"I'll hit ya with it! I will! I'll slam ya!" My heart thumped, and I could feel every pounding throb. I could feel thick, blazing rage in my system, like an intoxicant stealing my reason.

"Yeah, and that'll be the end of you!"

"I don't think so!"

"You don't think so, ha?"

"I don't care. You're not touchin' me anymore, Simon!"

"Yeah, but you like it! You know you like it!"

There remained this dense straining tension in that room. I heard cars on the street. Molly and her new house crossed my mind. I felt bolder, somehow unchained to this animal's cage now.

He came at me swiftly, with his forearms up, guarding, uncertain. He tried, in his lewd desire, to wear his mien of authority, his domineering psychology, like I was just some kid who didn't know any better, to persuade me that somehow he had this right, and I was under his control. I knew he was a liar.

"I said I'll swing it! I mean it!" My shouting carried.

"Ya want the whole neighborhood to hear ya, ya twerp! Who do ya think ya are! You're just some punk foster kid, and don't you forget it!" His huge gorilla hand reached for my face, to cover my mouth. It was then that I had enough. With my one hand still clutching my towel, concealing myself with insistence, and the other awkwardly holding the bat's broad end, striding back another step, I swung across, hearing the varnished wood whip through the room's agitated air. The hard, knobbed, thin end of the bat found its mark, stopping bluntly on his cheekbone. I could feel the humming vibration, then heard "Aaahhh!" as he shouted in agony. He looked at me, stunned, holding his face, looking at the bat.

"I told ya I'd hit ya! Now leave me alone!" I screamed. "Or I'll hit ya again! I'll hit ya right in the eye this time! I will!" I was frightened at this point. I knew his strength. I knew the potential of his wrath. Quickly I turned the bat around, holding the thin end. Instinctually coupling my right fist above my left, at the bat's base, as though I were stepping to the plate. And now my towel, unfastened, fell to the floor. I stood there, still somewhat wet, completely naked, disregardful of the absurdity, nearly cornered at this point, having stepped back repeatedly. The preposterousness of my holding the bat this way, naked, almost made me laugh in my emotional elevation.

I watched him. He was obviously in fierce pain. A long half-minute passed, then the blood began to pour. It was all over his hand, flowing down his cheek, into his goatee, dripping onto his shirt, staining like red oil. I thought this might send him into a state of terror.

"Ya bleedin," I said, still enraged. I thought he'd give up now. He didn't. He lunged at me again.

I quickly jumped onto the bed, then off on the other side; but Simon, as quickly, stepped around, holding his bleeding face, heated with fierceness. He came at me. I ignored my nakedness. His massive forearms and hands extended to overtake me. I eyed them. At this point self-defense slyly blended with my own fury. Concentrating, as though at bat, I swung, keeping my eye on his hand, as though on a speeding pitch. Perfectly, as though connecting with an inside pitch, meeting two-thirds up the bat, my swing smacked his atrocious hand. The crack could be heard distinctly. He howled and then snarled, succumbing to his knees beside my bed. He kept howling, crying. I watched, horrified, still clutching my bat. He leaned his face onto my bed sheets, pressing, aiming to stop the bleeding, holding his hand with his other hand, cowering, groveling, howling in horrified agony.

A long minute passed. Pity would not come to me. I was still filled with the consuming fire of rage. Violent tears dribbled down my face like candle wax as I just watched him.

"I told ya I would! Ya wouldn't listen! I told ya I would! And ya wouldn't listen!" At that moment I recalled that late afternoon, years earlier, when I'd beaten that dog to death. I felt that same appalling lack of control. I wanted to slam him, and slam him repeatedly.

"Call 911!" he groaned within his cries. "Silas, please call 911. Please! I can't see."

In my madness I shouted, "Okay!" turning, swinging, clubbing the wall with all of my strength, burying my bat into crumbling sheetrock, shaking the room, sending pictures to the floor.

I grabbed a pair of jeans, hurriedly stuffing my legs in, buttoning, zipping. I ran down the stairs and called the ambulance.

Simon made his way down the stairs, holding his bleeding face with his good hand, laying his broken hand across his opposite forearm. "Did ya get 'em?" He looked at me, trembling, shuddering.

"Yes, I called." I looked at him, horrified. He was soaked in blood.

He stepped outside and sat on the bottom step of the porch in his trauma, waiting, standing, sitting, standing, then sitting again. In minutes I could hear the ambulance's sirens. I glanced out the window. This blood-smeared human, this Simon, moved close to the street to flag down the driver. They arrived, pulled to the curb. An EMT stepped out and escorted Simon in. I watched them drive away.

I paced back and forth in the living room, feeling the vexatious burden of fear, wondering what would come of me next. Would Simon tell that I hit him with the bat? Would I be moved again? Away from this area? I wondered, feared. Abby crossed my mind. I wanted her near, longingly. I pictured her smiling face.

SUNBEAMS ABOVE THE BURROW

Early the next morning I, my trunk, trinkets, and bike were placed back into the Little Blossom van and driven back to the orphanage, which still remained administratively adjoined to the Brooklyn agency. It was that same center I'd twice spent stretches of time residing in, waiting in delay, lingering in interim.

Expectant of this, all that night I'd sputtered through broken sleep, through dreams in shallow spans of sleep, through dreams of plodding motion, of digging, of crawling, of tedious transit through a tight passageway, an illusory burrow. It was as though I were a human mole burrowing my way, aiming to find sunbeams and blue light and breathing air which I knew hovered somewhere just farther than a little more soil and stone. I clawed, pushed, pulled, dug, reached for breath. My asthma had me laboring to respire, and my eczema had me burning with prickling: I wheezed and scratched. And I didn't know if my heart hurt, were numb, or I were dead. That's how I felt.

Simon never mentioned a word about my violent "attack" to anyone. Certainly he was terrified that I'd tell all on him.

After carefully and casually inquiring, apprehensive of my own future, pretending that I'd been long expecting this, I said, "How come they picked today for me to go?"

Sandra responded, "I don't know why, but the Hellers, they say they can't keep no kids in care for a while. I don't really know any fine points yet. Mrs. Heller or her son—none of 'em—won't speak with me. I got a call this morning early from my supervisor." Looking at me, taking a deep breath, wearing that social worker look of compassionate concern, puckering her large lips, she added, "Foster parents—they do have a right to drop this on the county all of a sudden like this. It be unfortunate. My supervisor try to reason with Mrs. Heller. There ain't nothin we can do. On account a this we be reluctant to call on them in the future, only we desperate for foster homes." She shook her head.

I recalled the murmuring voices of Mrs. Heller and Simon last night when he'd returned from the hospital, no doubt stitched and in a cast. I didn't see him, didn't want to either. I don't know what he told them at the hospital, and who knows what he told his mother. I knew they were on and off the telephone through the evening. I thought about how much I hated Simon. I wished he were dead. I was so afraid, filled with a fear whose mortar had its footing in shame, so ashamed of anyone here—anywhere—finding out about his drunken sexual assaults on me. At the same time, I sort of knew that I had to tell somebody. I was half happy that I was out of there, but half in dread of where I was headed. I had this horribly fatalistic feeling that it was over for me.

It was a Sunday, a bright and sunny morning. I could hear resounding from somewhere in the outskirts, amplified church bells as they chimed charming old hymns over the graceful May forenoon, into the breeze which seemed to blow smoothly my way; hymns summoning a congregation to worship; ones I recalled once singing, or certainly hearing sung, when I'd attended with the Sparks'. It brought such a sudden flood of memory. I could envision those days; I could smell those smells; I could feel that brief feeling of security that had been so real, yet so fleeting; I could sense this all in one ephemeral moment. It was intoxicating. That moment somehow brought me an unknowable, almost mysterious sense of promise; but that moment followed with a predictable sense of longing, of painful craving for Mommy Lucinda's touch, for Daddy's shadow. I wondered who would want to take me in now, with my record of violent outbursts? I then thought about Abby. The hurtful fear of separation felt like an impromptu thrust of a knife. Panic pulled an impetuous inquiry out of my spirit: "What about school?" My voice had quick, demanding volume.

Sandra thought for a long moment. We stood inside the foyer. "Silas, there's less than a month before the school year's over. I am sure we can arrange at gettin' you to Richmond Ave school each morning till school's out, honey. Don't be worryin' 'bout that, honey."

I felt relief. I went into the huge kitchen and got some cereal for breakfast. Afterward, with my hands in my pockets, Yankee cap below my brows, head down, I moped around the grounds of the orphanage in this well-familiar despondency for about an hour. Sitting on the steps in the front, watching the yellow and white daffodils bobbing on the perimeter of the long circular driveway before the dandelion sprinkled lawn, smelling the familiar lilac fragrance, I noticed Molly coming up the driveway in her big white luxury car. An unanticipated flashback of yesterday, her face under the locust trees, the short drive, the view of her beautiful home, that same warm feeling of having someone care about me, which I'd had only late yesterday, returned to me in a twinkling. I stood, smiled, readjusted my cap so my eyes weren't so shadowed.

Braking, opening her door, rising, smiling, looping her handbag strap over her shoulder, walking toward me in bleached denim jeans and jacket and sunglasses, Molly said, "Sandra called me first thing, Silas. I wanted to come as soon as I could!" She looked so lovely before the vista of green behind her. "You okay, kiddo?"

"I guess so." I felt angry, strangely angry even with her.

She promptly hugged me. At fourteen now, I stood slightly taller. Her scent had always been the same, I thought, recalling these hugs at my smaller, earlier stages: beneath her chin with my ear against her heart; earlier at her waist with her hand on my back; earlier yet at her thigh with her comforting hand on my head and neck; and even earlier, recalling faded glimpses way back surrounding the time under those apple blossoms, at the height of her knee. How often I'd been comforted, how often her clothing had absorbed my tears. I hugged her, only this time I did not cry. I felt dead inside. I was on the verge of despondency.

"We need to talk don't we, kiddo?"

I didn't respond.

"Hey kiddo!" She moved her face closer to mine, trying to find my eyes. "Can we talk?"

I nodded, searching her sight where her shades veiled her eyes. She removed them, squinting, allowing me to see her eyes. "Can we go for a ride?" I said.

"Sure. Let me tell them inside. Hop in, kiddo." She ascended, stepped inside. She still had this commanding influence here, even though she'd stopped working years earlier. I sat, slammed, buckled my seatbelt, waited.

About five or ten minutes later she finally came out. I guessed she talked to Sandra and others about the Hellers and my case and all. We drove away. "Silas, what happened over at the Hellers?"

"Nothin'." My caustic tone stabbed.

"Silas!"

"Nothin'. Why?" I wondered if Simon told.

"You can tell me."

"Tell you what?"

"Silas, I know you. I can just tell, kiddo. Something's wrong. Something happened and I want you to tell me."

I felt the knot of anger in my chest. I was angry at Molly. I didn't want to be. I just felt it. I ignored her, remaining silent for minutes.

"Silas, I want you to talk to me. You have to talk to me. You know you can trust me."

This was what I needed. I needed to talk, and that's just what I did. I spilled my guts. I told her everything about what happened after she'd left yesterday. I told her about how I slammed creepy Simon twice with the bat, from both ends, and as I recounted, narrating, I became further ignited with anger.

"It's because he kept bothering me and I couldn't take it anymore! He kept bothering me! And that's why he didn't tell Sandra and the agency about how I broke his arm and smashed his face—cause he's afraid I'll tell all about how he kept bothering me!"

"What do you mean bothering you?"

I hesitated.

"What was he doing? What did he do, Silas?"

"Bothering me! Tryin' to do stuff to me! Always trying to do stuff!" I was too ashamed to tell Molly everything, about how far he'd actually gone in bothering me, about how often. Molly kept her vision forward on the road. As it was Sunday morning, the roads were somewhat empty. "Oh Silas, I'm so sorry, honey. See this is what gets me so angry," she said, slamming her palm on her steering wheel.

"What?"

"Everything. The whole messed-up system!" She kept driving. She grew quiet, thinking. I knew she knew things about this foster care system that I didn't know, and that the big flaws, ones in the big panorama, really distressed her. I think she also somehow knew, could somehow tell because she knew me so well, that Simon did go beyond an attempt, and did transgress, and that she knew, at least could imagine, of the shame that I was feeling. Once she placed her hand on my shoulder. "I'm so sorry about this, Silas."

"Not your fault."

"Those people will never care for another child!"

"Molly, I don't want to make a big thing!"

"I know. I understand. And I don't want to drag you into anything. Don't you worry. We'll leave it now. But for now I'm going to make sure the name Heller will be erased, for good!"

We drove to one of the ocean shore parks and got out of the car and just sat on the front of her hood looking at the crashing waves, smelling the briny air. It was so nice. The sun felt pleasant and mild and the breeze easeful, and the sand glistened in wan-white before the dark blue and sparkling white breakers of the Atlantic. We sat quiet. Beach grass shivered, shining, combed and woven in the slack fingers of the wind. Molly sat right beside me. She reached and held my hand, the same way a mother would, I imagined. I loved that. I didn't care that I was fourteen and that it might have been socially childish. It just felt so good for her to hold my hand in this maternal way. I let her hold my hand close, strong, steady. I didn't want her to let go. I once heard her take a deep breath, exasperated, and I looked at her face, noticing the rill of a teardrop beneath her sunglasses on her cheek.

This speechless reticence lasted some time, and then I said, "I'm sure hopin' I don't have to move to another school district next year. God, I hate that! I really like Abby too!"

Molly didn't say anything, but I knew she heard me. It seemed she didn't want to let go of my hand as much as I didn't want her to.

"Do ya think you or Sandra could make it so I could get in a place near Richmond Avenue School?"

Molly didn't say a word. The ocean kept whispering.

After a while longer we left, and Molly took me back to the orphanage.

At the end of the long driveway she shifted her car into park, "Silas, I'm going to come back later today to see you," she said with her car running before the concrete steps. "Why don't ya read awhile, kiddo."

"Doesn't do no good."

"I think it'll cheer ya up!"

I shrugged.

"Go ahead. Okay?"

I nodded.

"Good medicine! Ya know!"

"Okay, Molly. I'll be here. See ya. Thanks for takin' me to the beach. You don't have to come though."

"I wanna just straighten something out, Silas, and then I want to see you again later. I'm workin' on something. Okay, kiddo?"

I knew by the way she said this that something was up, and that she certainly would be back later that Sunday. It made me look toward the potential monotony of the day as something more sufferable, making the gloom of my situation less gloomy. I had something, as trivial as that something was, to look forward to for that day.

I did what Molly suggested. I got my New Testament and sat on one of the Adirondack chairs in the shade of the premises of that orphanage, and I read the whole Gospel of Matthew. What was strange was how I remained glued to that narrative and glued to that chair until I was finished, pausing only occasionally to discover with my eyes, my surroundings, and the sky. From clustering clouds sunbeams like a waterfall spilled like strands of filament, sputtering into drips and spray halfway down the long decline of sky. I could hear the steady elegies of wild birds from above in the limbs of the linden trees, lasting as though in a mysterious duration of withheld time.

From that shady covertness where I dug through pages searching for light like a mole in his burrowing, I allowed the print to steer my thinking. I don't know how long it was, maybe two hours. The fragrance of lilac and the tang of thawed, moist earth spread evenly in the air. The natural perfume was raw, pristine, clean.

Only moments after I finished, Molly returned, with Bob driving. As he parked, they spotted me waving to them from my linden shaded corner. I felt more electrified and in awe that Bob came with Molly. To me, he'd always simply been the busy, husband-lawyer whom Molly always alluded to lovingly. They walked briskly toward me. I stood, smiling, peaceful, strangely feeling like I suddenly lived on some newborn planet. Angelic beings encircled me, I imagined.

My focus fixed on Bob, who in his casual Sunday clothes, smiled at me, saying with a crescendo, "Silas, good to see you buddy!" His long arm sent his warm hand to grasp mine. He embraced me, compressing my frame, hugging, patting my back with honest warmth. He then held each of my shoulders, looking down into my eyes. His were a trenchant blue before his ashen sweatshirt, blue like the blue windows between the gathering pleats of clouds in the May firmament above us. Molly simply smiled with a constant, silent laugh.

"Sit down, Silas," he said.

We all fell into the depth of those hardwood Adirondack chairs.

"It's nice here," Molly said.

"Yeah," I responded a moment later.

"Quiet spot," Bob said, nodding.

We rested by this fire of each other's quiet company for a moment, and we spoke a few words into its warmth, simple words that seemed to sing songs that could dispel a dozen devils. I glanced to my side, across a short expanse of dandelion smattered green into the yard beside the county's real estate, and could see an old man sitting alone, beside his yellow-brown dog. The man's head nodded from side to side. His voice could be heard, but words hung inaudibly. The dog sniffed what I guessed were the flower-smells, the softened earth, finally rising and plodding away with a waving tail. The sound of a faraway electric horn of a ship could be heard above a farther siren and the many other well-known sounds of this city.

After a spell of absorbing that setting, those momentary glimpses of each other, flashbacks from the design of the past decade and a half, I noticed Molly, smiling, nodding to Bob. Bob then leaned forward from the sinking angle of his chair, weaving his fingers loosely together. His eyes beamed into mine with a paternal smile of tenderness. "Silas, we want to step out in boldness and take you into our home."

I felt my brows lift, my eyes widen with inquiry, conceiving in my mind a still life, a picture, a likeness of the wonderfully sullied, slippery, sculpting hands of the God in the New Testament tale I'd just read; of the face of Jesus, of his hands forming, holding this moment, the three of us, this situation, my life with its past and its future, grasping it all firmly and carefully as he does with all of creation. It was a mental portraiture. I saw in my mind his hands, his snow-whiteness. I could hear my own involuntary voice utter, "Really? You're not kidding?" I couldn't believe this.

"Really," he said, looking over at Molly.

Molly stared at me with a grin, a smile that, thrust from the stretching influence of her own years of suffering, had broadened, deepened. She looked away from me toward her Bob, sustaining that same steady smile. She remained steady with this beam which held the music always resounding from her heart.

"I want to be your dad." He paused. "And Molly wants to be your mom. I'm not talking about foster care. We want to adopt you, Silas! How does this all sound to you?"

I looked aside for a moment, then up into the music of the linden trees' limbs. I could feel the pleasurable pain of emotion in my chest, which seeped, which craved to spring pools into my eyes. I thought I heard a choir singing from some distant church. "Do you hear that?" I said.

"What?" said Bob.

"That singing."

He focused his ears, tilting his head slightly, looking at me as he strained to hear.

"It's like a choir, lots a voices—high voices, deep voices. Hear it?"

"No."

I adjusted my Yankee cap, thought for a moment, of their house, their hurts, this day. Once again tears filled the shallow pools of my lower eyelids. I felt this bursting rapture of exultation like an over-flowing pool. I briefly glanced at Molly, and could see the glistening in her eyes. Neither Molly nor I could say a word further. There remained this strange suspension of time, this peerless sense of wordless understanding as I leaned forward the way Bob leaned forward, and I covered my face with my hands. He placed his hand on my shoulder, compressing, comforting. I wept for a long time. Molly knelt beside me, hugging me, pressing the side of her face and temple against my arm, patting my back with her hand. I could hear her crying. I then knew what it meant to be absolutely speechless.

With my face in my hands I envisioned the three of us in our little huddle, the two of them surrounding me, touching me. I envisioned us in a gradually fading, slowly diminishing film-like image, our little cluster as it shrank, as it grew diminutive in the extending vista from an exalted lens above, moving into heights beyond the clouds, us huddled like the rest of the human race, huddled against the elements of the globe that for now breathed upon me fabulously favorably, upon us huddled like the rest of the human race, growing forward into this envisioned future where time grew evenly diminutive. I continued, in my mind's ear I suppose, to hear this beautiful choir of voices.

We three remained speechless, yet from the recesses of my being, in the silence of my center I kept saying beneath my sobs, "Thank you. Oh, thank you!" I felt so incredibly relieved.

THE LOOKOUT TOWER

I'm going to have to tell the rest of my story on some other rainy afternoon.

The sun just burst in the west, and its brilliant July beams reach from tens of millions of miles away across this wet island, beaming the way they had beamed that day twenty-one years ago on the orphanage grounds. They throw their feet through my screens and panes, onto my den's floor; and I can now hear the screen door in the kitchen slamming repeatedly as my ten kids—two offspring, two adopted, and six foster children—burst like those sunbeams one by one from their indoor imprisonment, out into the sodden yard.

Weak knocks on my door set foot in my ear.

"Come in," I say.

The doorknob turns; the door swings open. My three-year-old Gabriel takes three steps in, sneakers on, slightly pigeon-toed like me, scratching the back of his head, one blond curly lock hanging on his forehead, his eyes agape and shaped as lovely as my beautiful wife Abby's, and gazing aflame with thrill. "Daddy, the raining stopped!"

"Yes, I know!"

"And the sun come out!"

"I see. I see."

"Wanna come play band mittens?"

"You're playing badminton?"

He's nodding his head. "And... and Mommy said... um..." His thoughts drift with his gaze, recalling as I patiently wait.

"What did Mommy say?"

"Um, Mommy said to say to you there's a big... a big... um... there's a big rain bone in the sky!"

"There's a rainbow?!"

"Yep!"

"Okay! I'd like that, Gabe! I'll come see, and I'll play badminton. I'll be out in a minute, okay?"

"Okay, Daddy!"

Smiling, he reaches with two hands for the doorknob, closing my door, excited, hurried, stepping backwards, slamming. I hear him running, and then seconds later I hear the last slam of the screen door in the kitchen. The sundry voices of my family can be heard from the other side of the house. The resonance of a basketball's doused thumping on the wet asphalt driveway, against the backboard, and on the rim, beats its rhythm as I envision my older ones shooting.

I glance upon my desk. Paper. Much paper. Many things going on.

Sadly, things in the foster care system and in the family courts are little changed since I was stuck there. Twenty years have lapsed. Agencies continue to seek and receive state funds for each foster child placed within their charge, creating a discriminating reluctance to encourage adoption, as unremitting money is welcomed. And the bureaucracy is as monstrous as it was then, crammed with cases in court, with lifeless little laws that are loud enough to drown out the inexpressible cries of the lingering children waiting for a simple place of belonging. The facade of good intentions and the camouflage of nice words continue, while cases adjourn and adjourn, while countless foundling-castaways flounder.

Abby and I have been in court these days battling to adopt two more kids whose natural parents have been making no effort to reconstruct their own lives, and the child welfare system, like a crippled old man with a broken cane, carrying a hundred-pound package, drags its feet, pampers these broken adults who twenty years earlier should have themselves been adopted, who now, for the sake of their offspring's futures, ought to have their parental rights terminated by these feeble courts. It's simply sick, and sickly satanic.

The obesity and incompetence of this system suffocates, frustrates, exasperates the man who tries to budge it! More so, American church, each member amply fit to reach out and welcome a child into his home, in sleepy smugness and fat apathy lounges in lassitude like five oil-empty virgins waiting for a groom that will ultimately shun them.

Twenty years later Abby and I live and savor life with our quiver overfilled, in an epoch of unprecedented nationwide prosperity. We observe so many others—the do-nothings and do-littles and criticizers and stumbling blocks—driving to church in comfortable cars, with their 2.3 well-dressed children, from commodious homes, wearing fair, indifferent smiles and genteel clothes, holding their selectively read Bibles, quoting those verses interpreted exclusively as promises for their own self-indulgence, saying, "We're not called to that," or "You people are doing a wonderful thing," or "Taking in children isn't for everyone," or "I always wanted to do something like that," or "We tithe 10 percent," or "You know, you really have to use wisdom before you take someone else's child into your home," or "Gays and lesbians shouldn't be having rights to adopt children," or something even as ignorantly vapid and egocentric as "You know, by adopting a child, you might be inviting some other family's generational curse into your family."

The clarion shout from James' voice, to his pen, to ears that hear and hearts that sense, continues to cry through the ages: "Religion that God our Father accepts as pure and faultless is this: to look after orphans and widows in their distress and to keep oneself from being polluted by the world."

I make my way out of the house, onto the back porch. Immediately I notice the lucid quarter-circle of a resplendent rainbow situated toward a dark east, while the sun blazes in the west wet and glistening. I have a notion that both the bow and the sun will remain forever. I stare at the glory of color that treats my eyes with dazzling splendor after such a rainy-gray day. The cries of soaring gulls, the stroke of a summer breeze, and the scent of the briny ocean all lace themselves into this moment. In a new and unfamiliar way, I feel so grateful to be having life, so grateful to have been born, so grateful that my natural mother, Maureen, in an age when murderers keep crying for a right to choose to murder their unborn, chose to give me life.

I'm strangely grateful for my heritage, for the Rosenbergs, who'd made their way from Germany, and for the Dillons, who'd made their way from Ireland, so many decades into the past. I'm grateful for whatever derivation my African-American father might have had. I'm grateful for all the goodness that came my way from foster parents of goodwill. I'm especially thankful for Molly and Bob, who saw in me something redeemable, and saw that I myself was irreplaceable. I'm entirely grateful for the great God of the ages who chose me, who plucked me from the fire, who lifted me, who made me His son, who clothed me with clean clothes, who gave me a seat in a heavenly place with Jesus Christ, giving me such "a place to walk," in His courts, in His house, among those who stand there. Despite my childhood, I'm so grateful.

Morgan James
Speakers Group

↗ www.TheMorganJamesSpeakersGroup.com

We connect Morgan James published
authors with live and online events
and audiences whom will benefit
from their expertise.

Morgan James makes all of our titles available
through the Library for All Charity Organization.

www.LibraryForAll.org

CPSIA information can be obtained
at www.ICGtesting.com
Printed in the USA
BVOW04s0136050517
483284BV00001B/2/P